The Non/Fiction Collection Prize

Also by
Julie Hensley

Viable

LANDFALL

A Ring of Stories

JULIE HENSLEY

THE OHIO STATE UNIVERSITY PRESS | COLUMBUS

Library of Congress Cataloging-in-Publication Data

Names: Hensley, Julie, 1975– author.
Title: Landfall : a ring of stories / Julie Hensley.
Description: Columbus : The Ohio State University Press, [2016] ǀ "2016" ǀ 2015 winner of the Non/Fiction Collection Prize
Identifiers: LCCN 2015046938ǀ ISBN 9780814252697 (pbk. ; alk. paper) ǀ ISBN 0814252699 (pbk. ; alk. paper)
Classification: LCC PS3608.E394 L36 2016 ǀ DDC 813/.6—dc23
LC record available at http://lccn.loc.gov/2015046938

Cover design by Christian Fuenfhausen
Text design by Juliet Williams
Type set in Palatino Linotype

∞ The paper used in this publication meets the minimum requirements of the American National Standard for Information Sciences—Permanence of Paper for Printed Library Materials. ANSI Z39.48–1992.

9 8 7 6 5 4 3 2 1

For Bob, *go deo*

CONTENTS

ACKNOWLEDGMENTS

The author gratefully acknowledges the journals in which the following stories (sometimes in slightly different versions) first appeared: "Bread Pudding," *Crab Orchard Review* (Issue 8.2); "Landfall," *Hayden's Ferry Review* (Issue 32); "Lucy's Wake," *Santa Clara Review* (Spring 2004); "Accidents," *The Pinch* (Issue 30.2); "The Space Behind the Words," *Redivider* (Issue 3.1); "Olivia, the Rock," *Phoebe* (Issue 34.2); "Sugar," *Western Humanities Review* (Issue 59.1); "Naked Ladies," *Louisiana Literature* (Issue 21.1); "The Sound of Animals," *Fourteen Hills* (Issue 9.1); "Last Season's Growth," *Read Earth Review* (Volume 1); "Floating," *Shade* (Spring 2006); "Dry River," *Louisville Review* (Volume 70); "Seeing Red," *Indiana Review* (Issue 24.2); and "Expecting," *Blackbird* (Issue 10).

I also want to thank my husband, Bob, and my little ones, Boyd and Maeve: loving you makes life so beautiful that I have to try to capture it in words. Thank you for granting me time and space to write. Thank you for making life rich enough, always, to pull me back out of the words.

I wish to express gratitude to my parents, for turning off the TV and sending me into the woods, for bringing home grocery sacks of books from the public library, and for not even blinking when I declared English as a major. Thanks also to my in-laws (Kathleen Johnson, Robert Johnson, and Bernice Escamilla), to my sisters (Stacy Williams, Jenni McQuiston, and Carrie Beth Brown) and their families, and to my friends (the Dahls, the Parker-Noblitts, the Szabos, and the Frantzes) for all their support.

I will always be grateful that Michelle Herman and The Ohio State University Press believed in my manuscript and helped me polish it into a book. Special thanks to Taralee Cyphers, Laurie Avery, and Juliet Williams.

Many teachers had a hand in shaping early versions of these stories, including Jeffrey Pierson, Steve Heller, Ron Carlson, Melissa Pritchard, Mike McNally, and Alberto Rios. Classmates at Kansas State University and Arizona State University also deserve acknowledgment. Dustin Parsons, Jennifer Spiegel, Boyd Jorden, Alana Brussin-Hohmann: you continue to challenge and inspire me.

I'm lucky to have encountered amazing mentors outside the classroom, as well. Chris Cokinos, Kenny Cook, Charissa Menefee, Rilla Askew, John Morris, and Christina Lovin have offered invaluable advice on craft, publishing, pedagogy, and life.

I'm grateful to the institutions that have granted me the opportunity to teach in the discipline I love while allowing me the scheduling flexibility both to parent and write: Prescott College, Cameron University, and Eastern Kentucky University. Each has also provided essential financial support in the way of research grants. Special thanks to my colleagues, Nancy Jensen, Derek Nikitas, and Young Smith, and to my students in the Bluegrass Writers Studio—you treated me like a writer even before I had the book to prove it.

Without the generous support of the Kathryn Swarthout Award, Arizona Commission on the Arts, Berry College's Southern Women Writers Emerging Voice Award, the University of Central Oklahoma's Everett Southwest Literary Award, Kentucky Arts Council, Kentucky Foundation for Women, and Hambidge Center for the Creative Arts and Sciences I never would have finished this book.

I'm grateful to all the local coffeehouses which provided me with a quiet corner and a café miel over the years: Gold Bar Espresso in Tempe, Arizona; Prescott Coffee Roasters in Prescott, Arizona; and Purdy's Coffee Company in Richmond, Kentucky.

"Landfall"
(lănd'fôl')

1. *n.* The act or an instance of sighting or reaching land
after a voyage or flight. 2. The land sighted or reached
after a voyage or flight. 3. The reaching of land by an
oceanic storm or a part, especially the eye, of a storm
— *The American Heritage Dictionary*

4. *n.* within Appalachia, a misnomer for "windfall,"
something blown down by wind, as fruit from a tree

BREAD PUDDING

Helen 1965

This is not the story of my lover. And neither is it the story of my girls, although both their beginnings are gnarled somewhere in the thick of what I'm going to tell you. This is my husband's story because I label it so. I have never told my daughters, but I suspect if I could tell it to them—tell it the way it happened and the way it plays out in my mind—they would say it is first my story.

More than once my girls and I have packed a lunch and driven into the hollow, have climbed the washed-out logging trail that twists up to Cedar Creek Falls, and have had a picnic there amidst the ruins of an old farmstead. You can see, if you know where to look, the foundation of a cabin and the ruins of a family cemetery, limestone grave markers covered in nettle and moss. We've found tangled pumpkin vines, the remnants of an abandoned garden, flowering yellow in early summer. The plants continue to grow without reseeding or direct sunlight, even after a hundred years have passed. That is the way it is with this story.

I am allowed my secret. We all move around it carefully, knowingly. It grows larger and greener like the grass the cows leave untouched around last year's manure. The people I love radiate out from a season of loss.

The summer of my fifth wedding anniversary was the driest in forty years. By July, the corn still hadn't risen past the fence posts. The leaves pulled away from the stalks, shriveled, and curled toward the ground. My husband, Neil, who planted only about 20 acres of corn, grew it mostly for silage. But each week I would fill the back of the International with the best ears. This was in the time before the trees bore fruit, when my mother and I ran a roadside vegetable stand on summer weekends. I was strong then, and I would move down the rows with ease, cradling the crates of corn against my hip, sending the contents rumbling into the truck bed when I reached the end of a row. Cora, from the time she could walk, would sit in the shade of the tailgate sifting dirt through her fingers and sorting the pebbles into meaningful piles.

That year, instead of the quiet sigh of summer, the field was a hollow rattle around me. Forest fires were burning on the backside of Old Nag Mountain, and although the sky thickened gray in the afternoon, it was only ash hanging in the air. Neil worried for the fruit trees. The young orchard, which in ten years was to be our primary income, might not recover. Twice he filled five gallon buckets from the pump by the barn and drove—with water sloshing over the sides of the truck—through the lines of new trees, pouring carefully around the base of each one.

Neil brought home the fire truck and the man the same morning in July. The truck was already an antique, a 1934 American La Franc. Its red paint had faded to orange, and the words *Big Stone Gap Hose Company* stretched in a faded arc along each door. The cab was an open cockpit. Coiled in back were flat, gray loops of hose.

Rosario, who was short and thick, and all hands and shoulders, was to be the night irrigator. His hair was slicked back with water. It looked dark and clean in a way that reminded me of the old-fashioned men of my girlhood, my father and his friends milling around outside church. His skin was brown and mottled like pecan shells.

Rosario refused dinner, so when the rest of us gathered beneath the grape arbor, lawn chairs pulled up to the oak slab table, Neil told the man's story for him. Bees murmured overhead even though the grapes were small and hard from the lack of rain.

"He's originally from Chiapas," said Neil as he took the plate of cold chicken from my mother, "but he's lived in the states since he was nine. He says his family just kept working and moving. Always on other people's land. Christ, it makes you realize how easy you got it, don't it?" Cora was seated in his lap, and he had to pull her hands away from his tea. He gave her the cup with her milk, the one with dancing rabbits.

"Does he even speak English?" Dad wanted to know.

"Sure," said Neil. "And he really knows irrigation work. Been doing it the last few years out in California and Arizona."

"There's a good many of our boys looking for work right here."

Dad was right. Young vets, only recently returned, hung around on the sidewalk in front of High's Dairy Mart. Sometimes they waited with backpacks and cardboard signs along Route 38, thumbs extended in the wake of wind and horns from the rattling poultry trucks.

"Well, this one made himself known to me." My husband tore pieces of chicken from the bone and handed them to Cora, waving the flies away from their plate. He no longer worried about pleasing my father. "He saw me looking over the hoses, and he told me that he could rig up a pump and have the whole works going in two days."

"Where are we going to put him," asked my mother. The farm-house already felt crowded. The only bedroom not in use was clut-tered with boxes of seasonal clothes and holiday decorations. Her sewing machine was arranged there on a folding card table. In the end, Neil cleared out the tack room, and Rosario settled in the barn.

When I was a girl, things grew differently. We never had to wait for rain. Nearly every evening, summer storms shook the darkened win-dow frames and, for a moment, bathed the barnyard in blue light. Each morning, the ground was sprinkled with small branches and feathery leaves from the walnut trees. This entire valley is a flood plain for Dry River, and several creeks come down out of the hollow, forking like lightning across our pastures.

When my grandfather began farming this land, he had to build ditches and place drainage tiles beneath the earth to diffuse some of the ground water. He planted all sorts of things—soybeans, corn, wheat, barley, sorghum, milo. That way he could expect something to grow regardless of the weather. He crossed the farm with barbed wire fences, partitioning it into several acre plots. By my girlhood, the wind had seeded each fencerow with cedar scrub, blackberry bushes, and skunk weed. I tore up my legs following my brothers through that mess of bramble, searching for the snakes and field mice that teemed there.

When my father took over, he, like everyone else, began to rely more heavily on corn, selling it for chicken and turkey feed. Long houses for poultry had begun to appear all over the valley. We could see so many of them from the ridge at night, narrow strands of light in rows three or four deep behind the twinkling farmhouses. Some farmers began removing the fences and planting fields of corn so massive the women worried that children would become lost in the canopied rows. But we played hide and seek beneath the flutter of green light and insect wings. I can remember kneeling, breathless, in the silt and looking up through the layers of leaves to where the sun winked white and far away.

Neil and I changed the face of the land yet again. We grazed several dozen sheep where the largest creek drained into a pond, although that summer it had shrunk to a third its normal size and was covered in a gray-green scum. Every year, Neil ordered fifty more fruit trees—mostly Staymans—to plant on the east side of the farm. They arrived in September in two shipments, the roots of each tree poking through a hulking mound of burlap and crusted soil, and they had to be planted before the first frost. I had no idea there were so many varieties of apples until I read the descriptions off the waxy pages of the *Southern Fruit Co-op Catalogue.*

Dad teased Neil about the trees. "What do you want?" he said when he saw my husband bent over the book, "To be a gentleman farmer?" He was slowing down, and he wanted Neil to take over. But my father wanted things done his way. He didn't like the fact that Neil had a job at the muffler plant in Garrison. My husband worked a twelve-hour shift three times a week. He came home sweaty and exhausted, his brown hair matted from his hard hat and the creases on the back of his neck etched with metallic dust. My father couldn't understand why we wouldn't just stick with corn and farm full-time.

My husband grew up fatherless in a row house in Bayonne, New Jersey. He had to think about the land as a gift and keep it separate from the responsibilities he owed Cora and me. If he mixed them up, the blue line of the mountains might creep in and make him feel trapped. He loved his trees too much, but they were also his way of continuing to love me and our daughter.

When Neil came in, jeans wet from carrying water, my father always grunted, "How were your darlings?"

I had difficulty sleeping that summer. I would lie down with my daughter in her sleigh bed and breathe in her yellow hair. And later I would lie down with Neil. That was the only time he smelled like himself, right before he went to bed, the only time when the scents of work and the farm didn't hover—the tang of factory grease, the powdery sweet smell of hay, the musk of skunk that hung over the whole place early in the morning. We held each other as the ceiling fan moved the dry air across our bodies, but that was all. I lay in the long curve of his arm and wondered when we had grown this tired. After I'd seen everyone to sleep, I would move back through the dark hallways on bare feet, afraid of waking the others, as much out of selfishness as consideration.

I baked at night, since it was much too warm to turn on the oven during the day. Rosario's second night I prepared a cobbler. It was a silly thing to do—the apples were store-bought, out of season. As I rinsed the bowls and measuring cups, I stared out into the backyard. Moths fluttered against the window glass. The barn doors were thrown back, and inside, in the quiet, orange glow of an electric lantern, I saw the shadow of Rosario's back bent over some piece of machinery.

I carried a plate of cobbler and the small table fan I used in the kitchen. Underfoot, the grass was dry and prickly, except along the chicken coop where the dogs had run the ground slick. He stopped his work and stood up when I entered.

In the dirt and straw sat an engine from an old car, probably one of Dad's Studebakers. My father drove his cars until they stopped running and paid to have other people's junk cars hauled in. His automotive history hulked just past the crab apples behind the barn, stripped shells of vehicles covered in Virginia creeper. When we went for walks, Cora always wanted to climb across the cracked leather and mildewed upholstery to sit behind the wheel of one of them.

"Mrs. Ridenour." Rosario wiped his palms on his pants.

"Call me Helen, please," I said. "I thought this might make your room more comfortable." I set the fan down. "And here's some cobbler."

"Thank you very much," he said, taking the plate. His words had a sing-song, memorized quality.

Taking the fan in his other hand, he turned and stepped up into his room. I heard him pull the string, and a single bulb flickered on overhead. The tack room had a wood floor and an open doorway. Neil had fastened a yellow plastic shower curtain across the entrance, but it was pushed aside and held in place behind a large nail. I hovered on the threshold. They had moved the saddles up to the loft. The shelves had been dusted and the rough floorboards had been mopped, but the smell of saddle oil still lingered.

"You would like to come inside?" he asked.

I stepped just inside the door. The cot was neatly made with the quilt and sheets I had sent out the day before, and on one wall Neil had hung a small rectangular mirror. The silver had faded away from the back, leaving the edges tarnished. A wooden spool that had once held fence wire had been fashioned into a table in the corner, and it was there that Rosario set the fan and the plate of cobbler.

"Are you sure this room will be all right? It's awful hot out here." A tiny radio and a comb rested on the table, and I could see his empty duffel bag under the cot. I wondered if his clothing and personal items were stacked in the cabinet, the one that was usually cluttered with brushes and fly spray and a pink minty ointment. "We may need to get you another fan, a bigger one."

"No," he shook his head. "Everything is fine."

"You're certainly up late," I said. "When I saw your light I was worried you couldn't sleep out here in the heat."

"I work at night," he said. "In the sun, water will burn the leaves of the plants."

That night I returned to the house and was able to fall asleep in Dad's recliner. The light stayed on in the barn, though, and it was strange to know that someone else glided opposite me in my silent night movement, that we were together orbiting the house and the fields and the sleeping forms upstairs.

When I was seventeen, my parents sent me to New York to visit my brother. It was Christmas break, my last year of high school. Dad drove me up to Cincinnati, and I took a train from there. My parents purchased the ticket and gave me fifty dollars. I hid the money carefully in various pockets and compartments, except for one twenty-dollar bill, which Ma sewed, in case of an emergency, into the lining of my wool dress coat.

This was a lot of money, particularly in winter when everything was tightly budgeted. They were hoping that if I could see the city and the life James had there, I would come to my senses. They were offering me the same educational opportunities they had my brothers, and they couldn't understand why I was refusing them. "Your girl-friends don't have this kind of chance," my mother never tired of telling me. She wanted me to go to Mount Solon College and study to be a teacher.

James had purchased a guidebook and a pile of tourist maps so that I could keep myself busy during the day. He'd made an extra set of keys—one to his apartment, two to enter his building, and one to open the iron gate that closed the steps off from the street. "Maybe you should take the ferry from Battery Park today," he said. "I hear there's an awful line on the weekends." He circled sites on the map with a black felt tip pen while he drank coffee.

"Do you want me to make you some breakfast?" I asked him.

"I don't keep food," he said. "It just goes bad." He took some bills from his wallet and tossed them on the table. "Here's some money," he said. "Be careful."

I watched his departure through the barred window. He took off at a brisk walk, paused to check his watch, and then raised his hand to hail a cab.

There were things in the apartment I would have to commit to memory to describe for my mother upon my return—the stiff, green vinyl couch, the refrigerator with the working bulb, the muffled feel of walking over the thick rugs. Her back hurt her so in the car that she could never suffer the train ride up to see these things for herself. But she would be glad to know that her oldest son's tap water ran in one warm stream. In the kitchen back home we had only cold water, and two faucets had to be adjusted above the tub in the bathroom, one for cold and another for hot.

There were other things that would not interest my mother, even though these were the things that clarified most how much my brother had changed—shelves of strange records, with pictures of men who had black, moist skin; a desk littered with open file folders and yellow legal pads half-filled with my brother's masculine scribble; a rack of dark and ready wine bottles stacked in the kitchen.

The only reminder of home hung in his bedroom. Framed in raw wood above James's bed was an aerial photograph. Everything was gray and a little blurry, but there were the creeks, spreading like blue-black veins beneath the reflective surface of the glass. The ridge of bramble and curling cedars that one day would be our orchard. The house, dark and windowless from so far above, its courtyard sprinkled with familiar outbuildings. Perhaps he had commissioned someone local to take it, a crop duster or a patrol pilot during the fire season.

When I ventured out and down the block, I paused every so often, checking my hand bag for the keys and the map. I told myself I'd find one thing that day, make my way to one of the little black circles. First I stopped for a late breakfast in a diner not a quarter of a mile away. Over the door a sign said *Hot Food.* Inside was a small bar, a cash register on one end, and a grill in the back. I sat down on a stool covered in cracked vinyl.

Two men stood in front of the cash register, and the first ordered an egg sandwich to go. The young man behind the counter turned and, using one hand, broke two eggs over the grill. His hair was in a crew cut, and I noticed that his face and neck, even his ears, were covered in freckles.

The first man tapped his newspaper on the counter. The eggs sizzled and popped. "Goddamn, this is gonna take too long." He smacked the counter with his free hand, and turned to leave.

The freckled man shrugged and sort of smiled at the next man. "What can I get you?"

"Two eggs, fried hard, and toast."

Behind the counter, the man reached into an open bag of bread and dealt two slices onto the counter. He brushed them with melted butter and set them next to the eggs on the grill.

"I don't want those eggs. Those were his eggs."

"So, now they're your eggs," said the cook.

"I want my own eggs."

They clipped their words in a way that made everything aggressive.

"Suit yourself."

As the man with the freckles reached for two new eggs, the customer said, "Forget it," and stomped out the door. So I ate four eggs and two pieces of toast and a milkshake for breakfast my first morning in New York, and that's how I met Neil. I spent every day sitting at that bar. Sometimes I bought a magazine and flipped through it while he saw to customers. Sometimes I just turned and watched the people hurrying by.

Frustrated by my lack of adventure, James dragged me into the subway on Saturday morning. We came out of the ground somewhere on Madison Avenue and walked along the edge of the park, past the town homes, balconies wrapped with red ribbon and plastic pine boughs. It started to sprinkle. We rode the elevators to the top of the Empire State Building, and I made James put change into the telescope. The city groaned beneath us. The rain came in large, slow splats.

"Which way do you live?"

"Queens," he said, pointing. "Across the East River."

I swung in that direction and thought about Neil, grilling pastrami and rye bread.

I turned down my husband, inched away from the familiar pressure when, after weeks in that dry embrace, I felt him rise against me. He was not asleep when I left the bed, but he was not angry. Outside, chemical planes hummed overhead. At night, the fires moved in creeping orange down the mountain slope, an eerie volcanic glow. People, according to the radio, had refused to leave their homes. I imagined them rising every few hours and climbing on top of their houses, inspecting the progress from their glistening rooftops, hoses in hand.

Rosario turned the corn field, which Dad insisted was the more immediate loss, into a twenty-acre swamp. A new coolness arose from there at night, and you could almost hear the stalks nestling, drinking in the tepid water. Only after the water settled into the soil did we find the kitten.

Cora and I were stomping between the stalks, marveling at the deep prints our boots left in the soil, when she pointed to a damp mound of fur curled like a feather in the mud. There were flies, and I suppose if there had been any breeze at all, there would have been a stench. The heat had sunk the pelt over the bones. I had to fight the urge to find a stick and turn the thing over, knowing its underside was already swarming. I've always been that way—would make a point of going out to the pasture to see a still-born lamb.

"It's a kitten," I told Cora. "It must have drowned." I knew instinctively that if there was one, there were more strewn in the mud. My father didn't like cats, didn't let us make any into pets. But that didn't stop them from coming around. Often, I would open the barn door to find a white form slinking, haint-like, through the crack in the back stall. I forced myself to turn around, to lead her back to house.

After that, Rosario moved up the ridge with the fire hoses, and when they would no longer reach, he wooed each tree in careful bucketfuls. I brought banana muffins and crumb cake and warm wheat bread. I carried them in the linen napkins that one of Neil's aunts had embroidered as a wedding gift, and Rosario unfolded each item carefully, the same way my mother has always unwrapped a present, peeling back the taped edges, setting aside the paper to reuse on some other holiday. He ate what I brought him with a ferocity that made my heart swell.

Now, it seems like he was two different people during the month he spent with us. There was the man who rose just in time for lunch, who filled a space at the picnic table and offered polite yet evasive answers to Ma's questions, the Rosario with whom I exchanged everyday pleasantries as I picked up an empty plate or shifted Cora on my hip.

"Do you have children of your own," my mother asked him, "back in Mexico?"

"Yes," he corrected her, "in California."

"How many?" she wanted to know. When he told her three, she grew insistent, "You should bring them out here. Kids need to be with their daddy." He smiled and shrugged, and once, when he had left to run some errand for my father, she confided to me, "I don't really think he understands a word we say."

Then there was the working Rosario, clad in gum boots and overalls, leaning against the tailgate to pause for a slice of whatever I'd brought him. Never again did we exchange even as many words as we had that first night. I sat in the truck bed, watching him work beneath a series of hazy skies. There were no clouds, but the ash hung on the horizon, giving everything a fuzzy glow. From the top of the ridge the neighbors' turkey houses, the porch light, even the kitchen window, wavered as if underwater.

Rosario bent again and again. Mosquitoes hung around his knees, hovering over the fresh mud. He would not allow me to help, but he never sent me home. Sometimes, if I fell asleep in the back of the truck, he would wake me, his hand wet and warm against my bare foot—"Despiértate, Helen"—just as silver light was beginning to glow behind the shadow of Old Nag. Sometimes I woke confused. He would return the napkin, folded neatly, and nod toward the house. I walked back through the mud barefoot and, even before there was anything to hide, rinsed my feet at the pump.

On Neil's days off, the men moved together through the corn rows. The mud sucked at their feet as they fingered the leaves, marveling at how quickly they were softening and unfurling.

*

Neil and I were married, against my father's wishes, two days after my graduation in a civil service at the town hall in Garrison. To be truly blessed, Dad said, a marriage must take place in a church. But the minister at Conrad's Fork United Methodist refused to perform the ceremony since Neil had already been living with my family for several months. Only my parents witnessed our union. Neither of my brothers returned home.

We spent our first night as man and wife at Skyland Inn, the hulking lodge that hugs the mountainside just outside the Cumberland Gap National Park. We ate in the dining room surrounded by other vacationing couples. It was early in the season, and we were all allowed to linger over our meals. The evening sun came through the picture windows and cast a golden light on the giant chestnut beams that stretched the full length of the ceiling. The thought of leaving that space and walking across the terrace to our tiny room tightened my throat. I ordered blackberry ice cream and ate it slowly.

I locked myself in the bathroom. I sat on the toilet in my bra and slip, both white and trimmed in lace, far more delicate than my everyday fair. I was seventeen.

"Helen, honey, are you all right?" Neil's knock was careful and hesitant. "Come on out," he said. "We'll go for a walk and relax."

It did not happen that night. And when it did happen, days later, on the bed I had slept in since I first started school, we faced each other with a sweet and embarrassed reverence.

My grandmother taught me how to make a bread pudding. It's a recipe that requires a certain amount of patience, and because of that some people can never get the hang of it. The most important thing is the bread. It needs to be a large homemade loaf that has been left uncovered for at least a day, and you have to tear it into chunks about the size of a man's thumb.

You lay the pieces of bread in a medium greased pan, alternating it with layers of walnuts that have been crushed and shaken with cinnamon and brown sugar. Beat three eggs and add almost a cup of sugar. Then mix in four cups of warm whole milk, adding a teaspoon of vanilla and a pinch of salt. Pour that mixture slowly over the layers of breadcrumbs and nuts.

This is the secret: you set the pan inside another pan in an inch of hot water and bake the whole thing for at least an hour. The key to a good bread pudding is keeping it moist. The steam rises up and replaces what is lost to the heat of the oven. To make it really good, you cream butter and brown sugar and add milk, drop by drop, until you have a sauce the consistency of a good gravy. Once or twice, while the pudding is baking, pour a little of that mixture over it, and then when it has finished, pour on the rest.

It's a messy and decadent dessert, the kind of thing you have to sit down and eat with a spoon. When I made Rosario a bread pudding, I had plenty of time to think about what I was doing. I set the bread out early that morning. Once everyone was asleep and I began tearing the loaf and arranging it in the pan, the process took nearly two more hours.

The faucet above the tub screeched horribly whenever we turned the water on, so I crumbled a bar of lilac powder in the sink and sponged off while the dish was cooling. After that night, he always stopped whatever he was doing when he saw me walking up the hill.

I liked the fact that with Rosario there were so many questions. He had children out West. Although he never wore a ring, he probably had a wife or at least a girlfriend somewhere. I didn't want to ask, certainly didn't want to know the answers. I liked the thickness of the things unsaid between us. Neil and I had always talked, before and lying together for a long time after. We even talked during. In fact, sometimes we talked so much we talked ourselves out of it if one of us was tired or there were chores waiting in the morning. That happened right after Cora was born, and again the summer of the drought.

Rosario smelled of sweat and mud, but I didn't mind. I thought of it years later when my daughters, visiting from new lives out West, claimed the thing they most missed about the farm was the smell of good dirt.

Mama and I were boiling walnut shells and soaking strips of green wood, an end of August ritual. She would weave the materials into baskets to sell at the county fair in the fall. Our fingers were stained an oily, yellow-brown that nothing but turpentine could remove. We could not touch anything, not even Cora, who whimpered back and forth between each of us in turn. We had let the phone ring all morning because of the mess, but I answered it finally, exasperated, lifting the receiver from the wall with a damp dish towel.

"Am I speaking with Helen, Mrs. Neil Ridenour?"

"Yes," I stammered, somehow knowing already. The voice on the line was too calm.

"I'm afraid your husband was involved in an accident."

"Where is he?"

My mother stopped ladling the black mixture and looked up.

I steadied myself, grasping the back of a chair. "Is Neil all right?"

"I honestly don't know, Mrs. Ridenour. We haven't been updated on his condition. But I think I should tell you that his situation was critical. We've been trying to reach you for several hours. I suggest you go immediately to Garrison Memorial."

Of course, it was too late. The sleeve of his uniform had caught in his machine. He lost so much blood that he was gone before he even reached the hospital. Hours later, I signed paperwork in a quiet office. I left brown smudges everywhere my hands settled.

Rosario's departure was unceremonious. He walked to the end of the lane and waited, sitting on his duffel bag in the dust, until a van-load of workers stopped to pick him up. They were heading toward Westchester for the fruit harvest. I had no way to reach him and could not yet imagine that I would ever have any reason to.

The ears remained on the corn stalks that fall, and the stalks remained standing, unused even for silage. The rains that came the first week in September flooded the creeks, and Dry River threatened the bridge that connects Conrad's Fork with the highway. When the smoke cleared on Old Nag, a mean scar of charred forest split the skyline. The corn, which rotted in the field, tried to come back on its own in the spring, but it was choked with crab grass and Queen Anne's Lace. Not until the next year would Dad plow everything up and reseed it. The storms split a walnut tree, and it tore through the century-old grape arbor, destroying the table underneath. Although the wind shook the gray undersides of the leaves, the new fruit trees held onto the hillside.

We scattered Neil's ashes along the ridge on an Indian summer evening. They returned my husband in too small and too ordinary a box. It looked like it should hold take-out food. Only Cora was unafraid of the soft ash and hollow bits of bone. She trotted across the damp hillside, releasing her father into the breeze, her fingers spread in her own quiet vesper, an early sliver of moon hanging in the blue over her shoulder. We called a local collector to come haul away the fire engine, and then we retreated into the house for an entire season. Outside, though, the days pressed on around us.

To make sense of things, I tried to find the rhythms that had previously moved my life forward. I kneaded bread, I canned tomatoes, I hung sheets on the clothesline. And when solace failed to rise up out of my old rituals, I sought new ones—scalding baths, doses of mineral oil, hours chopping wood—hoping to work the secret out of my system before anyone could notice the change. But the truth has a way of taking root, and she clung there, like a sunken apple inside me, determined to find her way to the sunlight.

LANDFALL

Cora 1983

There are reasons why you should never get involved with a drummer, and equipment is as good a place as any to start. Undoubtedly he will own a full set of snare drums, at least two pairs of bongo drums, and a genuine Potawanami hunting tom-tom, along with a loud and fragile assortment of tambourines, cymbals, and wooden maracas—because, he will tell you, he is not a *drummer* but rather a percussionist. You'll have to move carefully through his apartment, and you'll never be able to fill the back of his car with groceries.

When the sound of his '78 Chevy Impala station wagon rattles down Casement Street and up through the sagging screened windows, you'll descend the fire escape. From the metal staircase, the evening air will smell like spent irises and swollen clouds as you watch him gingerly lift the black plastic cases and set them on the curb. He'll hand each case up to you with a trace of regret like a hastily made offering.

It's a popular misconception that drummers just fuck. Whether because of sensitivity or detachment, you won't be sure, but he'll never cinema-smash his mouth over yours and lay you across the American Novel notes littering your desk, no matter how many gigs it's been since you last saw him. Likely, he will want to make something like homemade salsa, want to relax with you. He'll ask you to share a joint and watch *M*A*S*H*.

You will wake shortly before dawn, tangled with him in the pile of quilts you dragged out to the fire escape to avoid the heat that gath-

ers in the loft of your apartment each afternoon. Notice the dark splay
of his thin limbs. Rustle the blankets off his back and watch the goose
bumps rise across his shoulders. Then clear your throat and stir in the
makeshift bed because, if he doesn't wake, you will find again how
impossible it has become to match the steady rhythm of his night
breathing. Awake and alone all night, you will remember how you
watched him through two jazz band seasons at the Mount Solon College, making your way to Miko's Music at least once a day to let him
ring up yet another box of clarinet reeds. You'll think about how for
the first three months he would only make love to you in bed with all
the lights off because he had never had a girlfriend who wanted him to
really see her.

This is what you know of men.

Your father died when you were four in an accident at the muffler factory, feeding razor sharp sheet metal into a machine. You know
that he was six feet five inches tall, that his truck made a cough-cough-
chug sound, that he kept work gloves made of canvas and kevlar on
the dashboard. That the change in his pockets jingled against his keys
when he came through the door in the evening, and if you could count
it correctly into stacks on the coffee table, it was yours. He spent the
first few autumns of your life planting more than three hundred apple
trees but never saw any of them drop fruit, never made it to the first
landfall. You can see Walker Manufacturing Company if you cross the
railroad tracks and take the county roads back home from your apartment. It's a windowless, yellow building. You can imagine the steady
hiss of the machine until it malfunctioned.

Your grandfather left your grandmother six years ago for a red-
headed waitress at Ray's, a diner on Main Street—the one that's
made to look like a train car although it's really only a trailer. You
can remember his steel-armed hugs, the crinkle of tobacco in his shirt
pocket, the quiet smack of him spitting off the porch steps. You won't
see him now, but you hear the waitress is expecting a baby soon.

The first date with the drummer will be arranged something like this.
He will ask you out only after you have given up all hope of ever
really knowing him, have ceased stalking him, and have begun dat-

ing someone else, someone completely different, someone who owns chinos. The drummer will not look up at you through his long lashes and shyly ask you to come hear his band play as you had imagined so many times. Instead, he will happen into Copy Co. during your shift to pick up one hundred concert flyers, which you were supposed to have printed an hour earlier on Orbit Orange card stock. Of course, as soon as you load the Orbit Orange, the ink cartridge light will begin blinking furiously.

"It'll be just a second." Look casual as you say this, and then tear into the back room. You'll have to move a wall of fifty-pound paper boxes to uncover a new powder ink cartridge. When you return, sneak a look over your shoulder as you tug at the foil seal. He'll be wandering around fingering the display of white-out bottles and paper clip boxes.

"When did you start work here?"

Try not to assume that he is passing judgment about your competency. Try to lean against the copier so you don't look so tall. "Oh, I guess about two months ago." You'll consider mentioning that you've seen him at the drum store, but don't. Why draw attention to the boxes of clarinet reeds hoarded in your closet when you haven't taken your instrument from its case since the tenth grade? You'll rip the foil from the powder ink cartridge with a potent cloud of jet black dust. If you turn back to the copier, you won't have to watch his fingers slide from the counter. But after you press START and hear the machine suck the first sheet of Orbit Orange from the drawer, you will have to turn around. Wipe your hands on your jeans if you have to because drummers notice people's hands. Their own are so lovely.

His brown eyes will be laughing at you, and you won't be able to tell if it is a good or bad kind of laughter since you can't hear it. He will tell you he's going to go get some coffee while you're finishing up his order. You'll be sure, and even a little glad, that you've blown it as you watch his figure flutter down the sidewalk, in and out of the sun-lit patches of window not covered with discount copy signs. Leave his order of Orbit Orange in a neat stack on the counter, and retreat to the back room. Exit cautiously only when he rings the counter bell.

"Yes?"

"I still need to pay for this."

Try not to notice that your fingernails are ringed with jet black ink powder as you hand him his change, and try not to answer too quickly when he asks to make you dinner on Saturday.

*

After more than a year and a half of searching the campus crowds for the rumpled flannel jacket and faded black turtle necks or T-shirts that comprise his wardrobe, you'll have invested nearly an hour digging through the closet for your Birkenstocks and the only pair of pants you didn't crease to impress the boy with the step cut and chinos, so don't pause too long before climbing the narrow wooden staircase to his garage apartment. Sit down on the sofa and note the various instruments arranged on the walls, leaning quietly into dark corners, skins stretched so tightly they seem to throb even without his touch. Ask him how he found such a great place, and he'll tell you that the owner of the drum store and his family live in the house and let him rent the rooms over the garage. Ask him if it's weird having a family ten feet away, and allow yourself to feel all warm when he explains how the kids come up to hear him practice.

He'll serve chicken and dumplings—yes, dumplings—rolled on a wooden carving block, and he'll refuse when you offer to pour him a glass from the bottle of wine you've brought. He'll say he doesn't drink, but later, on the deck that juts out from the garage roof, he will smoke GPC cigarettes one after another as the two of you lean back in old plastic lawn chairs. Tell yourself you will not leave until he kisses you and don't, even when you are alone in his futon bed and through the wall you hear him arranging a blanket for himself on the couch.

"I told you he was gay," is what your sister will say the next day.

When he finally does kiss you, you'll give up trying to maintain distance. When you hear the metallic ringing of him pulling down the ladder, more often than not it will be after hours. Think of the drummer ascending the fire escape from where the alley is spread with the hazy sparkle of street lamps shining on broken glass and turn off your computer. Wind your legs around him when he crawls through the window. The next afternoon you can grovel with your professor for an extension.

On Sundays, you'll have lunch with the drummer's family in a Mennonite farmhouse with a wooden barn. Like your home, only without the complicated history, without anyone missing. You'll marvel at how your drummer came from such simplicity. They'll hold hands and sing the blessing in four parts, and the harmony will con-

tinue to resonate in your ears over the quiet clink of silverware, even
after his mother comments on how difficult it must be for you to
compete with her son's music. She is, you'll remind yourself, from a
different generation. How could she understand the draw of an independent lover? Or even the fact that you like to think of him in just
that way—as your lover.

Place your cowboy boots, platform clogs, and T-strap stilettos in
a box for Goodwill. Swear off high heels forever since, without them,
you are closer to his height. Arrive late for your shifts at the copy shop,
your hair smoky and head cloudy from hours spent sipping Vodka
Gimlets in the back booth of the jazz bar where he plays; and when the
manager begins her speech about punctuality, quit. You don't really
need that job anyway. Carve the design tattooed on his left shoulder
into your notebooks with ballpoint ink pens. Open your stereo, your
oven, and the hood of your car to his male influence.

You'll think about your drummer when you have coffee with your
former favorite professor. You'll stare at this man's thinning shoulder length hair and ponder the times—was it really only a semester
ago?—you touched yourself and called forth the hovering picture of
his face. "You're a natural in front of the classroom." This is what he'll
say about the way you lead a discussion for his Hemingway seminar.
"Are you thinking about graduate school?" he'll want to know. "About
a career in academia?" This conversation will lack the rhythm of your
previous encounters with him. His gestures will seem too soft and
eager now that you know the drummer.

Your mother will say, "How come we never see you anymore? I'm
feeling good this week. Why don't you come out to the farm for the
weekend?" And you and the drummer will go on a Tuesday afternoon
because it's easier for you to skip class than for him to miss a gig.

You'll drive east along Route 38 until the mountains are tight
around you, no longer a set of softly sloping lines defining the horizon.
Try to warn the drummer before you get there. Try to tell him what it's
been like for the others. You'll fail to find the right word to describe
the feel of the farmhouse, filled for years now with the starched reality
of women's disappointments, folded over themselves again and again
like clean sheets.

The drummer will notice nothing because their eyes, those of your
mother and grandmother, will only seek yours in a kind of silent
warning. Walk with him along the slope of the hollow through the
orchards, then up to the top of the ridge. Each of you will remove one

glove. Walking with your hand clasping his inside the warm flannel of his coat pocket, you'll think how the skeletons of the empty apple trees are stretched like armor across the valley.

After your father died, your sister was a loud weight, something churning within your mother's belly, causing her to groan as she scattered chicken feed or put away the dishes. A rash of poison ivy swelled across her hands and neck, probably from bringing in firewood, and because of it she claimed she couldn't hold your sister for three weeks after the birth. A silence shrouded your sister that could touch you as well. As young girls you developed a kind of private language—the scrape of your Tonka trucks in the garden, the click of the plastic limbs on your model ponies, the nighttime intertwining of your small arms and tangled hair in the big sleigh bed you shared. The two of you forgot these things slowly, in the manner in which all languages are lost, and you think you will never know them again.

Sooner or later the drummer will want to play your body. Lie face down for him, naked on the hardwood floor, and allow him to sweep your hair to one side. Listen with all your nerve endings, first the sticks, then his bare hands softly tapping over the back of your neck and legs, crescendoing in the hollow of your back. You are not so inexperienced. You've let plenty of boys inside you—in the laundry room at a fraternity party, after prom in the Misty Mountain Motel— boys who you thought would believe anything. And they did because you're not quite pretty enough to be a slut. Your insides will soak up those drum taps like rain.

You'll grow tired of the drummer's gigs, of sitting for hours with the other girlfriends and groupies. You'll try telling yourself it's only the yellow lighting that makes these women look sad. Concentrate on him instead, as he works the cymbals with his feet. Every now and then he'll throw his head back, making his eyes dark, his mouth a wet sliver. Between sets he'll tug at your sweater until you stand up and dance with him to whatever album the bartender plays, but his hand will be a damp wash rag tapping time around your waist. You'll know the dance isn't really for you and him. He'll just be playing for the audience in another way.

Inside your mailbox you will find the familiar envelope with the college seal. When you unfold your midterm grades, you'll see that your GPA has fallen below 3.2, that you probably won't even graduate *cum laude*. Tell the drummer it has to stop. Tell him, "You may only take one class a semester, but I've got five to study for." Try not to be hurt when he shrugs his shoulders and says he understands but he still has to play every night.

Your sister will say, "What did you expect from a drummer?"

Weeks later, because it falls on a weekend, you'll agree to go to a show in Knoxville. The sky will be a pasty cloud cover stretched over Interstate 75, and you'll notice frozen groundwater icicling the limestone outcroppings. The Chevy will blow dry heat against your tights. His fingers will work their way up your neck, loosening your braid.

You'll be surprised to find one of the groupies at a gig so far from home, but she'll be sitting at the bar when the drummer leaves to go set up. The one with the tight jeans and the hair a shade too dark. You have never sat this close to her, and when she smiles, you'll see her face is deeply lined behind its foggy caul of cigarette smoke.

"I haven't seen you for a while, honey," is what she'll say once you are sipping your drink. "I thought maybe you let that wild thing go." She'll tap some glowing ash onto the cement floor.

Watch him piecing together his snares, and at that moment he'll seem beautifully quiet. "I've just had a lot of school work," is what you'll choose to tell her.

Later, when the guys have begun their second set, she'll lean over to you, and in a breathy beer voice she'll say, "Don't take this the wrong way, sweetie, but I think you better start paying more attention to your man. You can tell he likes for you to hear him play." Then, for emphasis, she'll point her Michelob Light in the direction of some giggly sorority girls. "All I'm saying is there's always someone else waiting."

Closing time will send you all out into a silent and swirling world of snow. Lean against the car, which will be glistening with frost, and feel the coldness start to clear the smoke from your lungs as the drummer struggles with the key against the half frozen lock. The piano player will walk over to you, sliding a little on the icy pavement.

"Hey, you two aren't going to drive back across the mountain tonight in that piece of crap, are you?"

"We were planning on it." The drummer will look at you to confirm.

"Listen, we already made reservations in a motel here, and there's two beds in the room. Why don't you guys stay too."

You'll look across the shining parking lot to where she'll be waiting, breathing steamy clouds out into the nighttime from the lit doorway. That woman from the bar. For the first time you'll realize that
this man, this married man, this father of three has been sleeping with
this woman for a long time.

It will be understandable for your stomach to tighten as the station
wagon creeps along the icy mountainside. After all, the caution lights
will be blinking around the signs before each curve. Tell him you are
scared, that you want to stop for the night if you can just make it to
Conrad's Fork, to your mom's house. Tell your grandmother not to
wake your mother, that the two of you just want to go right to sleep.
Beneath the quilts in the big sleigh bed, you'll imagine you hear the
branches of the fruit trees creaking outside, covered in ice and almost
cracking with the unexpected load. Then, you will wake him and tell
him you want to move in together.

The drummer's things will enter your apartment a few pieces at a
time. He'll bring an armful of jeans or a box of books and albums each
time he comes, and, in truth, he will sleep every night in your bed. Ask
him about his instruments, his furniture.

"I'm selling my furniture," is what he'll say. And you'll let it drop
because the only thing that matters is the wonderful curve of his bare
back when he moves to make coffee in your kitchen each morning. But
later, when the two of you are swinging your legs off the side of the
fire escape, watching your breath fog, he'll tell you how he can't really
ask his boss to let him out of his lease. "I'll still stay here, with you,
and I'll give you as much as I can toward rent, but I'll have to keep my
old place just as a sort of studio. After all, the people I give lessons to
all live on that side of town."

One afternoon, when the two of you get out of class, your sister
will want to go to a deli or maybe a thrift store in that same neighborhood. The two of you will look in on the drummer in his studio, and
this is what you'll find. His place will be all wood and light and music.
He will have removed the thick blue material that once served as curtains. The only pieces of furniture will be his futon, folded upright
like a couch, and one stool, on which he will be seated in front of his
snare drums. Note how the absence of the things he's moved into your
apartment only makes this place even more his own.

Lounging on the futon will be a girl, perhaps sixteen or seventeen,
with hard hips and slick, short hair. The drummer will introduce her

to you, and, after a moment, her name—something modern and mono-syllabic—will register her in your mind as the daughter of the family downstairs. Notice how, when he speaks, she worships him with her charcoal-lined eyes.

"Our asses will never be that small again," is what your sister will say as you are buckling your seat belt.

At closing time, bartenders let their friends stay, and the band members are always their friends. Although the drummer is not a drinker, he will prefer to stay and smoke and talk until blue streaks of light are creeping through your drawn blinds. On the nights that you stay home to do your reading, it will still be no good because you'll keep thinking about him. If his gig is somewhere nearby sometimes you'll pull on a cardigan and walk down, but more often than not, you'll close your books and burrow in the blankets. You'll eat mint chocolate chip right from the carton and watch the steady gray flicker of local TV.

When you try to sleep, the house's night noises will play all around you. The drip of the kitchen sink. The steady click of the space heater. The hum of the refrigerator. Your headaches will start right between your eyes almost like a tickle, then, as the pain grows, they'll curve back to the soft spot behind your ears. Until you can feel them swell whenever you swallow. These nights you'll formulate a mental list: he will never finish college, he will always have to live in the city, he has run up over $10,000 on his credit cards and barely brings that in a year playing. You are taken care of. The muffler plant set up trust funds for both you and your sister when your father died. You can afford the drummer, and that scares you.

You were never one of those girls who planned her wedding in middle school, but you've still always had basic dreams. A farm-house. A big dog. They will never win out with him. You will love the drummer more than anything you know, but not more than he loves his music. When you hear his key in the door and feel the bed sink beneath him, you will be too relieved and too tired to fight.

This is how the fights will go.

Wait until you are making dinner together, until you are crushing garlic and he's chopping wet basil for pesto. Ask him if in a few months, once you have graduated, the two of you can spend a week or two back in Conrad's Fork on the farm.

"I can't take that much time off right now," is what he'll say.

"Right now? That's four months away." Carefully, you'll peel the papery skin off the garlic. "And what do you mean 'time off'? You're self-employed—you can cancel your lessons for a week."

He'll say, "You don't know how it is. It's not even the lessons I'm worried about. I'm trying to make it. I'm lucky enough to get gigs just about every night, but that's only because I'm playing with three different bands."

Only then will you present him with your night-list, squeezing the garlic crusher until each bulb bursts and sprays pulp across the cutting board. When you've finished, he'll dry his hands on a dish cloth and say, "If you can't love me the way I am, then maybe we shouldn't be together."

His calmness will make you scream, make you sit down on the linoleum and kick the floor like a three-year-old. He will quietly continue straightening the counter. He'll gently slide the pasta into the water foaming on the stove, never looking at you until you tire and quiet down. When you stand up again he'll palm your face and wipe your eye with his thumb, saying, "It's not like you're in competition with my music. Besides, I spend every free minute with you. I'm here now, aren't I?"

You'll want to throw him off you then. To say that you never know when two you can go out. That you never do anything fun anymore because you're always holding every night open for him, but you will have cried until your chest feels so hollow you can feel your own pulse inside.

Your mother's illness began after your father died. It always begins with depression, is what the doctors claimed later. For the first few years came the headaches. They filmed over her eyes until her face was blank like the blind collie dog that sometimes wandered over from the farm across the creek. They silenced wherever she was. Your grandmother rushed you and your sister from the house, even off the porch, when your mother wanted to lie down, hurried you back inside whenever she wanted to go for a walk. In summer you traced her movements from afar, her shadow across the darkened glass of her bedroom window, her blond head bobbing through the young fruit trees.

For several months, she couldn't keep food down, and her room took on the smell of a sick person. On a rare afternoon, she left the

house and drove you and your sister to the park. She sat reading on
a picnic bench, nodding whenever your sister brought her a fistful of
weed-flowers. It was then that you noticed how thin her limbs were,
too thin for a mother's, and how her legs were spotted with blue-black
bruises. Her joints hurt so much from bending to gather the apples
into crates that she stayed in bed for weeks after the fruit harvest.

On autumn weekends you worked the fruit stand, filling paper
bags with Staymans and Granny Smiths, then handing them to your
sister to weigh. Your grandmother recorded every sale on a yellow
legal pad, and the three of you drank soup from the big metal ther-
mos that had been your father's. The apples smelled sweet in the bins
behind you, and whiffs of leaf smoke blew in from nearby farms. You
knew you could never be so sick as to miss this.

They tested your mother for cancer, food allergies, ulcers, diabe-
tes, lupus. These words were difficult to wrap your tongue around,
difficult to associate with your mother who still had good days, even
good weeks, who went sledding on the ridge during her up-swings.
Sliced apples for pies. Cleaned out the library. The doctors knew there
was something wrong with her, but they couldn't name it yet. Neither
could you.

You will actually count off the squares in your day planner since the
drummer has said he loves you. Since he's never said it first, you'll
stop saying it, and then nobody will say anything. Marvel at the ease
with which he continues to move through the apartment afterwards,
the way he slides off your wool socks to initiate a foot rub. He'll
behave as if he doesn't even notice this calculated silence.

You will not be able to stop yourself from testing him then. Try saying things like, "I think maybe monogamy is unnatural" or, "I might
be able to settle down in a house like that, if only it weren't here in the
city." Casually tell him, "I'm thinking of applying to graduate school
. . . faraway." He will sit you down then and wonder if that might not
be what's really best for you, tell you he has been thinking of applying
for a full-time position he's heard about with a jazz band at a resort
out by Lake Barkley, and that's more than three hours away. Go to
your advisor then and request applications for English programs in
the most startling places you can think of—Nevada, Kansas, Oregon.

How, you'll wonder, are you supposed to know when someone's
ready to leave you? You can't remember a time when your grandfa-

ther didn't want to be someplace else, and you've never begrudged
him that feeling. After all, there were moments you felt it too, once
you were a little older and could see nothing past the fruit trees and
the edge of the hollow. But for a long time you never thought he was
going anywhere.

He struggled constantly to turn a big profit. He called out masked
men with huge trucks to spray the fields with thick black fertilizer
and crop dusters to spray the locusts and aphids. You and your sister
had to play inside for days afterwards, away from the stink and white
powder. He would drive the hay rake all night to avoid the rain rot
that would halve whatever the going rate was for square bales. Your
grandmother used to say that it's the people who weren't meant to be
farmers who work hardest at it, that they work too hard. That eventually it made them mean.

The east side of the farm, the orchard, was always your grandmother's responsibility. She decided after your father was gone that
the trees would take care of themselves, and you think she must have
envisioned them rejuvenating your mother as well. A few pitchforks of
straw and cow dung around the base would be all the attention they
needed. The cold winters and wet springs made the valley's climate
ideal.

At the beginning of each harvest season, she drove to the labor
office in Garrison where there are Mexicans outside every morning
waiting for work. Sometimes they brought their whole families and
stayed for weeks up Route 38 at the Misty Mountain Motel. The chat-
ter of their brown children rose, foreign and melodic, from the shade
of the pick-up truck. Never any chemicals or rented truck ladders. At
first, your grandmother wouldn't even allow for the fruit to be picked
off the branches, only gathered off the grass. She said it was better to
wait.

The drummer will leave before the end of the semester. The night
before his departure, he'll tell you, "I know neither one of us would
be very good at doing the long distance thing." You'll help him pack
the station wagon, and he won't comment on the malevolent careless-
ness with which you drop his drum cases along the curb. "We are real
friends," is what he'll say when you are standing by the door, "and
that means we should always stay in touch." Of course his words will
launch you into a desperate final attempt to convince him to stay.

You will have always imagined how silence would fill the apartment without him, without his practicing, without his voice. But when you climb back up the fire escape and lie down on the bed, everything will sound unbearably loud. The flickering of the fluorescent light above the bathroom mirror. The steady swish of cars through the puddles on Casement Street.

When you drive back down the county roads, past the muffler plant, deep into the mountains, your car will be tightly packed. The only acceptance letter you received—on grayish parchment paper from Kansas State University, its creases soft from folding and unfolding—will be inside your glove box. The air will still be washed with the last of the apple blossoms when you open the car door.

As always, the apples will swell slowly. Your mother will read medical journals and self-help books and chart the biorhythms of each woman in the house. That summer your sister will keep an organic vegetable garden on the West side of the farm. The two of you will bend, brown-backed and dusty, amidst the rattling grasshoppers to pick bush beans. Your grandmother will weave daily through the maze of fruit trees with a basket, gathering the early apples off the ground, the ones half-eaten out by birds, buzzing with yellow jackets inside. She'll be waiting for the real landfall.

When the drummer finally calls, he'll come clean about what he'll describe as "a drunken one night stand last winter." Think about the groupie in Knoxville, the hard-hipped teenager downstairs from his studio. Casually remind him that he doesn't drink. He'll want to know what you think about what he said, about all the stuff in his letters, and you'll have to admit that you've never opened any of them.

"What's wrong with you?" he'll ask. "It's from being there, isn't it? From living in that house."

Tell him no.

He'll beg you to come to the Land Between the Lakes, to the resort. He'll say, "There are plenty of summer jobs here. Or just come stay for a week." Then, when you say nothing, he'll want to know. "Don't you love me anymore?"

Don't lie to him. Of course, you'll still love him. There may still be times you take the drumsticks out of your pajama drawer and rub the wood, which was oiled and smoothed by his fingertips. You'll only want something easier. You'll just be tired of trying so hard.

Wander out into the apples that are just beginning to get a trace of color. Lie on your back in the grass and try to feel the earth moving beneath you. Try to listen for it groaning on its axis. A bird will shriek up on the ridge, an early apple will fall somewhere nearby.

You'll watch clouds move across the narrow pocket of blue framed above the hollow. You will try to imagine a prairie.

DRY RIVER

1989

Lincoln followed a girl to the town of Garrison. Really she was a woman—four full years older than Lincoln, who was 22 that August—but he could not yet fathom that the world through which he moved might be adulthood. The girl, whose name was Cora, had magnificent breasts and only slightly crooked teeth. Her short, wispy hair changed colors every few weeks in a way that left Lincoln breathless. She was from the south, well from Kentucky, and that meant she had a kind of accent that she could turn on for antique dealers and waiters and state troopers.

They met in an empty McDonald's in St. Paul where Lincoln was eating 39-cent cheeseburgers and studying for his Ancient Civilizations midterm. Cora sat in the booth behind him, working her way through an order of large French fries and a Diet Coke. Before each sip, she would rattle the ice around in the cup a few times, and Lincoln, who had been growing more and more annoyed, finally turned around to say something. They didn't fall in love immediately, but they fell in love. Cora baked homemade bread and cooked dinners in a ceramic crock pot. By the end of January, Lincoln spent each evening on her sofa, forking mushy vegetables into his mouth and watching an endless string of sitcoms (she thought Lincoln a dead ringer for Michael J. Fox from *Family Ties*), just for the chance to work his way into the embroidered kimono she always wore.

Cora had been to graduate school in the Midwest, and what she said she really wanted to be was a writer. Not a junior copywriter at

Bergman & Horwitz Direct, the advertising agency where she worked in Minneapolis, but a poet. She composed poems about cottonwoods and prairie chickens and apples ripening—long, serious poems in sprawling free verse—which she recorded in a little leather journal. She would have Lincoln read them back to her while she painted her toenails on the coffee table. She wouldn't look at him as he read but would pretend, instead, to concentrate on the nail polish. He loved the loopy, feminine curve of her handwriting and the way something dark seemed to hover just behind the pastoral scenes. She had lost her father in some kind of accident when she was a girl, and that loss— Lincoln was certain of this—was what these lines were really about. He measured his tone and inflection carefully, wanting to please her with her own words, but she always took the book from him as soon as he had finished. "That one's crap," she'd say, shuddering dramatically. "I should've never let you read it."

They had some fights—incredible fights, really—with screaming and "fuck this" and "fuck that" and, sometimes, with a broken glass and, always, with Cora running out of her apartment. Lincoln was never really sure what these fights were about, but he ran after her. He would find her, hunched over and glaring, at the bus stop or seated on a swing in the park. They had make up sex in amazing places: ATM vestibules, the bathroom of their favorite bar, the amphitheater in the park.

When Lincoln completed his history degree at Concordia in May, Cora announced plans to move back to Kentucky where she was going to take a public relations position under the mayor of a town not far from where she grew up. There were several fights about whether Lincoln should go with her. In what Lincoln thought was true dramatic form, Cora thought it would make more sense to go alone. "There's really nothing there for you," she told him. "In fact there's really nothing there at all. It's boring beyond belief." She thought they should wait and see what happened.

In the end, Lincoln followed her. Well, actually, he drove the U-haul truck, and she followed behind in her Ford Tempo. He bought a set of walkie-talkies as a surprise, and every so often, she would buzz him. "Lincoln, sweetie," she would turn the accent on across the static. "Can we pull over at the next exit? I have to use the little girl's room."

Garrison was a medium-sized town. It was a college town and a farming town, but most of all it was a Christian town. When he and Cora drove through the wooded vistas that connected Garrison to Interstate 75, Lincoln was sufficiently awed. The wrought iron gates of Mount Solon College were ornately twisted into the shape of descending doves, and they were mounted on a brick base. From there a low wall snaked around the perimeter of the entire campus. Yellow and orange day lilies swayed on the other side. Why, he asked Cora, when they were stretching their limbs in the parking lot of Penny Lane Apartments, had she not stayed and attended graduate school here?

"It's a Christian school," she told him, and when he reminded her that she was a Christian, she said, "Not enough. Besides, they only offer Masters in Education."

Although there had come a time, back in Minnesota, when Lincoln had left a toothbrush and some clothes at Cora's apartment, this was the first time he had ever really lived outside his parent's home. When they began making phone calls, Cora had suggested they find something small, even a studio, but Lincoln had finally convinced her they should sign a lease on a renovated townhouse near the river. It was statelier than he had imagined, with green shutters and geraniums by the door.

He began to unpack immediately, and it thrilled him to see his history books next to Cora's literature anthologies on the shelves that were built into the living room wall, their shoes together in a heap on the closet floor. He loved the way his desk, the same desk on which he had studied back in high school, looked here in their spare bedroom. He loved the high ceilings and tall windows, the shady courtyard with the picnic table and grill.

They arrived in early August, and Lincoln took the only job he could find. One evening while he and Cora were lined up for custard-style cones in front of Bert's Dairy Bar, Lincoln overheard some parents commenting that a local private school still had several teaching positions left unfilled. Three days later he was able to sign a nine-month contract at Spring Creek Christian Academy. Classes didn't commence until after Labor Day, and by that time Cora had left their apartment and moved into a bungalow that the mayor had rented and furnished for her on the other side of Wildwood Park. She told him, quietly and apologetically, that she was leaving, reminded him that she had tried, for his sake, to come here alone. They carried her

things out to her car together. He wanted her to scream, to storm out
so that he could chase her.

Each morning, Lincoln walked to school along the flood mound,
an artificial ridge that Garrison had raised in the late twenties after
Dry River flooded and destroyed part of the town. Now the hill was
smooth and grassy, and the crest—where the people of Garrison had
taken to jogging and walking their dogs—was slowly flattening out
with time and weather. On one side rose Victorian houses and squat
cottages with stone steps and bright shutters, not unlike the one Cora
lived in now. There was Sullivan Street, lined with mossy brick sidewalks and shaded by sugar maples, and just beyond that the austere
brick buildings of Mount Solon. On the other side, half a mile of farm
land, mostly corn and alfalfa, stretched toward the river. Then, just
before Spring Creek Christian Academy, the swath of land on the far
side of the mound narrowed into a sparse forest of thick hardwoods.

The river continued on toward the new part of town, where there
were fast food restaurants and a shopping mall, but here on the outskirts of it all, Lincoln was able to lull himself into a kind of content,
which despite his loneliness, or perhaps because of it, he was able to
foster into hope. As he walked, he sipped coffee from a plastic mug,
and he took note of things around him that he would like to tell Cora
about, things that made him think about her poems: the black snake
sunning himself on the edge of the cornfield; the way one or two
old men were always casting their lines into the riffles where the old
bridge had collapsed; the pile of waxy poplar leaves left in the school
yard, the surface of each leaf punched by some girl's fingers to form a
smiling cat face.

Each evening after dinner, Lincoln walked to the house that the
mayor had arranged for Cora and stood for a little while on the sidewalk across from Wildwood Park. He never knocked or peered into
the Dutch windows. He didn't want to see her and the mayor in the
midst of anything that would make it more difficult to take her back
later. Once in a while, Lincoln recorded the things he had noticed that
day on notepaper, which he tucked beneath the windshield wiper of
Cora's car.

On Tuesday and Thursday mornings, when Spring Creek did not
hold early chapel, the day still commenced with the voice of the prin-
cipal, Rev. Jonas Baxter, reminding everyone to pick up the order

forms and "sell, sell, sell" those ceramic Christmas ornaments for the fall fund-raiser. The reverend started and finished with prayer, and he filled in some of the time in between with a daily Bible verse. These lines were nonoffensive and vaguely hopeful ("Now faith is being sure of what we hope for and certain of what we do not see, Hebrews 11:1"), and Lincoln sometimes recorded them at the bottom of the note before he pinned it to Cora's car.

Lincoln, who had muddled his way through English and barely passed his required mathematics courses, had to teach all subjects to the only sixth grade class at Spring Creek. He was an acceptable teacher. That is what Rev. Baxter wrote when he came to observe him during the second week of school. He wrote that Lincoln's attire was professional in appearance, with his belt matching his shoes; that he knew most of his students by name; that he seemed to be selecting appropriate worksheets from *A Christian Curriculum for Grades Six and Seven*; and that he was, overall, an acceptable teacher.

The day before the observation Lincoln pleaded with his students, "The love of my life has left me for a married man, and my position here is essential to winning her back." They stared at him with mild amusement. After school they played Asteroids or Missile Command in the back room of Boberia's Pizza, and during recess a gaggle of them always gathered around Jennifer, who snuck glossy-covered romance novels from a box in her grandmother's garage. They knew something about desperation, something about passion. And so, that is the way it went until the second month of school when something happened that changed everything.

Lincoln sat eating his dinner and flipping through a book that he had come across in the school library. The book was about the history of the Mennonite religion and its role in the settlement of Garrison, and Lincoln, a sucker for history's ridiculous details, was growing truly interested when the telephone rang. He pushed aside his box of fried chicken and faced the phone. His parents called on Saturday afternoons.

He wiped the grease from his mouth with a paper napkin and picked up the receiver. "Hello." His heart was pounding from somewhere down in his belly.

"Mr. Erdrich?" This was not the sultry fake accent that had been playing through Lincoln's mind for weeks. "This is Jonas Baxter. I'm terribly sorry to phone you at home, but we have a bit of an emergency. One of your students failed to return home after school today. Mark Lively was in attendance today, was he not?"

"Mark Lively?" Lincoln knew that in his class there were at least two Marks. He couldn't picture either of their faces, yet he felt fairly certain that one of them played soccer on a community league and sometimes wore his uniform to school.

"His younger brothers walked with him to school," explained Baxter. "And they waited for Mark, as they always do, to walk home this afternoon, but he never appeared, and now the boys' parents are starting to panic. Was Mark in your class today?"

Lincoln had not taken attendance, not once since Baxter's visit. He had planned on filling in his grade book later, fudging everything at the end of the semester, even using different colored ink pens the way he had in the weekly journal entries required as part of his freshman English class back at Concordia. "I'm not sure," said Lincoln. "I'll have to check my book tomorrow."

"Well, I guess that's all you can do," said Baxter.

"You know, I have a feeling he probably just ditched school with a friend," said Lincoln. "He's probably been smoking all afternoon behind the IGA. He'll show up within the hour like nothing happened."

Baxter sighed heavily into the phone, and Lincoln wasn't sure if the man was more disappointed by his inability to resolve the situation or by the prospect of one of Spring Creek's flock hiding out behind a dumpster and sharing a stolen pack of cigarettes. "You get there as early as you can."

The next morning, emergency vehicles had smashed a trail of flattened cornstalks through the fields. Two police cars were parked just shy of the water's edge, and they had turned up a wake of black mud. The early arrivals, mostly country children whose parents brought them by car from Conrad's Fork or Whitetail Gap, stood around on top of the flood mound. Lincoln told them to go inside.

"We're allowed to play out here," one of them said. "It's intramurals."

"You don't look like you're playing." Lincoln's voice, louder and an octave higher than usual, surprised even him. "Either stay on the black top and play some kind of ball, or go into the cafeteria and draw."

Lincoln found one of his students, Andy, amidst the dispersing crowd and asked him if Mark Lively was in school yesterday. The kid eyed Lincoln suspiciously and shook his head.

Rev. Baxter had already assumed the smooth and consoling demeanor of a eulogizer. His entire head moved in a subtle rhythmic motion as he spoke. He told Lincoln that early that morning fishermen had found a backpack and the detachable hood from a nylon jacket, along with various other personal items that Mark's parents had identified as their son's, scattered along the bank and caught in the roots of an overturned tree downstream from the school. "So far," Baxter whispered, "there is no body."

The search and rescue team came out, and they dragged the river bottom. Their yellow boat moved in long arcs across the deep and slow moving stretch of water above Wildwood Dam. They sent divers in below the old bridge and into the places water pooled dark below the rapids. Rev. Baxter led a chain of around-the-clock prayer for the next forty-eight hours. Students from the college stood in a line and fanned across the cornfield and then through woods north of town, moving across the ground like a beaded string.

Finally, the town of Garrison admitted what everyone knew to be true. They held a memorial service in Spring Creek Church of the Brethren, the chapel adjacent to the school. The mayor himself led the mourners in a prayer, which turned into an oration on the duty of the people of Garrison to protect the innocence of children everywhere. It was the first time Lincoln had gotten a good look at the mayor, who was younger than he expected, though not as good looking. He couldn't spot Cora anywhere among the man's suited entourage as it pressed out of the sanctuary. Throughout the boy's disappearance, which was heavily televised on the local news, Lincoln had been waiting for her to call. He walked by her house most evenings, but he could no longer bring himself to record all the events and observations of his days. Leaving such thoughts folded on her windshield would have left him feeling a little too out of control.

The family asked that, instead of arrangements of cut flowers, friends bring potted mums. They planted some of them on either side of the steps leading up to the main entrance of the school, and the others they placed in a flower bed with a plaque engraved with Mark's name and the verse, "Let the little children come to me, and do not stop them; for it is to such as these that the kingdom of God belongs."

After that, the days passed with a certain level of normalcy. The college lost its homecoming game, and the town began preparations for the annual Sugar Maple Festival. The world outside continued, and truly there were further-reaching losses: that autumn in China a group of student protestors were massacred in Tiananmen Square. The kids at Mount Solon gathered on the steps of the college library, lit candles, and sang "Imagine" and "Give Peace a Chance." But still Lincoln heard talk.

"The loss of her oldest," the guidance counselor said one morning as she poured coffee for the choir teacher in the lounge, "and she just had her tubes tied last year."

Roy, the janitor, was the brother-in-law of one of the fishermen who found Mark's belongings, and he recounted the scene over and over in mounting gothic detail for the women who worked in the cafeteria. "The boy's Bible," Roy said, "was spread like raw manure across the rocks."

The most disconcerting gossip came from the children themselves. When he headed into the boy's restroom to hustle along the stragglers who were playing in the sinks, Lincoln heard their voices, hushed and echoing off the tiled walls. "Lucy Breeden was with him. He told me they were going down there to do it."

The gossip sent Lincoln's mind reeling. He had viewed the eleven-year-olds with whom he spent seven hours each day as children. Mark Lively was tall for his age. He was an athlete and a bit of a smart aleck. He had a miniature pincher dog named Gumby, and he had read all the books in a young Christian horror series called *Spinetinglers*. Lincoln had encountered such details only after the boy's disappearance, and they had, admittedly, surprised him. Might Mark Lively have been sneaking down to the riverbank for an early morning romantic rendezvous?

There was a game that Cora used to play. Lincoln had always called it the "what if" game, and he hated it. Something, anything—a toilet paper commercial or a lady squeezing honeydew melons in the produce aisle—would trigger an emotional response that would start the questions. "What if I got pregnant? What would we do? Would we get married? Now—seriously? What if the opposite happened? What if we got married and we couldn't have any babies, would we adopt? Would we tell the child the truth? How old would it be when we finally came clean?" It could go on all day, and almost always what started in hypothetical fun ended in a real argument.

Lucy, whom he watched closely, was reclusive, but he couldn't tell if her isolation was self-imposed, if she scorned the other children or they scorned her. In some ways she reminded him of Cora. She had short, dark hair and a look that bordered haughty. He would catch her staring out the window for long stretches of time, but he couldn't bring himself to reprimand her.

Every day Lincoln thought up a new possibility. What if Mark and Lucy had gone down to the river to smoke pot? Lincoln couldn't remember when he had first smoked pot, but he was sure it wasn't until high school. Eleven years old was young, yes, but drugs were a growing threat. The majority of the business at both PTA meetings Lincoln had attended centered on the drugs circulating in the public school system and how it was the duty of every parent, every member of the Spring Creek staff, every citizen of Garrison, to keep them out of these walls.

What if Mark was secretly depressed and had weighed the pockets of his windbreaker down with the smooth stones that lined the river bank and jumped into the deep pool on the far side of the bridge. What if he had changed his mind but become caught on something. Dry River was deep in places. Its path carved in and out of underwater limestone caverns.

Lincoln considered mentioning some of the gossip to Rev. Baxter, but it would, he finally decided, be unwise to give such talk credence.

Suddenly Lincoln wanted to know his students. He wanted to see past their sneers, past the standard navy pants and white oxford shirts (the breast pocket of each stamped with the Spring Creek logo, the silhouette of a church next to a leafy sugar maple). So he put away *A Christian Curriculum for Grades Six and Seven* and began thinking about a special project for History and English. First he brought in the writings of Captain John Smith, Samuel Sewall's witchcraft tales, and Mary Rowlandson's captivity narratives.

"This is too hard!" His students complained mercilessly. "We can't read this stuff. My Dad doesn't even know these words. He thinks they're not in the dictionary." Lincoln, admitting that he had been a little overzealous, decided he would have to forego Thomas Jefferson, Benjamin Franklin, Margaret Fuller, Frederick Douglass, and Harriet A. Jacobs.

Although Lincoln's concentration had been in ancient cultures — Mesopotamian, Assyrian, Egyptian — and he had memorized long sequences of rulers and monuments and movements, timelines that began with Menses' unification of Upper and Lower Egypt and ended with Nekhtnebf's clash with Alexander the Great — his passion was American revisionist history. He loved the scholars who revealed heroes for what they really were, the ones who depicted the colonists responsible for the Boston Tea Party as a bunch of drunken rednecks, Molly Pitcher as a prostitute. He claimed to believe in the gossip of history, but, in truth, he read a lot of pop-culture biographies and trashy checkout magazines.

Lincoln decided to read to his class from the autobiography of Bill Veeck, the man who at various points in his career had owned the Cleveland Indians, the St Louis Browns, and the Chicago White Sox. Veeck, who was probably the greatest promotional genius baseball has ever seen, was, in Lincoln's opinion, fascinating and completely irreverent. The book, which was titled *Veeck as in Wreck,* was reprinted after the man's death in '86.

Lincoln purchased a box of baseball cards from the IGA, and when he began handing out packs the kids looked at him, confused. "Well, come on," he said, sitting down in the front of the room and opening the book. "Get over here, and tear into them. Let's see what you've got." He began to read, and they gathered around him in a half circle, squirming a little and comparing cards. He read for three hours, breaking only for lunch, glossing over some of the racier parts. They laughed at all of Veeck's promotional pranks, the way Lincoln had known they would — the exploding scoreboards; the 3'7" midget he brought to the plate for the Brown's; the "Grandstand Managers' Day," in which the fans determined the team's strategy by holding up large placards marked "YES" on one side and "NO" on the other — and they grew quiet during the part when Veeck was diagnosed with cancer and moved to New York to paint and meditate and await what he thought was his appending death. Once he'd finished the book, Lincoln instructed the kids to compose their own autobiographies, complete with pictures.

"Wait a minute," one student raised his hand. "You want us to write everything we've ever done?"

"Veeck doesn't include every detail from every minute of every day," said Lincoln. "He's obviously decided what's most important, what he wants people to remember."

"How long does it have to be?" It was Jennifer, the girl with all the smut novels.

"I can't decide that for you," he said. "It all depends on how much you have to say. Your story should build toward something, though. For Veeck," Lincoln held up the book, "the culmination was getting a second chance at life."

"We don't have anything like that." A couple of them started to groan.

"That guy had like a peg leg and was practically resurrected, like Jesus or something." Andy, one of the clowns of the class, hopped around, imitating Veeck's amputation. "I never even broke a bone."

"Look guys," Lincoln sighed, "For Veeck, I think his accomplishments show creativity and an open mind. He signed the American League's first black player and its oldest rookie. I'd say he's also selected events that illustrate his work ethic and the way he learned to deal with pressure and get along with people. What do your actions and accomplishments say about you?" Lincoln wasn't sure they understood, but he liked seeing them so agitated.

The Sugar Maple Festival ran the third weekend in November. The weather did turn decidedly colder, but nothing like the people of Garrison made it out to be. In Minnesota, Lincoln's parents told him, they had already had three substantial snows. Bundled up in winter coats, scarves wrapped around their necks, and hoods pulled tight, his students looked like cartoon versions of themselves. Most of the kids walked in the company of a friend, a good ten paces behind or in front of their parents. Sullivan Street was closed to traffic, and vendors set up booths that spilled over onto the college mall. There was kettle popcorn and candy apples and BBQ turkey legs. Artists laid out beaded necklaces and watercolors of the Appalachian Mountains. They smiled at him and asked where he was from. How, Lincoln wondered, could they still recognize him as an outsider?

A fortune teller was reading palms out of a family-sized Coleman tent, and Lincoln peeked inside just for fun. The girl who couldn't have been more than seventeen or eighteen sat on a folding chair in front of a collapsible card table. She had thin, reddish-blonde hair that hung past her shoulders. The ends were wild and ragged. "She needs a good trim," that's what Cora would have said. That's what Cora said about most women with long hair.

"Come on in," the girl at the table motioned toward an empty lawn chair. "There's no line." In the corner a space heater glowed orange.

"How much?" asked Lincoln as he sat down.

"Is this your first time?" she asked, and Lincoln nodded, smiling. "For you," she tilted her head and looked at him. She was heavily freckled. "Ten bucks."

Lincoln laughed.

"What?" she said. "That's a tremendous value. It means your fortune will be good. I charge more for the scary ones."

He pulled a ten from his wallet, and she took his hand. Her nails were bitten low, and the tips of her fingers felt like cold water on his palm. He thought about how it was with that sort of touch, the slighter it was the more you felt it. There was a girl before Cora, someone he remembered from high school, who used to lean in and brush her eyelashes against his neck.

The girl's fingers only fluttered over his palm for a moment, and then she held onto his wrist and leaned toward him. "Someone," she said, "someone you know extraordinarily well is going to make a decision that will bring you much joy." The heater buzzed in the corner.

"I don't know anyone very well."

"Well," she said, folding the money and pushing it into her coat pocket, "Perhaps you'll get to know this person better." Lincoln laughed and thanked the girl, but he thought about what she had said as he headed back into the crowd.

The highlight of the festival was the maple syrup, made from local trees and sold in tins depicting the college bell tower, framed by snow-covered treetops. Lincoln bought a tin for his mother and a tin for his Aunt Mare. He would take them when he visited at Christmas, and they would have a good laugh about southern syrup.

The local churches ran nonstop all-you-can-eat pancake breakfasts out of their fellowship halls. Lincoln made his way through the crowd to Spring Creek Church of the Brethren. As he waited in line with his Styrofoam plate, he happened to look up and see Lucy Breeden. She was wearing a wool coat, plaid with gold buttons and holding the hand of a man Lincoln presumed to be her father. They paused at one of the trashcans to dump their plates. When they turned to go, Lincoln saw Lucy recognize him, smile, and give a little half wave.

*

Lincoln spent Thanksgiving in Kentucky. He didn't really have enough money to fly back to St. Paul—he'd been paying the full rent on an apartment he'd originally planned to share—and, truth be told, he had not been completely honest with his parents. They knew that he and Cora were having some problems but assumed it was nothing that could not be worked out in time.

For his holiday meal, Lincoln took a taxi to Showalter's Mennonite Family Restaurant, a little place just before the interstate. The parking lot had posts where customers of the old order could hitch their teams, and a few buggies were already parked out front when Lincoln stepped out of the taxi. The horses snaked their heads and stamped their hind legs, rattling their harnesses.

It was a good thing Lincoln had come early because at half past twelve a hoard of families descended on the place. The line twisted out of the lobby and around the building. Women wearing prayer bonnets bustled in and out of the kitchen with trays of apple cobbler and shoofly pie. Lincoln found a quiet corner table and began working his way through his students' autobiographies.

Most of the kids had secured the pages in report binders or spiral-bound notebooks and decorated them with drawings and photographs. It seemed his students couldn't sustain a long narrative, so each page stood alone like one of Cora's poems. One girl, Ruth, had begun her own story with that of the Garden of Eden. There were all-star baseball picks, litters of kittens, high scores at Asteroids, births of siblings, prizes in costume contests.

Even if he hadn't been looking for it, Lucy's autobiography would have stood out. She had penned her stories on stiff, vanilla-colored paper. The pages were folded and hand-sewn, then bound with a wallpaper sample. She began with the story of her birth, which was also the story of her mother's death, and ended with the death of her classmate. In between these tragedies was the pith of Lucy's life: a father who traveled, a nanny named Ruby, swim meets and summers in the Outer Banks, her own rows in the family garden, and a photography award in the juvenile category at the Renfro County fair.

She wrote about how she had walked down to the river with Mark several times in the weeks before his death, how he had been teaching her how to skip rocks. "He had a secret hoard of stones," she wrote, "tiny, flat ones that he piled inside a rusty barrel near the old bridge."

There was no reticent confession, and Lincoln hadn't really expected one. Mark's death had made everyone very sad, Lucy said, but her father was letting her return to her old school in Conrad's Fork after Christmas, and now he was home nearly every weekend. Her father always said that God never takes away people or things that we love without sending others, so she was sure he would send someone to help Mark's family. It was, and Lincoln suddenly wanted to believe this too, guaranteed.

That night he dreamed he saw Lucy running along the flood mound, the dry cornstalks rattling below her. The sky stretched dark and starless, and the moon that rose behind her was ringed with haze, as before the first snow. It was a vesperal moon, chanting to the rhythm of her footfall, bathing the school yard in an eerie, expectant light.

When Lincoln awoke, he didn't make breakfast or turn on the television. He dug through a box that Cora had left on the floor of the hall closet until he found her special résumé paper. He sat down in front of the coffee table and started writing. He wrote about the summer his family had rented a cottage on Lake Superior, about the gulls and the rocks that were worn smooth as shells. He wrote about the times his father used to take him to see the Northstars play in the Met Center and how they would stand next to the glass to watch the Zamboni go by. He listed all the songs he had learned to play on the saxophone during high school. He wrote about the time he and Pam Bridges had gone to Tony's in their formal wear and shared a fourteen-inch sub before the senior prom. He wrote about the Fig Newtons his mother would put in his book bag each morning before he caught the transit for Concordia.

He wrote that he fell in love, for a while, with a girl who chewed ice and rattled her diet soda, and he described how Garrison had looked below him when they came up over the hill, shaded and secret and almost too perfect. I lost the girl, Lincoln wrote, and one student, but twenty-three others will be back from break this Monday.

Lincoln stood for a while on the sidewalk across from Wildwood Park, holding the pages he had written. The shaded patches of Cora's lawn were still gray with frost. He could see a miniature version of himself,

distorted and reflected in the Dutch windows. He imagined Cora coming out and picking each of his notes off her car as if they were flyers for some ongoing pizza promotion. He could see her tossing them
down, see each manifesto wilting curbside with the cigarette butts and
rotten leaves. He put his list back in his coat pocket. Behind him the
surface of Dry River had frozen into a slick skim of ice, but, underneath, water was still trickling through. The sound of it rose like bells
off the dam, and when he stepped backwards off the sidewalk, he had
the sense that things in front of him were moving away, downstream.

LUCY'S WAKE

Olivia 1995

I am straddling Jason Clement's lap. I'm still wearing my panties, but the tiny wet stain immediately burns into my consciousness like sunspots on closed eyelids. He tells me not to worry—that it's not even the real stuff—but I send him upstairs to bring the Family Medical Encyclopedia from his father's study. When we discover pre-ejaculatory fluid carries millions of sperm, I burst into tears and won't let him touch my breasts again for two months.

That is only one version of my story, one of many versions that circulated at Black Mountain High School, all of essentially the same story, the story of how I didn't do it. At least that story is mostly true. I should have told that one to Lucy. I should have called her as soon as I got home that night, shoved a sweatshirt under the crack in the door and whispered everything into the phone. But I never told Lucy any of the stories. We hung the things we should have talked about out of reach, like bathing suits over the shower rod, until they made the air damp and warm between us.

Now sometimes I try to think back and remember exactly when I met Lucy Breeden, but I can't. She must have always been there, and it must have been some need inside me that brought her into focus. So Lucy must have been among the ten-year-olds with whom I sat in a circle at slumber parties, half asleep and half awake, drinking flat Mountain

Dew at 3 AM. We already knew about things then. In fact, we had not yet realized we needed to pretend we didn't know them.

I picked at the pale green shag carpet in Treeva Dean's basement as we played "the question game." When Treeva asked how old we would be when we rolled our hair in hot curlers, wore mascara, or went all the way with a boy, we chanted, "Sixteen . . . sixteen . . . sixteen." It was the magic age, and we breathed the syllables in reverent anticipation. So Lucy must have believed in it too, then.

My first clear memory of Lucy is from a game of spin-the-pencil on the back of a chartered bus in middle school. The kissing game, learned from Treeva's big sister, was the latest thing. We had been spinning everything from empty pop bottles to television remote controls at all the coed parties we could talk our parents into, but as of yet no one had been doing any actual kissing.

This game wasn't different. I had a moment of panic when a boy whose name I can no longer remember, but who wore a lot of collared shirts and had to take allergy pills with his lunch, landed on me. We, like everyone else, shuffled around in our seats a little until someone cried, "He's not going to kiss her. Somebody else spin."

Hunched over the vinyl seats as headlights and neon burger signs flashed through the rain-soaked bus windows, we were all unprepared for what Lucy did. After spinning the pencil, she leaned across the aisle and kissed Toby Parker on the mouth. For one embarrassing moment, Toby looked as if he might cry, but he recovered quickly and later shyly followed Lucy to the very back of the bus, not to reemerge until we all tumbled out onto the wet pavement of the middle school parking lot to meet our parents.

Sometime that winter I think Lucy became my best friend, but not in the direct manner that most twelve-year-old girls assign their loyalty. We never matched our clothes or wore paired halves of a gold-plated broken heart on a chain around our necks. I spent the night at her house, a huge brick farmhouse a few miles away from mine. A plump, wrinkled lady in a lavender sweat suit fed us dinner. We ate off TV trays and watched *Fantasy Island*. It was the adult television hour, the time when, at home, I was sent to read in my bedroom.

"Is that your grandma?" I asked when the woman had shuffled back into the kitchen.

"Nope, she's just my Nana Ruby. My grandma lives in New York."

"Is Nana Ruby related?"

Lucy shook her head, "She just comes to take care of me when Dad's at work."

"He's working right now?" My dad, who was an attorney, was always home by 5:30 except when he was in court. He helped me with my math homework and emptied ice trays into dinner glasses.

"Yeah," she was squinting, concentrating on the television. "He works in D.C.," she explained. "He used to be a policeman, but now he's a consultant. He has his own company. Big cities hire him, and then he goes there and makes them safer."

I nodded, not really understanding, but not wanting to seem stupid.

"My mother's dead," she added before I could ask. "We live here because Dad says it's like the safest area in the whole country."

On the mantle was a framed photograph of a woman sitting on the edge of a fountain. She had hair that was so blond it was almost white and very soft-looking skin. She didn't look anything like Lucy, but I wondered if she might not be her mother.

Nana Ruby didn't reemerge from the kitchen until it was time for us to get ready for bed. She followed us upstairs, suspiciously watched us brushing our teeth, and then tucked us both into Lucy's big bed. As soon as the door clicked shut, Lucy sat up and turned on the lamp. "She won't come back in. Let's do something."

It was after ten, and I was tired. I looked across the room. "Could we play with those?" Across the far wall was a shelf lined with at least fifty dolls, all of them in various costumes. "They all look like you." Although they were different sizes, each doll had short black curls and brown eyes. There was a cowgirl, an Indian princess, a Hawaiian dancer, even a doll dressed in pajamas.

"Those aren't for playing," she said, "That's a collection. My dad brings those back from all the cities he goes to."

She pushed back the covers. "Do you want to see something cool?"

She padded across the rug to the window and flipped the latch. First the window, then the screen, slid easily open beneath her fingers. I climbed through after her, feeling the cold aluminum of the porch roof beneath my bare feet. I could hear cows groaning somewhere on a neighboring farm, and the air smelled bitter like someone had been burning leaves. The stars were very clear through the leafless branches. "Sometimes I sit out here when it's warm," she whispered.

I knelt carefully next to Lucy on the slanted roof. I felt my skin prickling beneath my flannel gown. "How did your mom die?"

"She died when I was born." Lucy stretched her night gown over her knees and hugged them to her chest. She spoke knowingly, like she understood it all and was a little proud. "Nana Ruby has been taking care of me pretty much since then, I think. She's not so bad. In the summertime she lets me help her in the garden." She stood up. "Wait here while I go get something."

I watched her slide back through the window, and then I looked out across the trees, the cold air emptying my chest. I thought about all those little Lucy dolls on the shelf inside.

She returned with a hair brush and, kneeling behind me, began to brush my hair. She moved the brush in long, slow strokes, and it felt like electricity in the cold air.

Lucy had several boyfriends that summer—boys from the neighboring county who had stringy hair and smoked cigarettes in the arcade at Elk Run Pool. I think I was jealous of these boys, of how she would sit on their knees for hours while they touched her hair and added her name to the others carved in the rotting wood of the picnic tables.

My mother worried about all the time I spent with Lucy. "Who is this girl," she wanted to know, "and why have you never mentioned her in the past? Can't we at least meet her parents?" There were other girls whom she would have preferred—Amanda, who lived in the three-story house across the street, or even Treeva. Mother said Treeva had manners despite the fact that her father drove a school bus and her mother worked at Piggly Wiggly.

It was my father who dropped me off at the pool each morning on his way to work. He couldn't understand why he should pay for me to go to the public pool when we were already members at Laurel Creek Country Club. "I don't get you, Livie," he said as he dug a ten dollar bill from his wallet. "The club pool has platform diving boards and beach volleyball." He shifted uncomfortably and surveyed the line of kids forming outside the chain link fence as I gathered my beach towel and sun block off the floor of the car. "Sweetheart," he said when I opened the door, "your mother said to tell you not to sit on the toilet seats."

It was the summer we ate grape snow cones and gooey microwave pizza, the summer we had "tea parties." Lucy and I would hold hands and cross our legs, letting our bottoms sink to the slick cement floor of the pool. Sitting there, bathed in sunlight streaming through cool chlorine, we would blow bubbles into each other's faces until we ran out of breath and had to kick back to the surface, gasping for air.

Lucy always laughed at me because I couldn't hold my breath as long as she could. Sometimes after I surfaced, I would look down to find her staring up at me through the water, her short hair floating like ripe seaweed and her eyes even blacker than usual.

Lucy forgot about the swimming pool boys once high school started that fall. We went to dances after football games every Friday night. It was easy to lose Lucy in the crowded gymnasium. I danced with boys who tried to slide their palms beneath my turtlenecks and wool sweaters, and by a quarter past eleven I usually found Lucy sneaking out from the darkness beneath the bleachers, her underwear in her back pocket.

She made the varsity track team in the spring. As far as anyone could remember, a freshman had never made it. After school I'd see her jogging down toward the track with a group of girls, their legs lean and moving in unison. When she quit, she told me it was because she didn't like the other girls, the way they all talked. She said they were jealous and I agreed, but I worried, secretly, that I might be too. I began to hear about things she did in the beds of pick-up trucks parked in the dead-end dirt road up from where the trestle crosses the river. I wasn't sure when she had crossed that line, but I was very aware that she had. And that somehow she had managed to do it without becoming one of those girls—the skinny, big-haired girls who left school to work at the Blue Bell Clothing factory and live with older men in the trailer park. All of us, even Treeva, were a little in awe of Lucy, a little afraid of her.

Her father bought her clothes—beaded jewelry from Arizona, a long leather coat from Texas, a thick wool sweater from somewhere in Scandinavia—all of which she wore with beat up jeans, then heaped in dirty piles around her room. All I had to do was say something was pretty, and she would offer it to me. I never took anything except a ring with a large amber-colored stone. I still have it, although I don't wear it anymore. The band is so intricately carved it looks like lace.

Even after she turned sixteen, Lucy's father wouldn't allow her to get a driver's license. He claimed she was too young and careless. I drove her

home in the Corolla my parents gave me for my birthday. Some afternoons Lucy was not waiting for me in the courtyard, and those days I
would usually pass her as I made my way through the lines of parked
cars. She would be seated on the hood of some boy's truck, watching
him dig through his backpack for his keys.

When she rode with me, we drank Slurpees from the 7-Eleven and
talked about what we thought would be on our U.S. Government exam
and whether or not our English teacher, Mr. Reed, was gay. One afternoon, she wasn't waiting for me, and I didn't see her anywhere, not
even after the buses had all cleared away from the front of the building and the parking lot had begun to empty. "Have you seen Lucy?" I
asked some kids who were passing a cigarette around in front of a blue
Suburban. They glared and shook their heads.

I called Brooke, a girl I knew from Spanish class, over from a cluster
of girls making their way to the baseball stands. "Sorry," she shrugged
her shoulders. When she rejoined the group, the other girls leaned in
for the news. One of them—younger, with a long, blond braid—looked
back and eyed me curiously as they trudged up the hill four abreast.

"Have you seen Lucy Breeden anywhere?" I asked a guy named
Jason who was pulling a ball bag from his trunk. He had shaved his
hair so that the number eleven floated like two caterpillars on the back
of his head. "I'm supposed to take her home."

He swung the bag over his shoulder and grinned. Like Lucy's, his
hair was dark and curly on top. "Well, let's see," he said. "She and my
buddy Rick ditched sixth period, so she's probably already made it
home by now. In fact, she's probably made it there twice."

He called me that night and apologized, sort of. He asked if I ever
found Lucy. "No," I said. "I haven't talked to her, but I'm sure she's
fine." He asked if I wanted to do something that weekend, maybe get
some ice cream and rent a movie. Although I was nearly seventeen, I
hadn't had many dates. A year or two later, I would come into fashion
the way girls who are too pale and too thin usually do if they wait long
enough, but at that time Jason Clements was more than I had hoped for.

Lucy said he was a pig and that I should probably cancel. I told
her I would think about it, but I curled my hair and wore eyeliner
instead. My parents acted like he was there to court me, made him
come inside and visit. I was mortified when Dad poured him a glass
of scotch, but then my mother made it even worse. She took the glass
from his hand and said, "Really, Vernon, this boy is going to be driving our daughter."

By ten-o-clock Jason and I were parked in the cemetery off Black Mountain Road. I had made out with several boys—in the empty hallway at dances and behind the arcade at the pool. But it was just that. We had kissed until our chins were chapped, let our hands flutter vaguely until something—the reverberation of a stairwell door or a car engine starting up—stirred us to wipe our mouths and return to the crowd. But there was an urgency to which I was unaccustomed as Jason's mouth worked at mine. Something about the closeness of space in the car, everything dark except a tiny light on the dashboard. When he began unbuttoning my jeans I sat up. "Christ," I said. "It's almost eleven. You've got to take me home."

I'm not sure what Jason's expectations were, whether he sought me out because of Lucy. We went out off and on over the next two years, and whenever we started at it, he would pull a condom from his back pocket and set it on the dashboard or the coffee table. I said no, always. Three times I let him get the rubber on first, though.

Sometimes, when the weather was warmer and the days were a little longer, Lucy and I would meet after dinner and go for runs. Nana Ruby had died that winter, and I think Lucy missed her more than she ever thought she would. Or maybe it made her start to think about her mother. Things were happening around us too. That April a bomb exploded in a government building in Oklahoma City, and we watched, again and again on classroom cable, the gaping mouth of cement and steel that had ripped open beneath a rising cloud of dust. Suddenly, the world, so unsettled, swelled just outside our periphery. As we jogged past the gray farmhouses and the spring smells of old leaves and new grass and damp worm dirt soaked through our windbreakers, she would ask me about things.

"Do you believe in God?" she wanted know.

"Sure."

"Do you believe in heaven?"

"Sure."

"Sure like absolutely, or sure like why not?"

She wanted to know if I thought time shot on forever or circled back around us. I thought about the plot diagrams Mr. Reed drew on the board. It had not yet occurred to me that maybe there wasn't a god or that maybe time wasn't infinite.

We never talked about boys, though, not the way I sometimes did with my other girlfriends. Treeva would tell me how she and Brian had parked in the church lot, and she had let him go to second, only to miss a button as she was refastening her shirt. I would tell her how I had touched Jason through his underwear beneath the wool blanket my mother draped over our couch. What I never told her was how often I let him come in my hands and how, after he left, I always scrubbed them with hot water and lava soap until I thought the skin would fall off. I was so afraid I would touch myself during my sleep.

The summer after we graduated, I told my parents I wanted to get a job and earn some of my own money for school in the fall. It seemed like a good way to get out of the house. "What do you think you want to do?" My father asked me. "I imagine I could arrange for a paid internship at the office." I told him I didn't know what I wanted to do, but I knew I didn't want to be an attorney.

I worked evenings at the Laundromat at Elk Run Campground, scraping the fluffy purple lint from the dryer screens, selling tiny boxes of detergent to the tourist campers. During the day I would sometimes lie by the pool. Lucy worked the flowerbeds, and on her breaks she would come and sit on the grass next to me as I slathered Coppertone onto my freckled shoulders. Her legs were brown and dusty, and her fingernails were stained with potting soil and juicy green weeds.

She sneaked out a lot that summer. Jason, who had broken up with me, was in boot camp somewhere in South Carolina. In his absence, I watched Lucy more closely. Sometimes I would see her as I was locking up the laundromat. Voices drifted uphill from the cluster of trees and sandlots where pale blue tents and white trailers were flickering behind lit fires. Some evenings she would be drinking beer with college boys there to fish the river for the weekend. Other times she would be climbing onto the back of a Harley, locking her arms around the waist of one of the strung-out coal miners from over in Wise County. I leaned into the railing where the cement steps cut into the hillside. I imagined she spent the night between the mildewing flannel of old sleeping bags or on the rocks up at Pinnacle Overlook.

One night as I was driving home, I passed Lucy on the road between our houses and the campground. I pulled up beside her, and she climbed in before I even offered.

"Where are you going?" I asked.

"Nowhere."

"You want me to take you home?"

"Sure," she said.

I couldn't find anything good on the radio, so I turned it off, and for a while we sat in silence listening to the slow swish of air through the cracked car windows and the click of insects against the windshield.

"You know, it hasn't been such a bad time here," is what I finally said. My father had talked me into attending Mount Solon, the local college, instead of going to one of the state schools or down to the University of Tennessee with Lucy. I didn't want to think about her leaving me, about her being almost two hours away. "Won't you miss Conrad's Fork?"

She laughed the silent kind of laugh people make through their noses when they don't want people to realize they are laughing at them.

"What's so funny? I'm serious."

"I know. I was just thinking about something from when I was little. Do you remember back in second grade when I tried to set the world's record for wearing a rubber band around my wrist?"

I have no memory of Lucy before middle school.

"Oh come on, Livie. Remember? I wore a rubber band for seven months until it was all dirty and stretched out of shape. Nana Ruby hated that thing. I must have talked about it at show-and-tell at least ten times."

I shook my head.

"Anyway, I wore it all spring and all summer, and then I lost it. It fell off when I was raking leaves with my Dad. At first I was all upset. That night before bed, my Dad wanted me to write a letter to the Guinness Book of World Records. He was sure that seven months had been long enough to set some kind of record. But you know what? I never did it. I wore the damn thing all those months and then I never wrote the letter. I couldn't believe it was over. For the next month of my life I was still extra careful with that one arm, you know, in the bathtub or on the swings. Does that sound insane to you?"

After I dropped her off, I turned off the headlights and waited at the end of her lane, but she didn't come back outside.

The last Sunday before we left for college, Lucy met me as I was closing up the laundromat to see if I wanted to go for a walk. She was wearing a loose white dress, but her feet were still dusty beneath her sandals, and I could see bits of weed in her hair. We took swigs from some bourbon she'd stolen from her dad, and walked with our arms linked toward the steady sound of the river.

She had built up a tolerance drinking with the guys down in the campground, but she had to steady me as we crept onto the iron trestle and sat, gripping the rusty bars, dangling our legs over the edge. It was terribly black outside, and all I could see of us was the reflection of her white dress in the water way below.

"Livie, you remember how we used to try to figure out how time moves?" she asked me.

"Yeah."

"Well, I think now it's not so hard to figure out. It's whatever you make it. You can make time move forward—you know, linear—or you can make it circle back."

I assumed she was alluding to the end of August, to the fact that we would be apart. So I said, "I like that last one."

"Yeah, I guess so. Only problem is when you don't want to make time move either way."

"What do you mean?"

"I don't know. You know what I think would be the best way in the world to go?"

"No, what?"

"I would like to fall off the deck of a ship—a ship where I had been enjoying sun and good food and beautiful men—and just decide I didn't feel like calling out for help. Then float down to the very, very bottom of the ocean where the waves would still be alive, swelling all around me."

"Jesus, Lucy, that's awful." I had thought she meant the best way to get out of Conrad's Fork.

I hated college from the beginning. I felt unanchored after moving so long in the safety of Lucy's wake. When my mother called with the news, I knew right then that I wasn't going to finish. Lucy had been found below the trestle, dead, with a four-month-old fetus cold inside her. You would think what she did would have made me even more scared, but I gave it up a few months later for the second-string forward on the basketball team, a skinny boy who smelled like Big Red chewing gum and Brut aftershave. It didn't really hurt as much as I had thought it would or feel as good as it was supposed to either.

After he had left my room, I opened the blinds and stared across the parking lots and brick gates to where the blue light from the tower at the regional airport was flashing across the winter fields, shiny silver on the frost. I thought about what my mother had said, about how the water there was shallow and rocky. Certainly, she had assured me, Lucy died instantly.

In a way that made it worse, to know the ending came so fast. Could it have been that simple? I wondered. Nothing more than someone shutting off the lights? I didn't want to think about her swollen and broken. Instead, I imagined her falling, the September night air rushing between her thighs and streaming through her hair, her white dress rising like a balloon around her body.

ACCIDENTS

Vernon 1996

At least once a week I tell my wife I am going to take a long lunch with friends at the country club. On these mornings, Altura's voice, full of nervous energy, bounces off the walls like a pinball. "Wait!" she says when I start packing up my notes and arranging them in my briefcase. "Give me five minutes." Then she begins opening cabinets. From my study, I hear the smack of the refrigerator or pans slamming on the counters, and I know that soon she will be in the doorway clutching a paper sack.

"Here," she says, "Take this."

This morning when I take the bag from her, I can feel fruit rolling around on the bottom.

"For the interns," she says. Altura, who hasn't spoken with our daughter for nearly four months, has somehow discovered where I go. I could have left my ticket from visitor parking on the windshield, or someone could have seen me. Or maybe she just knows because she is a mother.

In the car, I inspect my wife's silent peace offerings: microwave popcorn, peanut butter cookies, a fashion magazine, red delicious apples, and a package of ball point pens—fine tipped because Livie is left-handed like her mother.

We are not the kind of family you see on those television talk shows. I've come home mid-afternoon, just to relax for an hour and have a meal with my wife when I know I'll be pulling a late evening, and you would not believe the crap that is on the TV then. Yolanda, our house cleaner, leaves the shows on while she works. She keeps coming back and adjusting the volume even louder as she moves from room to room. Mothers who have become pregnant by their daughters' husbands. Fourteen-year-old girls who want to marry sixty-five-year-old men. Children whose mothers are strippers, whose fathers make methamphetamines out of the basement. Altura and I eat in the kitchen, but poor Yolanda, she's riveted. She turns off the vacuum cleaner and cocks her head toward the den if she thinks the guests are getting really riled up.

Altura and I have been married for nearly thirty years, and we have managed to raise our only daughter with very little conflict, relatively speaking. Livie was salutatorian of her high school. She never came home drunk. She never even got a speeding ticket. She was a happy child, not the kind to brood in the backyard or torture neighborhood pets. All the drama has arisen since she started college. Knowing that I'm in the middle gives me constant heartburn. I have to carry Rolaids in my pants pocket.

I know better than to call Livie and say, "Let me pick you up at nine, and we'll go shopping then get a bite to eat." I have to make it look unplanned. The second time I came to visit her I made lunch reservations at the Bluestone Inn. When she was maybe seven or eight, we took Livie there for her birthday and she finished off two adult orders of glazed pork medallions—mixed up her mashed potatoes and gravy and dipped them in that. Since it was her birthday, Altura let her get away with it. But that day she wasn't having it.

"I can't go that far," she said. "Just take me back to the dorm, Dad. I've got class in an hour and a half."

"Can't you miss one class?" She's failing half her coursework, my daughter who used to cry if she made a B. I really didn't see what difference one lecture would make. "We're already on our way, sweetie. It'll be fine."

"Oh my God," she said. "This is complete bullshit. What is this, a kidnapping? Is this some kind of intervention?" When I turned down the radio and looked at her, she yelled, "Turn around!"

Today I drive clear across Garrison, go past the college, and then spend a good hour or so just driving through the farmland outside of town. I guess I don't mind so much. When you cross Dry River, you are suddenly in another time. It is just one of a dozen forks of the Cumberland and Powell Rivers that crisscross that little valley, so the pasture is green and rolling. It's Mennonite country—salt box houses with nineteenth-century barns still standing behind them. Shiny black buggies sit in the yards like prehistoric spiders, and chickens wander up and down the long dirt lanes. Some of the people don't even own a tractor.

I've only just begun to broker farm deals, but I already know how this community works. When a young couple marries, all the families in the congregation pool their savings to help buy a piece of land. No mortgage, nothing. They'll come in with fifty thousand dollars cash.

Today I see a family making their way down a row of new bean plants—three boys in plain shirts, a young mother with her hair coiled beneath a gauzy bonnet. She looks up as I pass, lifts a hand to wave. And for some reason, I keep watching. I let my eyes flick to the rearview mirror and see her hand drift down to grace her stomach for just a moment, like a premonition.

I drive until 11:00. That's when I know Livie will be back from her morning classes if she has chosen to attend them, and at least awake if she has not. Mount Solon is a small private school with columned brick buildings and ornate entry ways, and it doesn't look much different than it did when I was there forty years ago. To get to Livie's dormitory, I have to walk the length of a long mall, grassy and bordered by more than two hundred maple trees. There are always kids out there, lying on their backs or tossing around a Frisbee.

One couple catches my eye—a girl on a bench and a young man sitting on the ground next to her. She has a handful of those little whirly seeds that fall off the trees, and she keeps dropping them in front of him. He reaches up and grabs them in mid air, throws them back at her. And I'm thinking that maybe things aren't so different now, despite what's on TV, when that girl sees me watching and she stares back, hard. I get embarrassed then, embarrassed enough to feel my face heat up. That's how I know I'm getting old. You get to a point where you think you're finally past most self-consciousness, but then it comes back full force.

Livie's window is third from the left on the back side of Dillon Hall. On the inside of the glass she has taped stickers that say things like *Meat Is Murder*. There is also a string of multi-colored Christmas lights that twinkle at night. I know because my wife, on several occasions, has insisted we drive by after an evening out. Just three days ago, we sat in this parking lot, Altura and I, watching the outline of that window, the rope of flashing color, like it was something we could grab hold of, something to help us navigate this ocean of silence.

When Livie was in high school, it was always her mother who handled the day to day, the little emergencies. Say she forgot her gym uniform or wanted to go get a bite to eat with friends after school. Livie would call home, and if I answered she would say, "Put Mom on the phone."

I figured out what I was and wasn't supposed to do as best I could. She wanted me to come watch her debate club competitions, but I couldn't walk up to the stage and congratulate her after they were over. If she had been on the phone and she came down to dinner with red eyes, I was not supposed to ask if she had had a fight with her boyfriend.

Her first months at Mount Solon, she called at least once a week. She would spend a good half an hour talking to her mother. Altura would hand me the phone for a minute, and I would say something like, "Hi sweetie. How's the car?"

And she'd say, "Fine. How's work?"

"Oh," I'd say, "same old, same old." Then maybe I'd ask, "Are your classes going well?"

She would say, "Good enough." Then we would exchange I love you's, and I would hand the phone back to my wife.

My first lunch with Olivia truly was an accident. I was advising the Board of Regents on purchasing land for the new science building. It had been over a month since we'd heard from her, and she wasn't returning any of Altura's calls.

I was cutting through the student lounge on my way back to the car, trying to get out of the sleet, when I saw my daughter in line at the snack bar. She was wearing her winter parka over a yellow sundress. I almost just walked on by. It took some convincing to get Livie to attend a school so close to home. One of the conditions we agreed upon was to give her privacy. We weren't supposed to show up unannounced or try to force her to come home every weekend.

I sidled up to the counter next to her and acted like I was concentrating on the menu, which was tacked overhead in moveable plastic lettering. It looked tasty, but really bad for my cholesterol—mozzarella sticks, French fries, onion rings. I asked, "How are the onion rings?" and Livie turned to look at me.

"Daddy." She wasn't smiling. "I guess mother sent you."

"Actually, Livie, I've just come out of a meeting with Dr. Sensibar."

She looked at my briefcase and eyed me suspiciously.

"What are you doing here?" I asked her. "Did you miss lunch?" We pay several thousand dollars each semester for her dining hall pass, which includes three square meals every weekday, brunch on the weekends.

She shrugged her shoulders.

It was maybe 2:00, the dining hall closed. I thought about how she must have just woken up. I said, "I have to get back to the office by 3:30, but if you want, I can take you to get something to eat."

"Do we have to talk about stuff?"

What, I wondered, could that possibly mean? "Olivia," I said, "We don't have to do anything you don't want to do."

I don't just go knock on the door of Livie's room. When I was a student at Mount Solon there were only a few visiting hours on Saturdays and Sundays. That was the only time a male visitor could even think about stepping outside of the sitting room area. If a couple was in a room alone together, the door had to remain open at all times. If you were going to take a girl somewhere in your car, you had to sign her out, and you had to take along an escort. When the weather was good, if a girl really liked you, she would say she was going to the library, and instead she would meet you out on the mall. You could hold hands and walk by the river.

I clear my throat to announce myself to the resident advisor, but she has some kind of aerobics tape going and just waves me on through. There is a courtesy phone in the hallway where you can call up to the girls' rooms, and that is the way I do it. On the side of the phone is a black sticker with a little dancing skeleton and the words *Social Distortion*. Today Olivia's voice sounds like I woke her up. When she finally comes down her hair is limp and going everywhere. Maybe that's just the style now. When she was in high school she wouldn't walk out to the mailbox unless her hair was done. Sometimes, if she didn't like how it turned out, she'd wash the front part of her hair two or three more times, blow dry it straight up, and start all over.

I've left the bag that Altura has prepared for Livie on the passenger seat. That way she has to pick it up when she gets in the car. She holds the sack on her lap and stares straight ahead. She is wearing that same

yellow sundress, only this time without the parka, flip flops instead of
snow boots. Altura hates flip flops, calls them rubber sandals.

"Is Showalter's okay?"

She shrugs and mutters something under her breath in French, as
she has been doing all semester. *"Pourquoi pas?"*

It makes me glad I never learned the language.

Showalter's Mennonite Family Restaurant is out on Route 38, in
the middle of nowhere, a little outside of Garrison, miles from I-75.
That's where we always go, but I know I still have to ask. It's a buffet,
another thing Altura hates, and it's glorious, better than Thanksgiving—roast beef, turkey, mashed potatoes, butter beans, stuffing, three
kinds of gravy.

When we get up to the hostess stand, Livie, who has become a veg-
etarian, says, "Just the salad bar."

I say, "Give us the works. I'll eat enough fried chicken for both of
us."

Livie fills one plate with salad and another with bleu cheese dressing. She picks up vegetables with her fork and stabs them in the dressing. I think she does this because the dressing has so much fat. Altura
has always just asked for lemon slices to squeeze on her salad. But
Livie really rolls the carrots around until they have a big glob of dressing, and today she cleans both plates.

I eat very slowly. Always, I try to remember things that we can talk
about, things that will make her laugh. Sometimes I tell her stories
about when I was at Mount Solon. There are stunts I know surprise
her, like the time my roommates and I made an anatomically correct
snowman on the president's lawn.

Today I say, "Yolanda hasn't cleaned the upstairs bathtub for two
weeks because she saw a spider in there."

She cracks a little smile.

And I think this is my chance. Dr. Sensibar told me that Livie has
been helping one of the botany professors in the greenhouse, and I
want to ask her about it, want to find some way to draw her out, but
then I can see I've waited too long. She's getting restless, starting to
look out the window.

I don't know what started this stand-off, and I don't know what
to look for to know if she's okay. She looks all right now, fuller in the
face. At the beginning of last semester Altura was certain Livie was losing weight. That was in September, after they pulled that local girl—
one of Livie's classmates—out of the river. Sometimes I worry that we
started all this too late. It was by no choice of our own—it was just the

way things happened—but Altura and I are nearly old enough to be Olivia's grandparents.

I tell Livie, "Let me just go get some pie. Then I'll take you back." I get a piece of coconut cream for me, and then I try something new. I go back through the dinner line one more time. I take a little salad plate and dish out a big helping of mashed potatoes. I pour gravy over it, making a little pool with the ladle.

Then I set the plate down in front of my daughter. "Dessert," I say.

She rolls her eyes at me. "Daddy, you know there's meat in that." But she doesn't keep the act going long. She stirs everything so the gravy and potatoes are all mixed together, just like she did when she was little. She takes slow bites and licks the spoon, and watching her, I think maybe I have more sway than I give myself credit for. So I say something I have been scared to utter these last four months, "How about you drive home with me this afternoon?"

"What are you talking about? You know I have class." Suddenly she is like a cornered animal, like that cat that somehow got into our basement a few years ago and gave birth to four kittens. She looks at me, eyes narrowed, a growl building deep in her throat. "You just said lunch. Don't you have to get back to work?"

But she hasn't said no.

"I've got a meeting in Conrad's Fork," I tell her. "I have to deliver some papers to a farm out near Sandy Bottom. The old Ridenour place. You know, where the orchard is. A Tennessee development company has been trying to buy them out for a year now. I don't think they really want to sell, but I think they probably should. I just want to make sure they don't get taken."

I could run the paperwork by this evening on my way home. In fact, that was my original plan. I keep expecting her to point that out, but she doesn't. She doesn't say anything, just chews on a hangnail, toys with the strap of her dress. So I keep talking.

"We don't have to run by the house if you don't want to," I tell her. "Just come along for the ride." There's no way I'd cart her all the way to Conrad's Fork without getting her and her mother back in the same room. But I'll say anything at this point.

It's a gorgeous day, sunshine warming up the car. Fluffy clouds, the kind that keep marking the mountains in shifting light and shadow. The lane up to the farmhouse is rutted from spring rain.

"Sorry," I tell Livie. "They need to spread some gravel."

She is leaning forward, palms pressed flat against the dashboard. "I'll say."

"It's just Mrs. Ridenour and her daughter now," I tell her. "They're having a hard time keeping the place up."

The house, built around the turn of the century, doesn't look much different from the farms I drove past hours earlier—two bedrooms upstairs, living room and parlor downstairs, kitchen built off the back. The paint is peeling, and the roof needs works. It has good bones, though, that's what Altura would say, if she could see the oak staircase I know is inside, or the wrap-around porch. It's a shame, really. If this deal goes down—and I feel certain it will eventually—this house will be demolished, along with all the out buildings.

"It's so pretty." Livie is looking past the house, to where the apple trees, heavy with blossom, loop the hillside in lacy, concentric rings. "They're going to sell this place?"

"They're going to have to, sweetie. Neither of them is in very good health. The mother fell, slipped on the ice last winter. Tough birds, though, both of them. They've kept things going all these years. The daughter, Helen, raised two girls on her own. And Mrs. Ridenour, the mother, well, her husband ran off with someone else years ago. The farm actually got more profitable after he left, if that tells you anything."

I pop a handful of Rolaids, and she watches me, worried.

"Morning, Ladies," I say as we climb out of the car. They've both come out to the porch to greet us. "This is my little girl, Olivia. Taking a break from college to spend an afternoon with her old man."

I'm ready for her to say I tricked her into coming or to mutter some obscenity in French, to at least roll her eyes. But she smiles and gives a little wave, says, "Hello."

"Oh," breathes the old woman, fingers clawing along the porch rail, "Aren't you lovely." Mrs. Ridenour's hands are so arthritic, she can't straighten them anymore—thick knuckled and brown as bark from all the liver spots.

And I can see my daughter for a minute, the way they must be seeing her. I can see past the pall that this depression—surely that's what we have to call it—has cast over her. She is pretty, our Livie, although I'm not sure she realizes it. Fair skin and gray eyes like her mother's, long, straight hair. It is her ways, though—she was such a kind and gentle child, just a little bit shy—which have always completed her beauty. As a little girl, she would move the worms off the sidewalk after a rain, carry them back to the flower bed.

"I'm Helen," says the daughter, "and this is my mother, Myra. Welcome." She looks at me then, all business, and I can see a little of why the two of them have been able to manage this long. "Well, what did they come back with?"

But Mrs. Ridenour's not having it. She raises her hand to silence her daughter, says, "Since when do we conduct business on the front porch?"

And Helen laughs, defusing that current which had begun to throb in the air between us. "Mom's right," she says. "Come on in. Let me get ya'll some iced tea."

"Oh, I don't want to intrude," says Livie. "May I walk up there a little ways?"

I have to do a double-take because she says it so sweetly, says *may* I. She is pointing up the ridge, past the orchard.

And I'm struck suddenly with the memory of playing with Livie in the front yard. She is six years old, standing on our own porch steps directing Altura and me in her favorite game.

"Take five scissor steps," she says because I am still her favorite person in the world and she always throws the game in my direction.

But before I can move forward and tap her hand, I have to say, "Mother, *may* I?"

I get a little lump in my throat then, I swear I do.

"Oh, sure," says Helen. "You're not allergic to bees, are you? The trees are full of them this time of year." And then she adds, leaning in toward Livie, almost conspiratorially, "Come back through the barnyard. There are six new lambs in the back paddock."

I'm thinking how great this is, that she is out of that dorm room, that she is outside in the sunshine. I'm thinking this is going to work, thinking surely she'll come on home and talk to her mother, she might even spend the night. But all I can say is, "Watch your footing, sweetheart. You're wearing those rubber sandals."

Helen has to move plant trays before we can even sit down at the table. They are everywhere. Around the corner, I can see more trays covering the floor in the mudroom, each cell sprouting delicate green leaves beneath the clear plastic—like hundreds of tiny greenhouses.

"What's in them?" I ask.

"Everything," she tells me. "Cucumbers, tomatoes, squash, eggplant, pumpkins, lettuce. Corn's the only thing we start in the ground, at least now anyway."

Mrs. Ridenour adds, "Now we really only raise what we can eat."

"You're planning on staying here, then. At least through the fall?" In my mind I start revising the contract, pushing back the schedule.

"Here you are." Ice clinks in the glass Helen sets in front of me. "Or would you rather have a beer? I think we may have some in the mudroom fridge."

"Oh, no. I can't drink at all anymore. Gives me heartburn."

I take a sip, and the tea is cold and sweet.

For her mother, Helen pours milk. Then she sits down across from me.

"They've upped the offer." I push the manila folder across the table. "Here. Have a look yourself."

As she scans the dates and figures, she starts to massage her temples.

I tell her exactly what they've asked me to: "They're also looking at alternative sites now, two properties near Bear Lithia Springs. One of the places is a dairy operation." But then I add, "That might just be talk. Even if it's not, they'd have to convince both owners to sell."

"We're not playing hard-to-get here, I promise you that. We understand this is a lot of money. I just thought some of this land would go to my girls eventually."

Mrs. Ridenour whispers, "Their legacy." She hasn't glanced at the papers, hasn't even sipped her milk.

I follow her gaze out the window to where Olivia is making her way up the ridge, a flash of yellow amid all that white. It is like setting course, like yearning into a telescope: my daughter moving slowly away from me as I watch through that tiny kitchen window.

She pauses at the top, and I know where she must be looking, down toward the river. And, of course, I wonder. I wonder if she can see the trestle from up there. And I think about that other girl's parents. Of course, we never met them. We hardly knew her, really. She was just a classmate of Livie's. But I think about them, just the same. Now, when my daughter seems to be bobbing, always, just out of my reach, I think about them in a way I never have before. What can it be like, I wonder, to have to go on without your child? I have that feeling again, that thickening in my chest, and I have to look away.

"We trust you, Vernon. What do you think we should do?" Helen, the daughter, is talking to me, drawing me back to business, back to the table.

Regardless of how little time I spend there now, I made my reputation in the courtroom. People will tell you law practice is all reading and research, and it is true there is a lot of that involved, perhaps even more with real estate law. But what it boils down to is what you do with the accidental information. It's a matter, really, of being always ready to receive. So, half an hour later when the three of us find Olivia out at the lamb pen, I am prepared.

The ewes are congregated in the far corner, chewing on the honeysuckle that is just beginning to bud along the fence. Livie has climbed through the wooden planks and is trying to coax the lambs over to her. "They're adorable," she calls to us. "I want to pet them." She lowers herself to her knees slowly.

"Will the mothers mind?" I ask.

Helen laughs. "They're practically pets. Tame as dogs."

They ewes look up, sleepy-eyed, and then, when they see we don't have grain, they go back to grazing.

Then Helen adds, quietly, almost as an afterthought, "How far along is she?"

And I feel it like I used to feel it in the courtroom, a sudden surge of electricity. There is just enough breeze to stir Livie's dress. The breeze is heavy with the scent of pollen and tilled soil and warm dung. In its wake, the yellow material, which has puffed out like a sail, resettles. And suddenly, I can't fathom how I couldn't have seen it before. I know it as fact. I also know that the decision has been made, that she has decided—that, sometimes, waiting is a kind of decision in itself. And I know, for the moment, to play dumb.

"She's a freshman," I say, "in the middle of her second semester."

"Oh," Helen says, not missing a beat. "Well, that's great."

The lambs are only a few days old. Their tails still flagging behind them, but they run and romp, chase the bees that hover around the clover. And in the middle of it all, Olivia kneels, still as stone. One hand flutters, smoothing her dress, the other is extended, palm up, reaching toward the lambs.

"Yes, child," Mrs. Ridenour calls, leaning heavily on her cane. "Just be still and wait. They'll come to you."

OLIVIA, THE ROCK

2001

Livie's five-year-old son is afraid of weather. He has no concept of black ice or ultra violet rays, but raindrops splattering against the minivan's windshield induce vomiting. When she wakes Eliot to a day of gray drizzle, he's clammy hot inside his pajamas and his hair, still toddler blond, curls in damp wisps. If she urges him out of bed, he steps willingly into a pair of corduroy overalls, even eats a bowl of Cheerios. But he's ghost-faced with his forehead pressed against the glass for the entire drive, and she's sure to receive a call from the school nurse before she arrives home.

Her best friend Fran, who doesn't want babies but owns a greenhouse, tells her to stop worrying. "Plants are always hardier than it says they are in the catalogue," she says. "I don't see why kids should be any different." If Fran were to have children, Livie knows, she wouldn't tolerate such silliness. When Fran finds kids plucking the blossoms off begonias or throwing rocks into the decorative ponds, she puts them to work. It's not uncommon to see three or four of them raking the gravel in the parking lot while their parents meander through the tables of annuals.

Other friends say their children invent all kinds of ailments to avoid school. Years ago, Livie did the same thing on warm days in May, arranging her symptoms late enough in the morning so that the string of emergency babysitters her mother kept on call would be unreachable, knowing her mother would take her along to the big swimming pool up at the clubhouse. She remembers leaning back into the crinkling paper that covered the sick cot, listening as the school nurse coaxed Altura, who has always insisted her daughter call her by her first name. Livie was an inexperienced liar back then and, as a consequence, suffered guilt, but it was worth it to listen to her mother's voice lilting with the others at Laurel Creek Country Club. To be one of those ladies, sipping pineapple juice from a glass topped with a green umbrella.

Livie remembers the morning she discovered she was pregnant. She had not spoken with Altura for months. She had been flitting back and forth between the most impractical majors: Earth Science, Religions of the Ancient World, Botany, French literature. At the time she liked to think of herself as disinherited, as wildly intellectual and severed from her conservative roots, but at the beginning of each semester her parents signed off roughly ten grand in tuition. She was failing required Algebra for the second time, and without her father's alumni donations, it would have become an issue, regardless of the fact that she knew the geologic history of the Cumberland Plateau and had committed to memory entire entries from the diaries of Collette.

That particular morning, Livie carried one of those boxed kits across campus in her coat pocket and peed over the plastic wand in the basement bathroom of the library. She thought she would find privacy amid the quiet tiles, surrounded by shelves of academic journals and bound periodicals, certainly more than in the communal cluster of showers and toilet stalls inside her dormitory. Livie waited, her thighs prickling cold against the slick porcelain. She wasn't surprised when two pink stripes appeared. It could have been morning sickness, but she thought she felt something turn over like a tarot card inside her. She knew then that Eliot had already rooted himself there, a molten mass of protein. He would be a way out, and she has never taken that lightly.

She rushes to her son's side as soon as the nurse calls. She carried a cellular phone with her to the market, even before they were fashionable, and she thinks nothing of abandoning half-filled grocery carts in the produce section. Her tires squeal into the bus lane in front of Conrad's Fork Elementary. She swoops him up from the sick room where three or four other children are usually congregated, then signs him out with a flourish. Last Friday a sealed envelope was attached to the folder in which Eliot brings his school work home. Inside, Livie found a letter from one of the Renfro County school district's rotating child psychiatrists requesting a meeting.

*

Livie carefully selects a gray button down shirt from the walk-in closet she shares with her husband and hands it to him when he exits the bathroom.

"Isn't this a little dressy?" Tom wants to know. The sweatshirt he's wearing—a navy blue one with *MERCK* printed in silver silkscreen letters—is from the pharmaceutical company where he works. They make everything from preventative pills for heart disease to deworm-ers for sheep, but most of Tom's lab work involves pills that stop baldness.

"I think we ought to at least try to make a good impression." Livie parts the blinds with her fingers and peers, past the terraced side yard, downhill to where streaky purple clouds are stretched across the line of bare trees at the edge of the park. They will be dropping Eliot off at her parents' for the course of the meeting, and she doesn't want any complications. "Besides I told Altura we're going to dinner with your boss and his wife." She doesn't want to subject her son's weather pho-bia to further scrutiny by her mother. She has been reluctant to tell Altura just how much school Eliot has missed in the last three months, how precarious his kindergarten enrollment has become.

Livie's relationship with her mother, which only resumed when she announced her pregnancy, is strained by the unexpected visits the aging woman makes on weekday afternoons when Eliot is home sick. Sometimes it's what she doesn't say that gets to Livie the most. The way she raises her eyebrows when she spies her grandson rolling his trucks back and forth over the living room carpet. The way she lightly fingers the laundered clothing Livie folds and stacks on the coffee table. The way she picks the mint leaves—which have been carefully cultivated beneath the back spigot—from her glass of iced tea.

Last April, Livie's parents sold the limestone Victorian home where she was raised in favor of a condominium in Cedar Creek Summit. Livie can see the lights along the ski slopes snaking down the side of the mountain as Tom drives down Route 38, toward the resort entrance. It's only November but unusually cold, so they must already be making snow. Making weather. She glances periodically to the back seat, imagining that Eliot can sense the snow machines blasting frozen precipitation down the side of the mountain.

Tom has had the foresight to bring Mr. Bing, Eliot's stuffed clown, in case their son doesn't want to be left with his grandparents, but when he and Livie slip from the room, the boy is already engrossed in the plastic models of WWII planes that Livie's father assembles and displays on bookshelves. To Livie's dismay, her son is fascinated with battle toys. "Guess what?" he tells his grandfather. "I get to carry a tomahawk at school for Thanksgiving."

Her mother escorts them back into the foyer where the floor is white Italian marble, buffed until it reflects their heels. "Where did you say you were meeting them again? Clancy's?" This is another thing that gets under Livie's skin, the way Altura always answers her own questions. "Are you sure you don't want me to have your father call the Bluestone Inn? It's not too late for him to get a table for four there. No, I guess not." Livie has been inside two of the neighboring condos, and their floors are exactly the same.

In the evening the elementary school is a different place. Livie is used to pushing her way through a crowd of sniffling children to find her son. Tonight the floors have been waxed shiny. The emptied hallways smell like glass cleaner and powdered soap. The room where Livie and Tom were directed in the letter is actually a teachers' lounge with two couches upholstered in faux leather. Eliot's teacher is already there. "It's good to see you again," she says smiling.

Back in August, at the registration meeting, Livie was pleased to discover that Eliot had been placed in this woman's class. It had been clear immediately that Darla Erdrich, with her red clogs and her shimmery blonde ponytail, was the youngest of the kindergarten teachers, and that had seemed like a boon at the time. The walls of her classroom were filled with bright artwork. In the corner, a white and brown guinea pig kicked cedar shavings around a little cage. And though it probably wasn't fair, next to her, the other teachers—older women with bifocals and graying permanents—had seemed grumpy. Back in the car that night, before she even buckled her seat belt, Livie turned and touched Tom's shoulder. "I'm glad he got her," she said. Now she wonders if Eliot would be better off with another teacher, someone with a little more experience.

Darla introduces the psychiatrist, Kenny. He, too, is younger than Livie expected, with a goatee, as if that would make up for his shaved head. The fluorescent lights shine luridly off his scalp.

A mini tape recorder rests on the coffee table. "Do you mind if I tape our session?"

The word *session* seems to echo against the soda machines lining the wall behind them.

"Of course not," says Livie. The words come out in a whisper.

Darla pulls a little book and a pen out of a leather bag. "My teaching journal," she says. "In case we want to review my notes." Livie guesses the bag must be imitation Prada and is dismayed—not by the lack of authenticity, but by the fact that she notices such things.

There is a quiet desperation in the way Tom's hands twist in his lap, like the potted English Ivy that Livie has to pull away from the mortar around the porch every few weeks. She takes one of them and clasps his fingers tightly in her lap.

"We've taken Eliot to so many specialists in the last two months." Livie looks at Tom instead of Kenny or Darla when she says this. "I still think it might be allergies. I know the doctors don't."

There is the click and hum of the recorder starting up. "Actually," Kenny says, "first, I'd like you both to just tell me about yourselves, your concerns about all this."

"They think we've screwed him up," says Tom an hour later when he and Livie are dipping breadsticks into plastic cups of marinara at Pizza Hut. Kenny has asked them each to keep a journal, tracking Eliot's bouts of illness and their own reactions to them.

Livie can still feel the man's eyes on her. "Many adults"—he'd looked up from his notes when he said it, looked directly at Livie—"as well as children are experiencing increased anxiety this fall."

But she doesn't tell Tom this. She just shrugs her shoulders and says, "Maybe we have. It took Altura nearly twenty years to finish the job with me."

He tries to reach for her knee but knocks the table instead, sloshing their drinks. "I'm just saying it's even more serious than I thought. I don't really think anyone's to blame." He steadies their sodas and sighs, "I wish he just wanted to carry a purse or something."

Later they are lying in bed where layers of gray light slink in through the wooden blinds making Tom look somehow older, and suddenly Livie's sure he does think she's to blame. For the last two weeks, her husband has taken the stance that they must not allow Eliot to stay home from school and they must refuse to pick him up early. But he leaves for the lab before she wakes Eliot. Tom doesn't know how the color drains from their son's face if it's raining. He doesn't understand how impossible it would be to just slip his knapsack over his shoulders and leave him ready to faint on the curb.

Tom's fingers are making little circles over her collar bone, and suddenly the motion—one he always employs to calm her—feels heavy and condescending. Normally she sleeps on her side, facing away from her husband. She likes the weight of his breath on her hair, his fingers brushing her nightgown, brushing her lower back like it's his secret. Her tattoo. When she was in college, studying French, Livie discovered that her middle name, which is also Altura's maiden name, means "Rock." So she had *Olivia La Roche* inked across her back in tiny ornate letters, framed by two inches of periwinkle vine. Olivia, the rock. It was like the real Olivia, the girl who had long simmered inside her, had finally broken to the surface. She would have carved the change into her flesh if she could have. Tonight she shimmies forward until Tom's hand falls back onto the sheet.

The next morning, after she has delivered Eliot safely at kindergarten, Livie takes one of the flip top tablets that Tom brings home from Merck and records the time and the date at the top of the first page. She checks the thermometer that hangs in the square of sunlight framed above the kitchen sink. Then she adds that it is thirty-eight degrees outside, there is a slight cloud cover, and Eliot is at school without signs of fever. She gnaws on her pencil for a while, then writes one word: *Relief.*

She knows that this, particularly that last bit, is not exactly what Kenny is looking for. She doesn't just feel *relief.* She wonders if, when Eliot was born, they left part of him inside her. Sometimes she feels like she has a bathtub drain funneling behind her ribs, and when her son's well—when she knows he will have a good day—it's like someone stops it up just in time. Then she can plant bulbs along the back fence. She can go to the park where all the trees have let go of their leaves, where frost lingers past noon in the shadows, where only a few dog walkers venture out. Then the day is a ribbon unfurling before her.

She doesn't know how to write all this without sounding crazy. Livie spends the morning removing the glass fixtures from all the lights and soaking them in ammonia. She saw a special on *Dateline* about children with seasonal depression. Actually, Altura, who calls Tom's research at Merck "hodgepodge" but lives by Stone Phillips's medical investigations, phoned two weeks ago and insisted Livie turn on the TV. There was an eleven-year-old girl who became so sullen during the winter months that she couldn't complete her school work. As her condition worsened, she turned violent, lashing out at her parents. They had to install special fluorescent lamps all around the house. Livie doesn't think Eliot's problem is anything so permanent. Besides—and this is the point she stressed for Altura—Stone Phillips said that sort of depression generally appears during adolescence. But nothing can hurt at this point, so she even dries the glass with the special chamois cloth Tom uses on their cars.

After lunch, Livie has to get out of the house. She waits for Tom to call, as he always does on his lunch break. His voice warms when he learns Eliot is still at school. He's a good guy, her husband. He was the instructor of her college chemistry lab, and she chose him because of the careful way he revealed himself over the months. He measured himself out to her a little at a time like the demonstration mixtures he heated over the Bunsen burner at the front of the room. Finally, she thought, this is a man whom I cannot hurt. He gave up his teaching assistantship, gave up graduate school altogether, to take the position at Merck when she told him. He's the kind of guy who restacks his weights at the gym and walks the grocery cart back to the curb at Piggly Wiggly. Lately, Livie has noticed television commercials for pills similar to the ones Tom has worked on the last five years. They warn that under no circumstances should pregnant women handle the drug. She tries not to wonder.

Livie drives faster than she is supposed to. Behind her, she can feel the clouds thickening and pressing over the blue line of the mountains. She turns after crossing the bridge, and for the next four miles every rise of the pavement reveals Dry River glinting up at her, cold green. Soon she's standing in the gravel lot of Outdoor Effects, where she can hear the clear plastic of the greenhouse snapping in the wind. Fran waves to her from the tables where rows of poinsettias are arranged out front.

"Got to get these in," she shouts. "That wind's tearing the flowers. Besides I think it's going to rain, and we already watered them this morning." She hands Livie two foil-covered pots.

When all the plants are arranged in a red mass on the wooden tables that border the greenhouse walls, Fran wipes her hands on her sweatpants and removes her flannel coat. She is wearing a pink, hooded shirt that says *Spring Creek Sugar Maple Festival*. Fran's clothing choices don't make Livie cringe the way other people's do. Maybe it's that they are so undeniably bad to begin with, or maybe Livie has just grown so accustomed to them. She makes sometimes two trips to Outdoor Effects each day from March through September. Her home has been on the Conrad's Fork Garden Society's annual tour three summers in a row.

"This is crazy," says Fran, hoisting herself up onto one of the tables. "I told Bryce I don't work winters. That's why we're in this business, so we can have half the year off." Olivia envies this most about her friend, the way she knows what she wants, the way it's never a secret. Fran and her husband are trying to stretch their business out through the Christmas season by offering holiday plants and greenery. They are going to suspend little clumps of mistletoe from the iron rings that hold the hanging flowers in the summer.

"When are they going to deliver the trees?"

"Not till after Thanksgiving," says Fran. "That's when we'll make the wreaths, too. If you set up that stuff too early, it always dries out. Besides we've got enough going on this week with the decorating. Bryce has two appointments out near your place today, stringing up lights."

"Are you going to get white ones?" Livie fingers the broad velvety petals of a nearby plant.

"That's all we're doing. I like those big colored lights myself, but it seems like people only want to hang up the white ones anymore."

"No," says Livie, "I mean the poinsettias. Are you going to get the kind with white flowers?"

"Not this year." Fran leans over Livie's shoulder, peering into the foliage. "You know, the red part really isn't even the flower. Those are just leaves. The little yellow part in the middle, that's the flower." She points to the golden berry-like cluster in the center of the plant. "You want to take some home with you?"

"You know I won't allow anything on the premises that won't come back," says Livie turning from the table in mock disgust. She refuses to buy annuals. She tells Tom they're a bad investment, when she could pay just a little more for lilies or peonies or any number of plants that will return every year. The truth is, she was horrified by the huge planters of geraniums that lined the porch steps when she was a girl. Altura often forgot to water them, and Livie had to watch the things shrivel up again and again since her mother just dumped out the talavera pots and filled them with a fresh batch of brightly flowered plants. Livie has cultivated her own garden in a series of levels and cul-de-sacs designed to allow different plants to bloom during different parts of the season. She has a shade garden and a sun garden. There's even a gazebo covered in a special morning glory hybrid that only blooms in moonlight.

"You can hold poinsettias over," says Fran. "It's hard to get them to rebloom, but you can. You just have to trim them all the way down in summer, then stick them in a closet for a few weeks in the fall." Livie thinks that is what she was back in college when she first met Tom, a wick, pared all the way down.

Fran probes the soil of one of the pots, then brushes the wet dirt from her fingers. "Me and Bryce have seen these things growing into hedges along the road down in Mexico."

Large raindrops begin a slow splatter across the plastic roof, and Livie knows it's just a matter of time. She chooses two poinsettias to set on either end of the mantle, then takes the cell phone from her coat pocket and waits for the sick call. Space heaters have warmed the inside air, which is moist from the plants. To Livie it feels like invaded space, like she's inhaling someone's breath.

Livie stops by the house to find an umbrella and Mr. Bing. The light on the answering machine is blinking, and when she presses PLAY she knows she will hear her mother's voice barking behind the speaker. This is why she has carefully concealed her cell phone from Altura.

"Olivia, are you there? I didn't think so, what with the rain and all." She whispers *rain* like it's something horrible and secret. "Your father and I were having lunch the other day with this doctor. Your father's been advising him on some sort of tax suit. Didn't I tell you he wouldn't know what to do if he retired? Yes, I certainly called that one. Well, we were telling Dr. Lowrey, that's the young man's name, about Eliot's 'problem,' and he expressed sincere interest in seeing him. You don't mind that we mentioned it, do you? Of course not, we're his grandparents."

Livie presses STOP and listens to the tape rewind. She clicks the machine off altogether. Then, with the deliberateness of someone yanking a shade over a window, she pulls the cord from the wall.

A double line of first or second graders files past Livie before she can cross the hall to the office, boys on the right and girls on the left, in route to the music room or the cafeteria. Their eyes shyly slide in her direction as they march by. One boy, who has a tuft of what must be original baby hair curling over his collar in a thin tail raises his hand and yells, "Hey, Lady." Livie sees he has drawn something on his palm with purple magic marker. He is wearing a different sock on each foot, but neither really matches his nylon windbreaker. There is something, though, in the face of this child and the others that makes her miss a breath. They are older than her son. Their features, streaked with ketchup and pencil dust, have begun to dissolve, just a trace, into their adult faces.

Moments later, on the school steps, Eliot burrows his face into her neck as she struggles to open the umbrella. When the spring doesn't catch on the third try, she makes a run for it. Eliot is sobbing by the time Livie has strapped him into the back seat. He wails and sucks on his fingers like a baby, and Livie drives. She doesn't stop until the rain stops, and by that time she's almost to Lee County.

Finally, the clouds break apart over the section of the Skyland Road that, after stretching up the mountain and past the Cumberland Gap National Park, descends amidst hunting cabins and abandoned summer cottages. The quiet buildings hug the curved road as if they're afraid of the open woods that radiate out around them. Olivia would like to crack her window and breathe in the smell of the wet asphalt and soaked bark, but she doesn't want the cold air to hit Eliot. He has whimpered himself into a restless sleep, clutching a Ziplock bag of animal crackers she found in the glove compartment. She turns the van around in the parking lot of a deserted fireworks stand.

On the way back over the mountain, the cell phone rings in her purse. She clicks it off without answering it, but one ring is enough to wake Eliot, and in the falling darkness he's confused.

"Where we going?"

"We went for a drive, Babe. Now we're on our way home."

"It's raining." Panic underlies his voice.

"Not anymore. That's just the tree branches dripping." In the rearview mirror, Livie can see him pull himself up and press his face to the window, then fall back, relieved. She feels a pang of guilt because she knows it must have been Tom on the phone, home from the lab and wondering where she and his son have gone. She doesn't know what she would have told him if she had taken the call. How can she make him understand?

Thinking about it now, months later, Livie knows it would have been better if Eliot hadn't been home. Only two weeks into school, and he had had strep throat. But he was over the hump, as Altura liked to say. The night before, his fever had finally broken, and he had slept late. The two of them were in the kitchen. She was loading the dish-washer, and Eliot, his appetite back, was working his way through a bowl of applesauce. The sound of morning talk shows rose from the television in the family room, the steady peal of a laughing stu-dio audience. When the news broke, she scooped Eliot up and carried him in there. For a few minutes, she stood, balancing him on her hip the way she had when he was a baby, and then she sank to the floor and held him close, whispering into his hair, "Sweetheart, what if you weren't home today? What if you weren't home?" And she had sat, holding Eliot tightly in her lap, unable to look away from the televi-sion set for the next three hours.

Tonight, she pulls off the highway at the park entrance. The gate-house is empty with yellow lights flashing on the edge of the roof, so she goes through and turns into the park. Sometimes she and Tom go hiking up here in the summer. Even though you're not supposed to, they take back wildflower samples to seed the side yard. It looks dif-ferent on a November night. She sees something shining off the side of the road like two eyes, maybe a raccoon or a deer, and she wants to show Eliot, but she can tell from his steady breathing that he has fallen back into sleep.

Livie turns off the van at The Pinnacles overlook and waits until her eyes adjust behind the extinguished headlights. Overhead, the tree branches look dark and oily. She opens the door and slides into the autumn night air. From the valley floor, the Appalachians don't look so big. She knows these mountains, formed from ancient volcanoes, once towered even the Himalayans, and that over millions of years wind and rain and snow have softened them into the smoky, rolling hills she sees each morning from her garden. She knows the earth's crust is in a constant state of flux, a truth that sounded sad to her in college. She knows the world erodes. Every day a loss.

She climbs out onto the overhang of limestone rock and stands shivering. More and more stars come out as she grows accustomed to the darkness. Livie moves a little closer to the edge away from the poinsettias tucked into the cargo area, away from the broken umbrella and the glove compartment filled with Happy Meal toys and Wal-Mart receipts. She feels Eliot behind her, head lolling, his breath gently fog-ging the glass. He is a tether. To the east, the second shift has clocked in, and Merck glows like a little city. Below her all the lights of the valley reflect against the haze, and in some hollows, narrow strips of cloud cover are still releasing rain. From where Livie is crouched, they look like pockets of steam, like something ready to erupt.

THE SPACE BEHIND THE WORDS

Altura 2001

We are leaving the Victorian houses that line Laurel Place in better shape than when we moved in nearly thirty years ago. There are privacy fences and aluminum gutters, granite counters in the kitchens. Still, you wouldn't believe the people who have put offers on these houses. (An unmarried couple, a single professor with three dogs!) We had to dress and put on our faces before breakfast because we never knew when they might ring the bell and ask to take one more look around. Now notices swing beneath the signs planted a season ago on each of our lawns. Sold.

And we've folded the last fifty years into Rubbermaid crates and collapsible cardboard boxes. We've catalogued our crystal, wrapped it ourselves in bubbled plastic. We've discovered things: horseback riding ribbons, toys from favored pets, beaded cotillion shoes, forgotten Christmas ornaments, folded and pressed and packaged with care because—we had been warned—they'll grow up so fast. We found our wedding dresses packed in yellowing tissue paper—of course, given her circumstances, Olivia couldn't have worn mine—and we resealed them in vinyl garment bags from the spring issue of the Spiegel home catalogue.

The rooms look larger now that we've begun to empty them.

Lillian Gentry and her husband have already gone to Florida, to a cottage on Sanibel Island. And Mavis Kieger, who lost Joe four years ago, will live in the basement of her son's home near Lexington, in a neighborhood of identical colonial style two stories. "How," she asks us, "will she be able to go for her walk?" She can't tell her son's house from the others.

Vernon and I, along with the Davenports, are moving into new condominiums in Cedar Creek Summit, a nearby mountain resort. We're too old to learn to ski, but there is golf and swimming. Our husbands tell us there will be thirty miles of walking trails and a full service spa when everything's finished. There will be fishing. "Don't you remember," Vernon says, "how we used to go fishing when we first married? How we used to rent a flat-bottomed rowboat from that man who lived up from the dam? How you used to make egg salad sandwiches?"

We have toured model condominiums, some overlooking the golf course, others overlooking the lake. The realtors had acrylic fingernails, and most of them—they were girls, really—wore suits of questionable synthetic blends. No one wears linen anymore. They're afraid of something they have to iron. My skin itched watching them push up their rayon sleeves and dig through their handbags. They carried large purses like the ones my daughter carries now—hulking, black leather things, with Labor Day still two weeks away—and when they looked for their cards there was a shower of broken crayons and crumbling Goldfish crackers. Made me wonder where those kids were. That's one thing I can say for Olivia. At least she's dedicated herself entirely to motherhood.

We have sat together in groups of two or three and flipped through the books these girls gave us, trying to decide on wall color and tile. They have such names now, even for plain white, things like "eggshell" and "dawn" and "vanilla mist."

We will be farther away from our grandchildren, and they need us more than ever. They start them to school so young. It seems too much to ask of a four-year-old boy, waking at 7:00 and not coming home until after 2:00. Our children didn't start any kind of school until they were six, and then only for half a day. Little boys need a softer discipline when they are so young. They need to roll through Piggly Wiggly with an open box of vanilla wafers, pointing and laughing from inside the cart. They need to sit on the porch and watch the potato bugs roll up when their grandfather lifts the geranium pots. They need younger siblings—a little sister, although, preferably without her father's high forehead—to direct and guide. One learns most through setting an example, and that is precisely what we insisted on from our children.

They attended fundraising dinners. At the country club, they sat on lounge chairs and read until we told them they could get in the water. Olivia was a little lady back then.

We open their medicine cabinets, just to see. We tell them they don't have as much time as they think. Vernon and I had given up for years when I finally became pregnant with Olivia. I was nearly forty, spent the last two months in bed, bleeding off and on, until they had to pull her out early through my belly. Think, we insist, on the risks of waiting. But now, now when she's married with a house and a comfortable income, now Olivia plans against pregnancy.

There are other people who need us here. Enrique Velasquez and his wife Yolanda. Twice a week they have come for years. It's true that the girl removes all the cleaning supplies from the closet and leaves them scattered room to room until she has finished the entire house—our mothers would have let someone go for leaving a tub of polishing cream open on the sideboard in the dining room—but she is more loyal than any other girl who has come to work for any of us over the years. She came an extra day each week once Joe really started to suffer, hand scrubbed the pots and pans that stacked up in the kitchen while Mavis waited on her husband, who, by that time, was confined to a hospital bed in the living room.

We can't remember who told us about Enrique and his wife or for which one of us they first came to work. We insisted on full interviews regardless of the recommendation. "Where are you from?" we all wanted to know, and Enrique told us Estill County. He remembered any little pieces of personal history we offered, saying hello with the Saints score every week in the fall, even though there was no team when I was a girl in the Garden District. At first, we eyed him suspiciously—such cheer for someone raking up hedge clippings. Someone who wore coveralls and was missing his left thumb. "Your Thomas Dempsey," he said when he caught me peeking at his hand, "set the record for longest field goal ever with one hand and a club foot." I just nodded my head.

Lillian says a film of sand coats the bottom of her bathtub down in Florida. "There is a full maintenance staff at Cedar Creek Summit," Vernon tells me. "You won't even be able to tell when the boxwood needs trimming; it will be done every week. And," he says, "there is a linen service. No more damp towels piling up in the wicker hamper. What do you say to napkins pressed fresh for every meal?"

"I don't trust laundry," I tell him, "when it's delivered off the back of a dump truck."

And what of Yolanda and Enrique? We can provide them with references that mean something, but will their new employers place out cold cans of soda? They might really stare at Enrique's left hand. You'd think that kind of behavior was perfectly acceptable now. We've seen eyes follow our own husbands, the slow shuffle our men make when they rise from their seats and head out of the cinema. And what if we've been too easy on Yolanda? All those years of pretending not to notice when she forgot to switch the nozzle and use the hose attachment to vacuum out the ridges beneath the sliding doors. We would just wait until they pulled out the driveway, a flutter of brown leaves escaping from the canvas tarp they stretched across the truck bed. Then we would pull out the vacuum and finish up ourselves.

In the last year we have attended retirement parties where very important men wished our husbands well. The former Governor Brereton Jones came to a dinner at the Bluestone Inn, where he thanked my husband for decades of community service. We bought new suits with brocade collars and accordion-pleated skirts. We sipped the cream of asparagus soup, even though asparagus always leaves our stomachs unsettled. We raised our glasses again and again, drank more champagne than we did at our own weddings.

We gingerly descended the steps, each of us, on her respective evening, clinging to the familiar arm of her husband. The sidewalk looked oily from the weather and street lights. We worried about the mist and fingered out hair. We'd had new permanents done. Our husbands gently touched the top of our heads, guided us into the waiting taxis. Years ago we used to drive home after cocktail parties, after fundraisers. Everyone did, then. Rupie's son will have to go to jail if he is arrested driving home again. She says he's so lonely since the divorce that he can't get through the day sober.

In the rain, the taxi windows sweated around us, and, because we were unaccustomed to having them so close beside us in the car, we let our heads lull into our husbands' sloping shoulders.

We had to walk up our own sidewalks, past the "for sale" signs, and unlock our front doors. We entered under a kind of spell, standing in the foyer and fumbling for the light switch like that. "Don't wash your face off." Our husbands' voices were candied with champagne. Each word pushed warm and heavy against our necks. "Don't make tea tonight," they said. "Let's go get in bed."

And that is what we wanted to do, but, always, there are things to attend to. I had to feed the cat and take care of my suit. I took it off in the powder room and hung it there. It would have to be dry cleaned. When I took off my girdle, a red mark snaked across my waist from the elastic band. Just below it, the start of another line—fainter, but always there—the one where they took out Olivia. When I pulled back the comforter, my husband didn't stir. He was already asleep.

"We can plan a trip to Europe," our husbands say. They bring home brochures for senior citizens' bus tours. How about this—they point to pictures of ocean vistas and rolling pastures—from the Ring of Bearra to Connemarra in three days. Olivia tells us to go to France.

"There are supposed to be cave paintings," she says, "and canals all along the Perigueux River Valley."

The waiting is what I remember from our first trip abroad. Standing on the curb with Vernon, trying to hail passing cabs from beneath a dripping umbrella. Sitting at a table so small our knees touched, making eye contact with the waiters again and again, finally having to ask for the check. Back then, such moments were gifts, time and circumstance pressing us closer to these men with whom we would be spending forever. So many of the rooms they gave us had twin beds, and although we would spend the night tightly wrapped in one, we always pulled back the sheets on the other before the maids came in the morning.

We felt the worst for Mavis when we saw Joe yellowing against the bed that hospice set up in the living room. We brought scented candles and sheets woven from Egyptian cotton dyed pale blue. We took turns. One of us stayed with him, and the others took Mavis to lunch. She wouldn't go far, though, so there was just the Valley Vista Grill. Mavis looked at the menu a long time, but she always ordered the fresh fruit platter. We felt horrible watching her unrolling the rubbery cold cuts and pushing the scoop of cottage cheese around the cheap plate. But it was worse when we had to stay and sit with Joe. "Look here," we said shaking out the paper, "would you like to know how the construction is going on the new high school?" We just tried to keep talking. The room was so full of the smell of sickness. Those times, we felt worse even than we would at the funeral. We felt the tug of our own moorings.

We don't want to have to think about what would happen now in Florence or Bruges if we found our husbands had rented one of those rooms, high in some pension. Would we both lie awake but silent, in his and her beds, listening to sirens passing in the street below?

Our health is starting to go. It's so much easier to correct aging from the outside. They can do things now with lasers—the eyes, the veins pinching up on the back of the legs—all outpatient and relatively affordable. We still look pretty good. They ask to see our driver's licenses when we request the senior citizen's discount on Tuesdays at the club. But we're a far cry from what we were at sixteen. Mavis found a picture of herself when she went through Joe's wallet. She's wearing a tweed jacket with a heart shaped collar, looking back over her shoulder at the photographer. She had sent it to Joe when he was over in Korea. She'd signed the bottom of it. *All my love, forever.*

Between us now we share only two uteruses and six breasts. They cut the breasts away years ago, right after Rupie Davenport turned forty. Once she caught her daughter, Sarah, trying to make it out the door with her spare prosthetics squished inside her brassiere.

The things our children do make us aware of all we can't. They can shop all morning, pricing items from store to store, buying two weeks' worth of groceries in one trip and toting it out to the car themselves. Olivia spends hours on her hands and knees, rooting around in her flower beds. Entire afternoons of hard labor, with bare hands and cut-off dungarees, when I have to cover the bathroom tile with a foam pad to bend down and rinse the soap off my grandson. And more likely than not, I need to sit on the couch and rest for half an hour afterwards.

It started years ago when they came home from college in the summers. They parked themselves on our front porches and read. They sat there thumbing huge books—philosophy books, French novels—wearing undergarments you could see through their clothes or wearing no undergarments at all, wearing all black in July. They took jobs—not positions volunteering at Garrison Memorial or at the art museum in Knoxville—jobs waiting tables at Ray's Diner, disinfecting rental shoes at the bowling alley near the university, shelving books at the public library.

"Jennifer Ann's going to legally change her name," Lillian told us. "From now on she's Jenni with an 'I.'"

Rupie's son eloped in Las Vegas, and her youngest girl said she might be a lesbian, even though she eventually married a military man and moved to Texas.

Through the back windows, we watched our children read. We watched them smoke cigarettes and hide the butts beneath the planters. We listened to them come and go at odd hours. We lectured them on all they shouldn't do. They were not to wear white shoes before Memorial Day. There would be no phoning young men unless they were returning a call. Their escorts must always ring the bell and come inside. We all had to compromise.

"Please," I begged Olivia, "don't wear rubber sandals on your date."

"There is," I told her, "absolutely no reason for your boyfriend to follow you up to your bedroom."

We modified the rules: If you two must go up there to study, at least keep the door open. And we made rules that would have been impossible to foresee. *Never, ever, accept a collect call from a prison.*

When they refused to talk to us, we talked to each other.

Our husbands insisted on taking us to see the construction sites up at Cedar Creek. We had to go late at night. We had to walk on our toes to keep our heels from sinking into the soil. "I didn't go in," Rupie tells me later, "there were no steps." I don't tell her how it felt when I took Vernon's hand and he pulled me up next to him, how the earth fell away behind me.

"Watch out for nails," my husband told me when I reached out to steady myself on the skeleton of a doorway. The ground was pushed up all around so that the frames of our houses looked like something breaking out of the mud. Porch lights twinkled in a twisting line just off the road that curves down the mountain. As we stared at them, they seemed to glaze over and sink down into the valley.

I thought about a night in Louisiana some forty years before, riding to Algiers Point. We both knew it was the last ferry, that we would have to wait until dawn to ride back, but we pretended we didn't. The night air hung heavy over the river, pressed us into each other. I felt scared and safe at the same time as I watched the lights of Canal Street shrink and spread over the Mississippi. Vernon had to return to Kentucky the next day, and it would be more than a month before I could see him again.

My husband sat down in the sawdust. I could tell his back hurt him. "So, this is going to be it," he said. I went over to him and I wanted to sit down too, but I knew my stockings would surely snag on the rough wood. I asked him if he thought we'd be able to see Olivia and Tom's from up here. I moved over so that I was standing right behind him. "Maybe." He leaned against me. "Maybe in the winter." The back of his head was resting on my skirt, so that only layers of cotton separated his white hair from my scar. Then, after he thought about it, he said, "Probably not. But we should be able to see the river."

I was glad when we were back inside the car. I didn't want to be up on that mountain anymore that night, but I didn't want to be back in the house with the newspapers and boxes yet, either.

He turned to me with the keys in his hand. "Do you want to stop and get some ice cream?"

"Oh," I said, "I'm not hungry."

But he knew, because it's been more than forty years, and forty years is long enough to know the difference. I felt better then. I knew that's where we were going to stay, always, in the space behind the words.

"Altura," he said, "we don't have to be hungry to eat ice cream."

SUGAR

Amanda 1996

Let your five-by-seven homecoming portrait be evidence that you need to leave this town before the end of summer. In the photograph, you are standing next to Jeremy in an Asian-cut dress with frog buttons on the right shoulder. The gown was tailored, along with his tie, to match the decorative fans and papìer mâché dragons suspended from the ceiling. There is a silk screen with the words, *An Evening on the Orient Express: Black Mountain High's Twelfth Annual Homecoming.* There is also the tiara.

Remember how the photographer, as he arranged the two of you in a simulated embrace, said, "These are good days for you, the best days of your life."

And rest assured that staying here will only make that true. Compose a list of reasons why you should break up with Jeremy. Let it start something like this: he's no good on the phone, he freaks out whenever you kiss somebody on stage, he calls your friends "drama fags," and he's been developing a belly since the end of football season. You know that lists are the only way to make sense of your life. It isn't the first time you've allowed their power, the collective force of words on a page—or a napkin or a gasoline receipt—to direct you. Consider a list outlining why you should stay with Jeremy, but don't expect more than: he has a sweet mouth, and you love his golden retriever.

Contact your father's California relatives. You can stay, at least for a few months, with Mason, the second cousin you've never met. Try not to be alarmed by the strange science fiction montages on his answering machine. Have head shots done at the trendy photography studio in Garrison, and purchase new bikinis, stringy ones, the kind girls wear when they live on the beach.

Ending things with Jeremy is more difficult. Your relationship has wound on for more than three years, with all the normal high school milestones from first car date to first car fuck, and, in the end, you can't exactly do it. As a last resort, behave in certain ways. Stay out all night with cast members of the show at the community playhouse. Stop returning phone calls. Master a sullen stare out the window of his Nissan Pathfinder.

When he comes by on the morning of your departure, so the dog can at least say good-bye, try not to lean into the hug. Stand around kicking at the clumps of grass that swell over the brick walk. Let the dog press his nose wet against your palm, and then watch him lope off to sniff around the flowerbeds. Listen as Jeremy talks about what it's going to be like for you out in L.A. and him up at Eastern Kentucky University come September. It seems as if he thinks everything—even your long trip West—is some big party.

On the road, you stop by 5:00 PM, and you eat in the same sort of diner each night. You order the grilled chicken breast and seasonal vegetables—sometimes it's the lite dinner, and sometimes it's the heart smart meal—then phone your parents and watch TV until you fall asleep. You never even swim in the motel pools. There was a time when you and Jeremy were good for one another. Admit it. Not until Tucumcari, New Mexico, can you think about that last conversation without crying.

You were raised a starlet. A leggy child with shiny dark hair and watery blue eyes, who, at the age of four, began reenacting movie scenes for your grandfather's camcorder. Your parents were amused and decided their baby girl might very well have a future in film.

You have always lived in the big house on Laurel Place, an old house with oak banisters and a dumbwaiter in the dining room. It is a house meant for a larger family, and it was hard to keep up, but your parents—who had lost another child, a boy, in infancy—loved the drama of it. They sanded and varnished, beat rugs on the clothesline, searched the local farm auctions for antiques.

Your bedroom is in the attic, and it is the bedroom of an only daughter: a canopy bed with Irish lace, sheets emblazoned with rose sprigs, a velvet boxed window seat street side and a round window, like a porthole, facing the backyard. In one corner sits a dollhouse crafted by your dad. It rises three and a half feet high, a replica to scale of the house around it.

Throughout adolescence you prepared. You took ballet in the basement of the church next to the elementary school. Miss Cozette, a gray wisp of a woman, would measure your waist against a black mark on a curl of satin ribbon—nineteen inches: the appropriate waist size for a professional ballerina. You donned jodhpurs and leather boots for lessons at Mountain Meadows Stables. Every other Tuesday, you stood in the parlor next to the upright piano, breathing from your diaphragm, moving up and down scales in an alto staccato for Geoffrey, the scarf-clad voice instructor your parents paid to drive all the way from Richmond. Over the years, you practiced guitar, tae kwon do, cotillion, assorted romance languages, tennis, sign language, and fencing, and when someone asked what you were going to be when you grew up, you replied, "Famous."

At eighteen, you wore a sequined leotard and twirled a flaming baton in front of the high school marching band. You played Annie in *The Miracle Worker.* You had a white Rabbit convertible, and sometimes you drove it over rocky dirt roads to the secluded pastures where your friends held late-night parties. But you always passed when they offered you a hit on the bong because you didn't want to become wrapped up in any scandal.

You know immediately that the apartment isn't your cousin's. Mason, whose hair is sort of long and sort of curly, wears a T-shirt with a picture of a girl in lavender wings and thigh-high boots. He leads you down the hall, and although you've only just met him, you recognize that the furniture and photographs cannot belong to this boy.

"This one's yours." He flings open a door, revealing gauzy window treatments and a pale blue duvet.

Demand to know what's going on. Grab a fistful of the expensive curtains and say, "Whose stuff is this?"

"Technically," Mason says, "It's Todd's."

"Todd?"

"This guy I work with at Darkside Comics."

Feel the heat of rising panic inside your chest. "Does he even know I'm going to be staying here?"

"Oh, he doesn't care." This comes to you over his shoulder, flippantly, as he heads back toward the front door. "His dad's loaded. He's been paying for this place the full six years and change it's taken Todd to get his marketing degree. After you." He holds open the door, follows you across the patio and into the street. "I'm house-sitting while Todd backpacks through Eastern Europe."

"It's a gorgeous room." Watch as he struggles, then maneuvers one of the larger boxes out of the back seat.

"Yours is his hook-up room," Mason explains. "He sleeps in mine except when he brings someone home. Then they stay in yours. He even keeps fresh flowers in that vase on the dresser."

As the two of you make trips back and forth from where your car is parked in the alley, you learn that the apartment's owner is a sexually ambiguous alcoholic and that, when he finally returns, he'll be the new manager at the comic book store.

"Why are you house-sitting for this guy if you don't like him?"

"Oh, I didn't say I don't like him."

You feel relief when Mason leaves for work and all your things lay in a heap on the now ominous blue duvet. From the balcony, you see a kid on a scooter circling the alley, and on Newport Boulevard, a woman digs change from an enormous beach bag while her dog winds his leash through her legs and around the parking meter. A block beyond her, a narrow strand of gray pavement is teeming with more dogs and bicycles and girls with long hair and roller blades. Then it is umbrellas and sunbathers and the ocean glittering less than a quarter of a mile away. Let yourself sink into the edge of a patio chair. Foggy from days of driving, you sit and stare for nearly an hour, telling yourself, "This is the Pacific."

When you were young, your parents would drive to Sandbridge or Buckrow Beach just for a weekend each summer. Mostly you sat and dug holes until sand strung your hair and clumped heavy in your bathing suit bottom. Once you were in middle school, your family stayed in a hotel at Virginia Beach for a full week. You remember painting your toenails until they were lumpy with layers of polish and following boys around the damp arcade pavilion.

Later, your parents invited Jeremy, and once it was dark, the two of you would hold onto each other outside as long as you could. You would lie behind the lifeguard stand until your bodies had made an impression together in the sand. Back in the hotel he would have to sleep on a pull-out cot. It was so hard to fall asleep when you could feel his presence magnetizing the air of that hotel room.

Your father always said, "Smart people will go far in this world, and good looking people will go far in this world. My little girl is smart and beautiful, so there will be no stopping her." It's true that the things you desire have always fallen into place with relative ease, but you arrive in Los Angeles expecting some amount of rejection. Your parents were not so blinded by their starlet daughter's talents as to agree that you should forego college, but they thought it couldn't hurt to put it off six months, maybe a year.

After searching the L.A. and Orange County papers and growing leery of seedy advertisements for agents located in the outskirts of Santa Monica, you choose an agency on Wilshire Boulevard. Revel at the buildings as you drive to your first appointment, the patios with terraced fountains, the walls of reflecting glass. Palm trees rise in street-side columns, and when the road widens fruit trees line the median, avocados dangling like Christmas ornaments from the waxy branches.

"You've got very nice skin." Celia, who conducts your interview, is maybe fifty, with too much chin and too much powder. She spreads your photos across the papers and loose office supplies already littering her desk. "You can never tell until a girl's actually in the office." She picks up one of the headshots, holds it beneath the light. "They're all touched up, air brushed." She looks at you then and says, "So, what's your deal? Why are you here?" Stare back at the woman as she shuffles through the mess on her desk until she asks, "Why do you want to be an actress, dear?"

This is a question you have long anticipated. "I love being able to be someone other than myself." Your voice needs to assume the right quality of decisiveness and karma.

Celia leans back in her chair and narrows her eyes. "All you girls come out here for a reason. Missing fathers, that's a big one." Watch as she ticks off the remaining problems on her fingers. "Sexual abuse, deserter boyfriends, various addictions. Everybody's got low self-esteem and something to prove. What's your story?"

"I just like to perform," you say, "since I was a little girl."

"You have a dad?" The woman rubs her fingers into her temple. You are giving her a headache.

"Yes, of course."

"At home?"

"Yes."

"Do you do anything, even pot, even every once in a while?" It seems that no matter what you answer she's not going to believe you, but shake your head anyway. "Just remember I can demand to see your arms at any time." Remember how your mom used to sniff your forearms to be sure you had used soap in the bathtub, how she would turn your hands palms down to check for dirt beneath your fingernails.

"Do you have a job?" Celia asks, and then, when you open your mouth, she adds, "Not this one. This is not a job."

"I've saved some money, and my parents are willing to help me for a while."

"You've got to have a job." She leans forward as she says this. "It's too easy to leave if you don't. Something at night—in a store, or in a restaurant as a hostess—so you can audition during the day. You need to have friends here and a life here." She shakes her copy of your resume. "Away from this."

Tell her you can get a job. Say, "I'm already looking."

"We're going to have to change your name," she says. "Most people have to do it. Amanda, huh? Christ, that sounds too much like a homecoming queen. Did you use that name in the work you did back in," she checks your file, "Kentucky?"

Nod your head. You may have said too much already.

"You haven't even thought about a stage name?" She won't wait for an answer. "Look, for now, let's go with Amandra. It sounds classy, a little exotic. We'll keep McClintock. That shouldn't be too confusing. If I line up an audition for you this week, that's the name you'll have to sign in under."

You can't remember a time when you weren't acting. You did your first commercial for Lloyd's Steak House when you were seven. In high school you sat on top of a convertible from Myers Ford and smiled and waved to throngs of prospective car buyers for the full course of the Conrad's Fork Harvest Days parade route.

Acting was a natural progression of things. In high school you perfected it, not in the shows you did, but in each daily performance—flipping through the card catalogue in the library, washing your hands at the bathroom sink.

Perhaps it was the inevitable result of being an only child. You remember moving the miniature version of yourself through the upholstered rooms of your dollhouse, and you recall that each of your stuffed animals had a special voice, a specific personality. Surely, these activities were not so unusual.

You can't be sure, though, if your talent stems from an abundance of imagination in your play or a lack of reality in your life. The distinction starts to gnaw at you if you dwell on it.

Answer this ad, "Learn to tend bar. Immediate cash, no experience necessary," and begin working at Sugar, a bikini bar in Westminster, a windowless dive of a place with cement floors and framed prints of cigar-smoking hounds. Behind the bar, the girls, all of them beautiful in ways different from you, move in platform sandals. Tell yourself: It's more preparation. It's not so different from tennis.

You and Mason develop a routine in which he drives you to work. He says you never know what kind of crazies could be hanging around the lot at closing. Wear gym shorts and a University of Kentucky sweatshirt over your bikini, so that you only have to step out of your clothes before going behind the bar. Of course, Phong, the manager, makes all the girls go to the bathroom to change. "It ruins the mystique," he tells you, "when paying customers can see you peeling off your street clothes."

Take a moment before stepping out of the car. Reapply your lipstick, something thick and matte and cherry-black, something called *Vamp*. You bought it at a cheap jewelry stand the afternoon Mason took you to see the street performers in Venice Beach. When you turned the silver tube over to read the label, and said, "Racy," the woman behind the counter misunderstood and confessed that she, too, thought the case looked like a miniature vibrator.

"What time should I come back for you?"

Tell him to come back at two unless you call. Then lift your sweatshirt and give him a quick flash of your bikini top. "How do I look?"

"Pretty trashy."

This is what he always says, but you know it isn't true. You are the innocent one, still tanless, your dark bob pinned to the side. Get a feel for this role, and don't fight it. Every girl at Sugar plays some kind of part. Jennifer's mother is Korean, so she wears sticks in her hair and red lipstick like a geisha girl. Leslie, the girl with whom you usually work, spent four years in the Marines and attends Cal State Fullerton on the GI fund. The top of her arms muscle up when she shakes the tumbler, and the words *semper fidelis* snake blue below her navel.

You come to recognize the sound of Mason's car as it pulls onto Beach Boulevard, the whir and whistle of some loose belt as he disappears into the mess of commuters pouring off the freeway.

Inside, the women's bathroom is twice as large as the men's, and Phong has decorated it with you girls in mind. The paint is dark green, and a full-length mirror with a gilded frame hangs on one wall, the kind of thing your parents are always dragging home from flea markets back in Kentucky. An antique wardrobe sits in the corner, massive and crafted from walnut, with perfumed lotion, hair spray, new toothbrushes, a box of tampons, and various cosmetics inside.

In the bathroom each night, remove your sweatshirt and shorts and dig your character shoes out of your backpack, the leather ones you keep for stage auditions, black, single strap, chunky heel. They look like something Mary Poppins would wear. Leslie wears aerobics shoes or, sometimes, black combat boots that lace half way up her calves. Mason is particularly fond of these. They remind him of the warrior footwear of his comic book women. He tells you how his only real girlfriend was a soccer player—shin guards.

Don't even try to pull off that look. Tell your mom to send some of the shoes you wore to dances in high school, the strappy ones with sequins and sparkles.

"What on earth do you need those for?" she wants to know. "Unless you're going to clubs every night." She thinks you're waiting tables at Shoney's.

Before going on the floor, unscrew the top from a plastic container labeled *MoonGlow*. These are the products with which you hope to perfect this part—body glitter, floral henna tattoos, toe rings, a jingling belly chain. Dip a powder brush into the silvery dust and swirl it over your chest, then down your belly.

Try not to think about the messages Jeremy leaves on Mason's machine, the sweet way his voice catches as it strains over background party noise. "I know you must be doing well out there. I miss you. I've gone out a few times, but nobody is as real as you are."

Although you live by the beach, you don't spend much time there. The water is colder and rougher than in the east. Mason, twice caught in a rip tide and plucked from the surf by the life guard boats, has water issues. If you didn't have to work the night before, you get up early and jog to the end of the strand and down Pacific Coast Highway. Sometimes you see the low, glassy domes of jellyfish and the bulbous roots and wet, gold leaves of kelp drying in the sand, landfall from an evening storm. At high tide surfers bob in the water, waiting for waves where the Santa Ana pours out into the ocean, and when the tide is out, Mexican boys leave their coolers on the sand and wade into the mouth of the canal to fish flounder. You like the beach at this time of day, the empty lifeguard houses and the quiet expanse of wet sand.

After breakfast, Mason spreads his art supplies across the patio table. He shows you his drawings, notebooks full of characters whose musculature and weaponry he has rendered in incredible detail. They look naughty and mythological at the same time. He has a string of story lines too, but you don't find these as interesting. You learn that Mason dropped out of Orange Coast Community College and that his mom, Peg, worries constantly for his future.

She lives in a duplex in Anaheim and works for Merry Maids, but every other week or so she finds an excuse to drive out with a bag of groceries. If Peg drops by in the afternoon, you have to suffer an embarrassing barrage of questions. "Does he bring any money home from that job or just more comic books?" She probes unabashedly about her son's sexuality. "Don't you think he's a good looking boy? I don't know why he doesn't have a girlfriend." Or worse yet, "Why do you think that Todd guy is letting him stay here for free, really?"

You enjoy mornings at the apartment, sitting out on the patio and reading. You begin making your way through the list of novels you didn't finish in high school, and when you have a call-back coming up, there are lines to memorize. Look at Mason when he bends over his drawing pad. Notice the way his hair curls up when it is damp outside. He dips old-fashioned pens into a pot of indigo ink. He tells you that what he really wants to be is an inker, and at first you don't understand why. Tracing over what other people have drawn sounds boring. But then you start to see the way his drawings change as he inks them, the way the blackened lines suddenly take on more shadow and depth.

Lure Mason to the ocean. Drive away from the crowded strand to the state beach, the one where you like to run. In the car when you wonder if maybe you should have invited some other people, he says, "Who would we ask?"

Mason knows how to make a fire. He refuses your bag of quick light charcoal briquettes. Someone has left a splintery pile of scrap wood by one of the fire rings. Kneeling next to the cement circle, Mason pushes aside the feathery ash and begins arranging the sticks into a careful pyramid. See the lanky arc of his back as he leans in, nursing the flame with his breath. Don't tell him that your hot dog is still cold in the middle.

Once the beach has cleared, you show him where the tidal pools form at the mouth of the Santa Ana. He finally removes his T-shirt, revealing the wash of freckles across his shoulders. He lies down in the center of the pool, eyes closed, hands pillowing his head just above the water. Sit down next to him and watch the sun start to leak into the ocean. When you lean over to see if he's awake, Mason spits a stream of water into your face.

Your first role in California, a commercial for Angel's Indulgence candy squares, comes more quickly than anyone, even Celia, had expected. They film you in a bubble bath unwrapping the foil from a piece of Angel's Indulgence. A halo and a feathery pair of angel wings hang from a towel rack in the background. You say, "Everyone has to indulge sometimes," and then you place an entire square of Angel's Indulgence into your mouth, giggle, and lick your fingers. After the seventh take, hold the candy—delicious chocolate with a hazelnut creme center—in your mouth until the director has called cut, then spit it into the waste basket.

To celebrate, Mason takes you to Junior's, the deli where Peg claims to have seen Rick Schroeder, Florence Henderson, and Lisa Bonet. When you get up to go to the ladies room, he convinces the people at neighboring tables to ask for your autograph.

In Conrad's Fork, when the Farm Bureau had its annual sidewalk sale, they wheeled the racks of hunting coats and coveralls into the parking lot, and if it didn't look like rain they left them out all night. The only time your parents locked the house was when your family went on vacation.

There is no trust at Sugar. The cameras concealed in the light fix-tures and suspended behind the bar unnerve you with their blinking red eyes. The girls have to count money for a camera above the cash register—set the bill on the counter, count out change next to it, place the bill in the drawer. The video images are continuously broadcast on television screens in the back office where Phong sits smoking. If, during a rush, you begin pouring shots on a three count instead of first measuring the liquor in the aluminum exacter cup, he appears suddenly behind the bar, sucking his teeth. "Ah, Kentucky, you have to measure," he says, pulling the bottle from your hand. "How can I make money with you pouring whatever you want? You girls are sending me to the poorhouse."

Each girl is assigned a bucket and a stack of plastic tip trays. When you bring a man his drink, you have to leave his change next to it on the tray. "Make sure you write your name on those," Leslie says. "You don't want anyone to get the tips mixed up. You have to watch some of the girls here."

Take your trays home and write "Kentucky" on them with black magic marker; everyone at Sugar calls you that, never Amanda. You just go with it, even though it's not a name, not like Virginia or Georgia. Mason offers to decorate them with dominatrix pictures, but instead you paint a heart on each one with *Reddy to Wear* nail polish.

At the end of the night, after the bar has been wiped down with sanitizer and the pint glasses have been polished and stacked along the wall, each girl takes her bucket of bills to a corner table for counting. Try not to feel uncomfortable with the way they look over their shoulders, measuring their shifts against each other. If you empty your bucket directly into your bag, they look up and ask you how you did.

"You're never going to make anything if you don't stop feeling guilty," Leslie says one evening, resting her hand on your shoulder. "You leave the bills on the tray so long your customers take them back."

"What do you mean?" You are uncomfortable around the other girls. At home, the only time you see people in bathing suits is at the river or the pool, and those suits are nothing like the ones you see in Sugar.

"If they give you a ten and say, 'That's for you, honey,' that means it's all yours. Don't even put the change back in front of them. You're supposed to laugh and say, 'Thanks, baby,' and put it in your pail."

"I know that." But you know that she's right. You are not playing along.

"You don't have to feel bad," she tells you. "We earn the money."

You learn that on her first shift someone left Jennifer a one hundred dollar tip, and it set the standard for the summer. Sometimes Phong comes up behind Jennifer, puts his hand on her shoulder then looks at you. "What would you do, Kentucky," he says, "if someone left you a hundred dollar tip?" You'd follow the man out to the parking lot for fear he'd meant to leave a ten.

You lost your accent the summer after the tenth grade. You were playing Portia in the *Merchant of Venice* for Hillandale Park's Summer Nights with Shakespeare. Most of the other cast members were students who had come down from Ohio. The director said you sounded like Loretta Lynn. "It's really a problem of vowels," he said, "Nothing a little speech therapy can't fix." He made you repeat words like "night" and "book" over and over again into a hand held tape recorder. Your words grew more tinny and hollow each time you played them back.

That same summer, after a lot of wallowing—on the sofa, in the sand, in the back of his Pathfinder—Jeremy said the two of you had figured out how to do it, and that now you really ought to do it right. He waited until his parents went to visit friends up in Lexington and you two had the entire weekend. He bought three dozen roses and scattered the petals in his bed so that it looked like a music video or something. Hours later, after you had told your parents you were spending the night at a girlfriend's house, you got creeped out. You sat up in bed, the wilted petals sticking to your damp back, and demanded that Jeremy take you home.

Back in your attic bedroom, you turned your dollhouse around so that the inside rooms faced the wall.

You start to wonder if the Angel's Indulgence commercial was a fluke. At auditions you begin to notice the same girls—thin girls with fair skin, hair medium brown to black, anywhere from fifteen to twenty-five. You sit with these girls for hours each week in reception areas that look like the waiting rooms outside doctor's offices. You watch them flipping through magazines and turning into corners with their scripts. Mothers wait with the younger girls, smoothing fly-away hairs, picking lint off their daughters' slacks.

Sometimes two or three in the room know each other and congregate to discuss, in hushed voices, whatever they've heard about the casting director. Then the rest of the girls stop reading or fidgeting, and their necks prickle toward this conversation, trying to glean some advantage from the gossip.

The Amanda with the flaming baton knew what she looked like. Always, when entering a room, you have moved with grace according to the picture you hold of yourself in your mind. Think about the way you would leave the salad bar and carry your tray across the crowded cafeteria. In California, it is more difficult to find that picture, and that vacant place starts to change everything. You wish you could pick up the photograph on your dresser back home.

One afternoon, as you wait to audition for a commercial for a new volumizing shampoo, you remember your lists, composed to make a decision or just to pass the time in Math Analysis or church. Sometimes they helped you remember what you had to do that week: homework, or dance lessons and voice. You made lists of vocabulary words and things you thought it might be a good idea to know, like your favorite songs at any given time or the names of your best friends. Suddenly, you need a California list to motivate you.

Turn to the girl next to you and ask, "Do you have a piece of paper and something to write with?"

With a great deal of suspicion, she digs a tiny notebook and a pen from her purse. Turn away from the girl, who is watching intently, and cover the paper with your cupped hand.

Write this down: one part, three call-backs; Junior's, McDonald's, House of Pancakes; Mason. For the first time in your life, you are failing.

Your first kiss—with Randall Hansboro at church camp—was wild and messy and not something you wanted to immediately try again. But kissing Jeremy became so familiar that you can call to mind the taste of it, the feel of his hair where he kept it clipped tight at the back of his neck. You kissed him to say good luck when he went into the locker room to dress for a game, or good night when it was time to climb out of the car and go inside. You've learned to channel whatever emotion is necessary into a stage kiss—frosty and defeated for the Baroness in *The Sound of Music,* happily-ever-after for the finale of *The Pirates of Penzance.*

You are unprepared for what it's like to kiss Mason, the desperation of who he is to you. Not just the son of your father's first cousin. You are more affected by the fact that he is the only person you really know anymore, anywhere. Kiss him after you paint your mouth in *Vamp* just to see the stain you leave.

He begins sleeping in your room—Todd's hook-up room—beneath the blue duvet. All you do is sleep, although he asks for more. The two of you wake in the middle of the night, when the answering machine clicks on in the living room and the desperate voice of one of Todd's admirers floats down the hallway. You find yourself reaching for him. Desire roots like kelp inside you when he says, "It's not illegal," or "Let's just see how we fit."

At Sugar, you learn to use your accent to your advantage. You buy a red and white gingham bikini and pouf your hair like the girls on Country Music Television. Over the course of that summer, a man cuts lines of coke on the counter and bends to sniff them in front of you. A woman comes in off the street and spends the better part of an evening servicing customers in the men's room. Four men exit with flushed and nervous faces before Phong catches on and throws her out.

One night you mix margaritas for a well-dressed man. Every time he orders another, he motions you closer. "Come here, Kentucky," he says. "Do you know what I really want?" Each time you move your ear toward his cologned neck, he lets the back of his hand brush your hair. "I would like some straight up Kentucky bourbon, but I'll settle for another Margarita."

The fourth time, he reaches out and pulls the bow holding up the top of your bathing suit. It feels like you've been shot. Phong and one of the regulars lift the man off his seat and push him towards the door as you clutch your loose breasts. But he yells back over their shoulders, "Why don't you go back home, you little tease? You cunt. Go sit on the porch swing and fuck your cousins."

When you climb into Mason's car, turn down the visor to look at yourself in the mirror. Your lips look empty and swollen where the lipstick has worn off. You start crying, and he wants to know what's wrong, but you aren't exactly sure yourself.

Don't protest when he drives to the row of empty parking spaces at Huntington Beach. A few people still cluster beneath the darkened doorways of bars, holding onto bikes or each other. Walk away from them with Mason toward the place where the cement silhouettes of fire rings rise darkly out of the sand.

Holding him feels different because now you know you can't just go home. Stay there until you see a light lumbering up the beach, pausing, and then moving toward you. A truck materializes from the darkness, and workers exit, scraping cinders from the fire pits, shoveling them into the truck bed. The ash is not yet cold. Watch the gray clumps shatter into gold as they fall.

THE SOUND OF ANIMALS

Cora 2001

When my husband finds me sprawled across three heating pads, watching *Designing Women* reruns and stirring a honey stick into a mug of tea, he says, "Good Lord, Cora, you could have at least rinsed the dishes." How is it that he can't understand that I have cramps, but he can detect the slightest hormonal fluctuation in any one of the 230 Hereford cows pressing against the back fence? He charts the rising and falling estrogen levels in these bovine—his girls—on a piece of poster board thumb-tacked to the back of his office door. It looks like a seismograph or something. Lately, I like to imagine myself creeping in there while he's at the barn, finding his pink highlighter and filling in my own ovulation cycle.

I'm a patient woman, and although—like all the women in my family—I am, by no means, a small woman, I look young for 39. (What really skinny women don't realize is that they're going to wrinkle early.) I still get carded at Piggly Wiggly if I pick up a six-pack for Elden. But I'm starting to realize that no matter how long Oil of Olay holds off the wrinkles, there's nothing that can hold off what happens inside. I saw my sister, Jane, marry at nineteen. She moved with Steve to a new parish in Indiana and pumped out a baby a year until they had the front pew half-filled and she'd swelled up bigger than one of Elden's girls. She faked a family crisis and came back to Kentucky to get her tubes tied and her stomach stapled on the sly. She had to tell Steve she'd had an emergency appendectomy.

When I first got to thinking about a baby, I would call Jane, expecting her to advise against it. Instead she'd tell me how she wouldn't change anything if she could, and how she had never doubted I'd want to be a mother, too, in time. "What are you on, Cora, like career number three? All this time your clock's been ticking," she said. "Fact of life."

Since the day we met, I've known what my husband wanted to do with his life, and I'm not the kind of woman to be unsupportive. At least not anymore. After a while, you have to grow up, pare down your life to what matters. Elden's a little younger than me, and that fact is always in the back of my mind. When we met, he was fresh out of Murray State driving around a refrigerated van full of bull semen, traveling from farm to farm. He limped into the emergency room, his knee swollen to the size of a softball after a well-placed kick from a skittish heifer. On our first date at Lloyd's Steak House, over London broil, he explained the wonders of artificial insemination.

"Some people think my hands look girlie," he said. He displayed his hands one at a time, and I have to admit that, at that moment, as he sat, palms suspended in the air like a magician's, nothing about him looked terribly masculine. His limbs were slender and soft. His hair flopped over his glasses in the front and curved across his collar in the back. His key chain—a rabbit's foot dyed to look like a spotted cow—lay next to his steak knife.

"You've got to have small hands, though, to maneuver the syringe inside. It's all about finesse."

I pulled one of his hands directly beneath the decorative lamp that fanned out from the wall next to our booth. His nails were tiny half moons arching over each finger. There was a strange translucence to his skin that made his fingers seem to glow, and for some reason—I'm not sure why—I was tempted to press my lips to his wrist. Maybe that moment, although I had no concept of it at the time, planted the seed for now. Regardless, I knew then those hands would win me over.

Now you have to understand what that meant. Before I met Elden, I'd call it quits when a man started talking commitment. Once I went so far as to date a married man because I knew we'd never have to have that conversation. Elden knew it was all about timing. He was patient and waited until my heart was ready to receive him. Still, there was a time, even with Elden, when I shifted uncomfortably in the pew if a shaky wail arose from the back of the church. I would roll my eyes when those commercials came on with the baby wriggling inside the tire. I would give him a look that said, "I'm glad we're not there yet," mostly because we weren't.

Back when he worked project to project, paychecks were sporadic, but he made his own hours. We could take off and drive to Lake Barkley for the whole weekend. He used to park the van in a campground and spread a sleeping bag in the back. We'd fall asleep with the damp air curling through the cracked windows and the little drawers with the vials of semen sealed tightly all around us. In the morning we'd go to Krispy Kreme and ask for a dozen of whatever they had hot, then feed the plain ones to the ducks.

When Elden took this job with Les Monger, we moved into the herd manager's house, a two-story with strawberry beds in the back and a swing hanging from the porch. When you grow up on a farm, there is something about land, even if it's not really yours, that grounds you. All of a sudden I get a flutter in my chest whenever someone pushes a stroller past us in Wal-Mart. Only I don't say anything outright since Elden's girls consume so much time. Jane tells me that being the herd manager's wife doesn't sound all that different than being a minister's.

I take my pills between seven and nine each morning, even on weekends and even the sugar pills at the end of the pack. The ones that are green like tiny wedding mints, there to make sure you remember. I keep the plastic case in a little mug with our toothbrushes. Each pill is small and tasteless, so I don't even need water to take them. I can pop one through the foil backing and onto the surface of my tongue with one motion, but this morning I hold the pill, a yellow one, between my fingernails thinking I just want to examine it. And, at first, that's all I do—stare at it as the fluorescent light clicks faintly in the background.

I wonder how something so small could do the job. I have been on the same kind of birth control for more than ten years. My friend Amanda had those tubes inserted into her arm a few years ago, and I thought about doing it too, but she fell off a step stool and landed kind of funny on her shoulder. It didn't break through the skin, but one of those tubes bent upwards at a weird angle. She had to check into Renfro County Memorial and have them all removed. In spite of a few months that felt like close calls, my pills have always worked.

I start to exert increasing pressure, imagining the splay of yellow powder like spilled eye shadow across the porcelain. The pill flies out of my fingers, and years of conditioning lead me to frantically sweep my palms over the linoleum until I find it. But then I flick it into the toilet and send it swirling into our new septic tank.

Elden is flushing his girls. They are all in the east pasture. He and Les's teenage sons round them up in groups of fifteen and herd them into a corral for vitamins, a bran mash, and two hours of total darkness. One of the boys records the numbers off the plastic orange tag in every cow's ear, which is not really necessary since my husband knows each animal by her markings, even from our upstairs window. He has his favorites, and sometimes he calls out to them as we pull in the driveway. "We're coming Myrtle," he shouts through the open van window. I know he sets up a folding camp stool in the foot or so of mud- and urine-soaked straw that cover the cement floor of the barn and talks to them while they eat in the dark. He listens to them snort and stomp as they lick their mash out of the troughs. Three weeks of this and he claims they will all ovulate at the same time.

I tell him, "It seems like that sort of thing should just happen naturally." During my freshman year of college all the girls on my floor started their periods about the same time every month. Open boxes of tampons lined the stainless steel shelf in the hall bathroom. Everyone slammed doors and glowered behind their books in the study lounge.

Elden says, "Contemporary agriculture is a calculated science. You can't trust anything to nature anymore."

My husband works at least fourteen hours a day once this process begins, so one evening Amanda comes over to do my nails and keep me company. We sit out on the porch and drink white zinfandel mixed with 7-Up. The mountains are darkening against the lit sky. The sound of the girls groaning around the tractor carries over the hill. It scared me a little the first time I rode along, feeling the animals press against the wagon as my husband rhythmically sliced twine and tossed hay. Each bale accordioned out in mid-air. They ate the hay right off each other's backs.

While Amanda uses a wet brush to spread acrylic powder across my plastic tipped nails, I try to explain how I've been feeling without confessing that I've stopped taking my pills.

"I think you just need more responsibility at work," is what she says as she adds more wine to her glass. "You only go in three days a week."

I quit at the hospital when Elden became the herd manager. I took a job as a part-time medical assistant at Black Mountain Manor.

"You're not using either of your degrees, and you're the kind of woman who needs to do something for herself. More than rinsing out bed pans and serving Jell-O."

Amanda has been trying to convince me to go back to school and be an RN. She took off for Los Angeles right out of high school and spent two years out there—doing some acting, learning the business—before returning to Conrad's Fork. Now she's the make-up artist at J & Company, the salon on Main Street. She gets a lot of customers during the prom and wedding seasons, and once, when they were filming part of a movie over in Wise County, she led the make-up crew.

I met Amanda when the director of Kyger Funeral Home called her in to work on Mom. She was so professional, so poised for someone so young, especially in a situation that delicate. She asked me to bring in my mother's make-up bag. "Using her own cosmetics," she explained, "will help me capture her as she was." Amanda's so young, young enough to be my daughter, yet she's always got a plan. Besides Elden, she's the most driven person I know.

I wonder sometimes what's wrong with me. Even Jane, who never finished college—Jane with her PTA meetings and her meals-on-wheels and her plot to take control of her body—is more focused, more ambitious than I've become. It's not like I've never been anywhere. I went away to graduate school. I worked for a while at an ad agency up in Minneapolis, mostly just running out to Starbucks and taking notes during creative briefings, but still, that's more excitement than some people around here see in a lifetime. It's not that I'm lazy, or, as my mother liked to say, that I'm always settling. Maybe I'm just not wired like other people. Or maybe it's that I tried too hard back then. Maybe I got tired.

"The thing is, I'm not sure I'm even cut out to be a real nurse," I say. "I've seen three people go in the last month, and it's awful watching that. I try not to get too close to those folks. That's part of what's made me feel this need." This isn't completely true. I feel a connection to my patients at the nursing home that I never could have imagined when I was filling out medical charts for all the people moving through the emergency room. I can close my eyes and remember exactly the pattern of wavy liver spots on the last patient to pass on. They are all going to die, but I try to bring them things to make things better right now, things they can't get inside there, even things they're not supposed to have like real chocolate chip cookies to crumble up in their fortified milk substitute. "I need something permanent in my life," is what I tell Amanda.

"I'll tell you what's permanent, Cora. The weight. This girl I worked with out in California gained 72 pounds with her first kid and never lost any of it." She looks up at me, raising one carefully penciled eyebrow, silently warning me that I, like my sister, could go hurtling into obesity.

What I don't tell her is I've seen how people look at pregnant women, and it's nothing like the way they look at fat women. Once a woman has had a child, she's considered matronly. No one ever says that such-a-shame, such-a-waste, such-a-pretty-face crap. A pregnant woman can order an extra scoop of vanilla on her cobbler.

"So what's Elden say?" Amanda wants to know.

"Nothing. I can't figure out how to bring it up."

Fertilization is actually more effective without a bull. That's what my husband says.

Standing in front of the mirror, I hoist up my blouse. I push out my belly and hold my breath. I try to imagine how I would look with my girth stretched tight, my navel inverted like a plug.

I can remember standing in front of the mirror like this more than ten years ago. My stomach was flatter back then, but my hands were spread across it just this way. I was trying to fathom how it could have happened, what it was going to mean. I couldn't see any difference, and I never felt sick at all. Otherwise, I know I wouldn't have been able to do it. I've never told anyone, not even Elden.

I fold a pillow in half and try to lower my shirt over it.

Sometimes I tease Elden, "Your poor girls. They never actually get to do the deed."

"They're better off," he says. "I've seen a bull nearly kill a heifer. Besides, you've got no idea how much it costs to keep a bull. You've got to put up stronger fencing, and they eat almost twice as much. They're completely unpredictable and they're 50 percent of everything you have. Imagine your livelihood depending on just that one animal."

As I fluff the pillow and place it back on the bed, I start to think about what it means to be keeping this thing that really isn't a thing, but more like a feeling, from Elden. I'm not doing anything wrong— we haven't had relations since he started flushing the herd. But I've stopped bothering to toss my pills into the toilet bowl each morning, and now more than a week's worth of unswallowed ones have lined up in the plastic packaging next to our toothbrushes. I threw away the tiny box of condoms Elden has always kept next to the flashlight in the night stand, and I left the J. C. Penney Spring catalogue open to the section with playpens and TYCO toys. Although Amanda calls it the victim network, on my days off I sometimes get pulled into those afternoon movies on Lifetime. I've been behaving like the husbands who, wanting their wives to catch them cheating, leave little trails of restaurant receipts and hotel match books.

One of the emptied rooms at Black Mountain Manor is filled by a tiny Filipina woman. Mrs. Sanchez is nearly eighty. Her waist-length hair is only streaked with gray to her shoulders. The rest of it is shiny black, looped around and around her face. She lost her husband in a fishing accident, and now she has been brought here by her one daughter, an anchor on WVPT in Garrison. They wheel her out after I leave at 6:00 PM to watch her girl, slender with a burgundy-tipped shag, talk about the Main Street Renovation Program and safety in the county schools.

Mrs. Sanchez has stacks of *Redbook* and *Woman's World*, which she refuses to look at. Next to her bed two pairs of new dentures rest in clear plastic cups of blue fizz. There is a rosary, an assortment of sea-shells, and a heavy silver hairbrush with soft and yellowing bristles. She smacks her gums and fusses over the shells, smoothing her fingers across their pearled insides, holding each one to her ear in turn. Jane and I used to do that as girls with huge shells my grandfather brought back from Florida the one time he and Mamaw actually took a vacation, but I don't think Mrs. Sanchez listens for the ocean.

I think she's straining to hear her daughter. Not the strange voice that says, "Good Evening, Appalachia." She wants to call up the girl voice she cooed to, the child she once held to her chest as she lay on a mat on a faraway island.

When I sit with Mrs. Sanchez, she calls me by her daughter's name. She tries to brush my hair, and she takes a pair of dentures from the table. She holds my fingers and tries to file my nails with the dripping false teeth. Her hands are cool and soft.

I wait for my husband on the swing, wrapped in an afghan my sister sent me. She's in charge of the Crochet Crusade, a glorified knitting club that pumps out blankets, scarves, and hats for needy Midwestern families. She occasionally sends me items that don't make it through her rigorous inspections. It is the kind of clear spring night that we have in the valley after a few days of drizzle. The swing groans with my weight, and every now and then the cows call out from the back field. Elden has gone to a farm in Virginia for the semen.

Tomorrow is the day. I have seen Elden work. I admit I had a strange fascination with the whole process at first. I remember kneeling next to him and holding the stethoscope tubes to my ears, amazed at the strumming of a fetal calf heart. The actual insemination is different, though, and I stopped going along after the first few times. No one needs to continue to see her husband's cheek pressed against a cow's rear end, both his hands inside, his face lined with calm concentration like he's digging a dress shirt out of the back of the closet.

The van pulls into the lane, its headlights reflecting off the wet gravel. AM radio leaks out the open door, and I see my husband silhouetted in front of the van as he pulls the gate open. He seems stretched out like an afternoon shadow.

"I have to talk to you," I say as he climbs the steps.

He crinkles a drive-through burger bag into a ball and sits down on the middle step. "How was work?" he wants to know.

"Fine."

"Nobody break out?" He smiles. That's Elden's way of asking if all the patients made it through another week.

I shake my head.

"What's going on?"

I concentrate on the concern in his voice, even though I know he might just be worried about the cows. I need some sign to build my confidence for this conversation. My husband is an understanding man, a man who wants to please. He bought me a new gas stove and had our closet walls lined with cedar paneling when we moved into this house. He thinks I'm beautiful. He's never asked me to lose weight, and he's never touched my body the way some men have—with curiosity or, even, aggression, instead of love. But he is careful and scared of change.

Moths are circling the porch light, making shadow-flutter above his head. I come down from the swing and lower myself next to him. He reaches one arm around me and lets his hand rest at my side.

"What would you say if I told you I was pregnant?"

"Pregnant. Are you?"

His finger traces a black scuff on the toe of his boot as he waits for my answer. He won't look at me. I realize that I am playing a kind of game, that what I'm doing isn't very nice.

"I don't think so."

"You don't think so?"

"No, I'm not."

"Did you think you were or something? Is that why you're wanting to know?"

Once again, the full extent of my husband's ignorance of my body amazes me. For weeks he has been orchestrating the ovulation of an entire herd of animals, yet he is always surprised to roll over searching for my mouth in our darkened bedroom, to hear me say, "Elden, honey, it's my time of the month." Then his hands, those hands that over the next three days will work in and out of over two hundred cattle, spring back from my thighs in a kind of quiet fear. Those nights, he just strokes my hair until one of us falls asleep. I realize I could be late—maybe several months late—before he would wonder.

"Well, why are you asking me that?"

"I've been thinking about it lately, about having a baby." I watch his face, wanting to wean something positive away from his stare. He exhales in a long slow whistle and enfolds my hand in both of his. It feels numb and swollen inside his long fingers, and I know I don't want to hear what I know he's going to say.

I don't offer to help the next day. I don't walk back to the corral with a cooler of sun tea, even though Les Monger has come down with his sons to watch my husband double the value of his herd. I've seen the drama before. I know the drill. Elden will remove the large silver containers from the drawers in the back of the van. The canisters break down like stacked communion trays. When it's time, he will draw out the inner vial, releasing a cloud of steam that will roll across the barnyard.

Elden is good at what he does, among the best on whole east coast. Les tells me—when I hand him a to-go cup of coffee and hurry him off the back porch that he technically owns—that my husband has an 80 percent success rate on the first try. Next year, they might order embryos from a farm in Wyoming and place them inside the scrub cows, the ones that aren't the right shape for maximum beef production. Then even the worst ones will bear award-winning calves.

I call my sister and ask her, "Isn't that somehow wrong? Doesn't that seem outside the natural order of things?" I've heard worse. Elden's told me about how when embryo transplanting was still experimental they used to insert cow embryos into the uteruses of rabbits for easy transport. They could survive about a week, and that was enough time to ship them to South America or Australia if they had to. Now they can freeze embryos and spare the rabbits. But even the thought of the freezing appalls me all the sudden. I need agreement in the form of an old-fashioned Bible verse or parable.

Instead, Jane says, "I think you're talking to the wrong person. I had half my stomach removed so that I wouldn't exceed the acceptable dress size for a minister's wife. I can no longer drink a can of soda in one sitting, but I'd have to say my marriage has improved."

When I hang up the phone, I dial the number for J & Company. The receptionist who answers tells me Amanda has no openings until the day after tomorrow.

"I don't need a color consultation," I explain in no uncertain terms. "This is a full out emergency. I need a fool-proof seduction face by 9:30 PM Tell her it's Cora, and I'm sure she'll work me in on her breaks."

It's just beginning to get dark when I return home. Amanda and I had dinner at the Tastee Freeze and formulated a plan as we watched the high school kids cruise Main Street. Perched on the red vinyl stool, I confessed my fear that Elden might be wary after our conversation the night before.

"He might not even want to do anything," I said.

"Just don't act horny, whatever you do." She tapped her French tip on the Formica counter for emphasis. "Let the eye makeup work its magic, but make sure he thinks it's all his idea. Men are all about the challenge."

"Here's the thing," I explained, "Even if we do it, he might not do *it* inside me. I threw out all the condoms a week ago, and he's liable to suspect I haven't been taking my pills." I thought about the special shocks on Elden's refrigerated van and how he's always been as careful to deactivate our encounters as he has been to keep all that bull semen safe and strong.

"Well then, you know what you have to do," Amanda said like it was the most natural thing in the world. "You'll just have to put it there yourself."

When I shrunk back, she said, "Oh come off it! It can't be that hard if he can do it to a half ton animal."

Les Monger and his boys have gone, but the van is parked in front of the barn. Elden must still be cleaning up. In the hallway I pause, inspecting my face in the mirror above the antique coat rack. Amanda says the kind of make-up one uses does not matter, only the brushes. She buys Rite Aid cosmetics and orders special brushes from a company back in California. She spent about half an hour working those brushes back and forth across my eyelids dabbing smoky purple colors onto my skin, then stepping back like a painter to inspect her work, and I have to admit the effect is really something. I look kind of like Liz Taylor did back in the day.

I wonder if Elden ever came in and got anything to eat, so I decide to make him a couple of sandwiches. I set them on the table in the kitchen with a slice of two-day-old apple pie and cover everything in plastic wrap.

Upstairs, I put on the nightie Amanda and I agreed on and prop the pillows up in what we decided would be a casual yet sexy backdrop. I climb in and pretend to be flipping through a copy of *Country Journal.* I lay my hair, which has been teased and fluffed and coated with Bio-luxe Shine Spray, back against the pillows. I listen, heart thumping, tendons straining toward the creak of the back porch or the click of the screen door.

I go to the bathroom, where I take the Lysol Mountain Meadows candle from the back of the toilet. I light it and toss the match into the bowl, hear it sizzle behind me. Back in bed, by candlelight, I read an article about mailbox stenciling and tear out a recipe for dill bread, then fall asleep. When I wake up a little later, the candle has burned down to an oily purple mess. I rub my eyes, and when I feel the mascara flake beneath my fingertips, I pad across the wood floor, scrub my face clean and apply Oil of Olay.

When Elden slides into bed, even later still, his hair smells faintly of shampoo. Even deeper is another smell, the smell of cows—of hay and manure and dried mud—which is also the smell of us. He reaches for me, and I say, "How did it go?"

"Good," he says, "Real good. Les says we're going to have some perfect little ones this year. You sure were gone a while," his lips brush my shoulder. "Are you peeved at me?"

"I don't think so. Not anymore."

When his mouth covers mine, I lean into the kiss, spreading it out carefully like pie crust. His arms wrap around me, and each breath seems to catch in his throat for a second. His fingers start to tangle in the hem of my gown, and I have to tell him. I say, "We better not Elden. I threw out your condoms, and I've missed too many pills."

Then the breath hangs warm between our faces like at night at the beach, and he says, "Let's see. Let's just see what happens."

I can't fall asleep right away. Outside the wind chimes are clanging over the deck. I step outside and pull them down from the hook next to the door. I pause for a moment, letting the wind flap my gown against my legs as I peer across our dark backyard. Behind me is the pull of Elden sleeping through our bedroom window. It feels like we are connected by a string, like the rising and falling of his chest tugs gently on mine. There are no stars, so I know the clouds must be swelling overhead, getting ready for another rain. I listen through the thick air that hangs around the farmhouse, and I inhale the sound of animals brushing against each other in the dark.

LAST SEASON'S GROWTH

Mary Joyce 1992

It's hard to say whether Francesca Trigiani, as she was known back then, ever cruised Main Street or siphoned gas or stood around in a circle of headlights sipping wine coolers in some pasture. I know so little of her life with her grandmother. Likely, she did not participate in these activities—although she may have wanted to at times if, as she rinsed off the dinner plates, she heard the swish of tires over the wet pavement outside or, on a clear night, the clank of tailgates rising from near the river. Francesca never marched with a baton in the Harvest Days Parade like most little girls in Conrad's Fork. But, then again, neither did my daughter.

As far as I can tell, Francesca was rarely allowed out alone except, of course, to trudge over the broken sidewalk and up the street to Cook's Laundromat with a wicker basket of soiled clothing on Saturday mornings or to cut across the vacant lot between her house and O'Dell's Grocery if Nona ran out of olive oil. More than once on my way into the office to meet a client for a weekend appointment, I stooped to help her collect the scattered handkerchiefs, the white cotton underpants with gaping leg holes and loose elastic. Twice each week, on Wednesday evenings and Sunday mornings, the girl and her grandmother backed out of the carport, which was scattered with dead leaves, and drove all the way to Garrison to St. Isadore's for mass. She went to and from school, her forehead against the clouded glass of the bus window, her fingers resting on a canvas satchel. The one her grandmother claimed had belonged to her grandfather. She told me once that she liked school, but as far as I can tell, she did just well enough to escape reprimand while avoiding praise.

Francesca's life was uneventful until her eighteenth summer, specifically until an afternoon in July—an afternoon she once described to me when we sat together in the office basement, sealing and stamping envelopes for a bulk mailing. On this afternoon, as she hurried back from O'Dell's, the jar of pepperoncinis she carried was slippery in her warm fingers, and grasshoppers hurled themselves up from the dry weeds, bouncing off her calves. She was careful to shut the screen door behind her, and she paused only a minute in the sitting room to kneel in front of the fan, turning into the breeze and holding her thick braid up off the back of her neck. In the kitchen she found a pot of water boiling over onto the stove top, and Nona sprawled across the linoleum. The old woman's lips and fingernails were an eerie blue. So, three years after her confirmation and two months out of high school, Francesca found herself alone.

I'm afraid the insurance policy her grandmother had selected—not the one we recommended—covered the funeral expenses with little left. So the girl, who didn't want to sell the house but could hardly bear so many hours there alone, began to look for work. Janelle, the owner of J & Company, offered her a position immediately. Personally, I think she harbored plans to chop the girl's dark, wavy hair for a before and after shot, then enter it in one of those design shows she's always talking about. She set Francesca up as a shampoo girl, lathering and rinsing in the back of the shop, but she never gave her time to get the hang of it. The stylists were always hollering for her, "Frannie! Be a doll and run and get me some sanitizer out of the back." Or worse yet, they'd send her across the street to the Valley Vista Grill for sandwiches and coffee.

Janelle fussed at the new girl for not rinsing all the shampoo out of customers' hair, for not making any conversation with the men, and for letting the towel snag on the women's earrings, but it was difficult to find a girl willing to sweep up hair and scrub the base of each chair with Pine-Sol.

Never a graceful girl, Frannie was accused of breaking the air pump that raises one of the swiveling chairs and knocking over a 24 oz. bottle of coconut creme conditioner. The cats were the final straw. Frannie bumped the display shelf above the sink and sent Janelle's collection of 114 miniature porcelain cats crashing to the floor. Only about a third of them were broken—and I'd been after her to have them all appraised, so she could start thinking about our special collections insurance—but that was the end of Frannie's salon career.

That night she scanned the want ads, and the next morning she drove to Walker Manufacturing Company. Frannie wasn't sure what exactly happened in a muffler factory. I don't think she even knew what a muffler was. She may have paused for a second, parked safely in the visitors' lot, but she took a deep breath and decided not to dwell on such uncertainties. Someone was waiting at the entrance to usher her along with others, lured by the printed offer of seventeen dollars an hour, into an air conditioned conference room with blue Berber carpeting. She watched a safety video. She allowed a rubber gloved nurse to snip a lock of her hair for drug testing. Two days later she went on the line spot welding metal doughnuts around pipes.

Frannie's new job wasn't that difficult. Really, she only had to set up the pieces and then push two buttons. But the man on the neighboring machine tossed the pieces into a basket at her feet quickly, and she was expected to keep up. There was a foreman who drove a little golf cart. He came around every so often to shake his head and mark his clipboard. Each line had a quota.

Frannie had a navy blue uniform with a clip for her plastic ID card. She had leather boots with steel toes, but she would have preferred to wear tennis shoes because standing on the cement floor all day made her feet ache inside. She was issued kevlar gloves, but they didn't let her fingers move fast enough, so she never wore them. By lunch time, she had a ring of blue-black metallic dust around her fingernails. On her obligatory ten minute breaks, she went to the ladies room, and the snot she blew into tissues was strung with the same dark powder.

Entering the cafeteria at noon was like surfacing from deep in the ocean. The room was clean and crowded, veiled in fluorescent lighting, not unlike high school. When Frannie pulled the plugs from her ears and left them dangling around her neck, she was immediately washed with voices. The workers lifted their thick goggles onto their foreheads or lay them on the table next to their trays, and suddenly—with eyes visible and blinking in the brightness—everyone looked human again.

Only a few women worked at the plant. They gathered at a corner table for their breaks, smoking and talking about KT's, a bar where they liked to meet for line dancing on Friday nights. Frannie sat by herself, grateful to be lost in the noise. Sometimes she would flip through a *Readers' Digest* if she could find one in the box of complimentary magazines next to the fountain drink island. More often than not, she would stare outside. It was still dark when she left her house in the morning, and the sun began sinking down behind Old Nag Mountain as she drove home. Huge glass windows lined one wall, and after hours in the dark factory, she just wanted to drink her thirty minutes of sunlight.

Once, that I know of, another worker tried to talk to her on break, a boy from across the mountain in Virginia. He sidled up to the cafeteria table.

"Hello there," he snapped her ID card from its clasp on her breast pocket. "Miss F. Trigiani." I imagine he stumbled over the name a bit.

Frannie made a grab for the plastic card, but the boy was too quick. "What are you doing after work tomorrow, Miss Trigiani?"

"Laundry." This was not flirting. She had pulled the box with her winter sweaters out of the attic and was actually planning on washing them out in the bathtub with Woolite the following evening. She made another swipe for her card, and this time she got it.

"How about you go see a movie with me instead?"

Frannie looked at the boy and sighed, not the come closer-sigh of a typical eighteen-year-old. "I'm sorry," she said. "I don't even know you."

He took her right hand in his and tapped his name tag with his left index finger. "Sure you do," he said, pumping her hand up and down in a mock handshake. "I'm J. Klawon."

I imagine she looked unamused and pulled her hand away quickly.

"Seriously, I'm Joel, and you're . . ." he pulled back and studied her dark eyes, her hair knotted heavily at the base of her neck. "Felicia."

She shook her head, and I'll bet she smiled a little, giving him license to try again. "Fredrica? . . . Faynette?"

Something—a brush of the elbow or shoulder—jarred her then, and sent her hurrying away to hide out in the bathroom. Once, she saw him again in line at the time clock, and he smiled and said, "Fern?"

Despite her job, Frannie still had too much time to fill. She worked twelve-hour shifts but worked three days then had three days off. So, she planted mums in the boxes along the porch steps and meticulously weeded the herb garden the old woman had started around a solitary bird bath in the backyard. For the first time ever, the carport was swept clean. In the beginning of October she finally went through Nona's things. I saw her make three trips to Conrad's Fork United Way Thrift Store in one day. She went right past my office window, lugging plastic bags of nightgowns and old woman loafers. She walked for hours in the evenings—down to the boat landing, up to the baseball fields. One person told me they saw her walking along the old River Road out by Bear Lithia Springs. I felt a strange kind of connection if I passed her on my way home with Charlie buckled in next to me and bent over one of her comic books. After all, we knew something about loneliness. There were still nights when I didn't want to have to go home.

It was on one of her walks that Frannie met Wade Rogers. Every October, the Black Mountain Independent Pentecostal Church throws a huge carnival in the town park. They don't call it a Halloween carnival because they don't want to participate in any kind of celebration that honors Satan or anything evil, even indirectly. Instead, they call it a Fall Faith Festival. They bob for apples and pop kettle corn, and some of the kids still wear costumes. Wade, a Black Mountain Independent Pentecostal elder, was in attendance and he had invited my daughter to keep his boy, Nick, company. Charlie came home toting a plastic bag emblazoned with Biblical scenes and bursting with miniature candy bars and plastic spiders, so she and Nick must have hit the games as soon as they arrived, leaving Wade to wander through the booths alone. Eventually Wade climbed the hill overlooking the park and sat down on a bench, nibbling a caramel apple.

Wade, at 35, had vowed never to remarry, and as far as I knew, with the exception of an occasional matinee with Charlie and me, he did not date. I'll admit, there was a time when I wanted Wade for my own. I had tried through subtle forms of persuasion to mold my relationship with him into something more than employee or parenting advisor. So, something must have shaped his mood that night. Perhaps, as he stared down at the picnic shelters, which were strung with Japanese lanterns and teeming with cake-walking youth, the indulgence and complication of it all overwhelmed him.

When he turned his face to the crunching of leaves and saw Francesca walking toward him, hands deep in the pockets of her brown barn coat, she looked simple and familiar. Although Frannie had been in and out of the office a few times in the previous months, he couldn't remember meeting her there. He struggled to place this face, free of

lipstick but dark and lovely beneath the street lamps, and his mind
halted suddenly on an afternoon at the very end of the summer, on the
sound of ceramic shattering and this girl's termination as he sat in the
front room of J & Company awaiting his haircut.

"Frannie," he said, because that is what the owner had yelled after
the shelves crashed down.

She was, of course, startled. She probably pulled her hands from
her pockets and smoothed back the frizzies that fell from her braid, a
gesture I have seen many times since, whenever she's nervous. "Do we
know each other?" she asked.

"Well, you used to work at the salon. You used to shampoo my hair
before you . . . well before you left." Although it may seem impossible
in a town as small as Conrad's Fork, Wade knew nothing of the young
Francesca, the one I watched trip back and forth through the vacant
lot. His married life was so tumultuous that, from the beginning, his
gossip was limited to keeping track of his wife's indiscretions.

Frannie, able to remember only the most dreaded appointments—
the old men whose limp comb-overs required two applications before
she could even work up a lather—failed to place Wade's carefully
groomed head. She squinted at him and shook her head.

"I was there," he insisted, "your last day."

"Oh," she stomped her feet against the cold that seemed to hang
just over the grassy hill side. "I was fired. I found another job, though."

This is how I picture them: facing each other, their breath coming
in puffs, until Wade breaks the silence and points with his caramel
apple to the swirling mass down in the park. "I need to find my son.
Will you let me get you some hot chocolate?"

I have no doubt she hesitated at first, and he had to explain, "It's a
faith festival, not a party."

That night Wade did not sit in his idling car, as was his habit, and
wait until Charlie was safely inside and he could see me waving him
away from the lit rectangle of the doorway. It was a kind of premonition of the months to come, the brief courtship that would bring the
girl into the office on her days off. The afternoons when she would
bend to remove the lids from steaming single-serving Tupperware
containers and feed us—she always included me in these lunches—
pasta with pine nuts and basil or sandwiches with thinly sliced roasted
red pepper. The Friday afternoons when Wade would call and say, "Is
there any way you could watch Nick for a few hours tonight? There's a
bluegrass festival I want to take Frannie to up in Berea."

If you'll believe it, masochist that I am, I bit my lip and said, "Sure. In fact, why doesn't he just spend the night."

I think Frannie had some nerves before their wedding. The afternoon before the ceremony, when Wade had driven to Garrison to pick up his tuxedo, she showed up at the office. Years ago, when Wade set up shop down on Main Street, he went all out. People are anxious when they purchase insurance. He knew the atmosphere would have to make clients comfortable and trusting. The building is one of those tall ones with the facade fronts. It used to be a grocery store or something. He replaced the display windows in front with big bay windows that fill each of our offices with sunlight during the morning hours, and he chose a heavy, old fashioned door of solid oak.

The door swells whenever the dampness outside warps the wood. It sticks a bit, but if you are patient and put pressure in the right spot, it swings open without too much trouble. I was on the phone interviewing someone about a cracked windshield when I heard the familiar thumping, and I knew it was Frannie struggling to get inside.

I opened the door to find her breathless and flushed. I said, "Wade's not here. He had to run to town." Everyone here calls Garrison *town*.

She threw herself into one of the leather wing-back chairs in the waiting area. "I know. That's why I came today." She looked up at me imploringly. "I need you to do me a favor."

"Sure," I said. "I mean, if I can." *My God,* I thought, *she's nineteen, Wade. Nineteen.* Although I was younger when I married Larry.

"I want you to cut my hair." She pulled her braid over her shoulder and looped her fingers around the end of it where it was fastened with one of those plain rubber bands, the kind the newspaper comes wrapped in. "A sort of surprise for the groom."

I tried to imagine her face without that mane. When Charlie was born and I cut my hair, Larry came home drunk one night and told me what a grave mistake I had made. "Of course I liked it better long," he said with disgust. "All men like long hair. We want to smell it and touch it and get all wrapped up in it." I tried to picture Frannie with a springy bob like mine, or worse, a shiny bald head like that Irish singer.

"I don't think I'd do a good job," I said. "Why don't you go across the street?"

"I can't go in there. I've not been back since Janelle fired me. I haven't trimmed my hair in more than a year." Frannie has the most peculiar voice. English was her first language. Her mother didn't push her off on her grandmother until she was four or five, but the old woman spoke a strange mixture of English and Italian in a heavy, lurching accent. Frannie's voice, maybe to compensate, has always moved across words with a fluidity she could never achieve with her body. It's musical, really, so different from the steady twang of most of the locals I talk to. "You need not take off much. Just neaten up the ends a little."

I sighed and directed her into my office, told her to get the scissors from my desk. She pulled a drawer all the way out in her haste to find them, hurling an array of ink pens and paper clips across the rug. I took the drawer from her gently. "Frannie," I said, "just go get me the spray bottle we use to mist the plants. It's probably under the sink in the bathroom." I gathered everything up and then spread newspapers over the floor all around my chair.

When she was seated in front of me, I took her braid in my hands. It was heavy and alive beneath my fingers, like the flinching tail of some animal. I unwrapped the rubber band slowly, snapping it around my wrist. When I loosened the plaited hair, it was a curtain hanging down the back of the chair, still warm with sun from her walk down the hill and smelling earthy like mulch. I thought how she was probably one of those girls who only had to wash her hair once a week.

When I pumped the spray bottle, I watched her hair curl up against the mist like worms on a wet sidewalk, as if it knew what was about to happen. The first cut was the most difficult—I stood for a moment with the scissors open. Her hair was coarse. It felt like the wisps of horse hair my brothers and I used to yank out of the barbed wire fence behind the cemetery. But after I worked the blades through that chunk of hair, it became easier. Her hair collected in six-inch tufts on the newspapers underfoot. I was careful, working my way around the crown of her head, measuring each cut against the previous one, although with wavy hair it doesn't matter as much.

"Are you ready for the big day?" I asked her.

"Yeah, I guess so."

"You guess so?" I looked down at my watch. "The florist truck will be pulling up to Black Mountain Independent Pentecostal in about fourteen hours. You better be ready."

She smiled up at me. "Were you completely ready?"

I pulled damp sections of hair down around her chin, measuring the sides. "Frannie, at eighteen, I was living in a shotgun shack with my parents and three brothers. Larry had a motorcycle and I needed to go somewhere." I sat back on the edge of the desk. "My marriage was a complete disaster," I said. She looked down, picking at her cuticles. "But I got Charlie out of it. If I'd had a lick of sense I would have known it wouldn't last." I started to tell her how I was barely out of high school, but I caught myself. Instead I said, "Wade's an entirely different caliber of man than Larry will ever be."

"It's not Wade," she said, snapping her eyes back up to mine. "I know he's the one for me. I'm just a little nervous because I always thought Father Daniel would be the one to do my service when the time came. Everyone's wonderful at the Pentecostal church, but it's still strange." Her eyes started to water a little, and I got worried that I had broken in somewhere I didn't want any part of. "I'm not sure Nona would approve," she whispered.

"You can't worry about that, honey," I told her. "You've already made lots of decisions without your grandmother, maybe some decisions you never would have made if she was still here. She did her best to give you your own sense of what's what, and you have to just go forward based on what feels right to you now."

I fluffed up her hair—which now fell right at her shoulders, more curly than before—and helped her out of my desk chair before she could say anything else.

The next afternoon everything went off without a hitch. Wade wanted it to be a simple affair, nobody but him and his bride standing up there this time. Charlie and Nick handed out programs and ushered guests into the church. Of course, my daughter refused to wear a dress. She stood outside the congregation hall, scrawny and serious in velvet pants.

Father Daniel actually came to the service, at least I assume it was him, sitting near the back of the sanctuary in one of those white, cardboard-looking collars. Frannie wore her hair down, which is always nice at a December wedding, and the reception went about as well as a dry celebration in a church basement can go. The couple honeymooned in Chattanooga and made it back in time for Christmas.

Larry came into town for the holidays, as well. He parked his rig on the street outside his mother's house, a peeling two story with dogs running patches of grass bare circling around their chains in the back. I felt obliged to let Charlie see her dad, so I dropped her off in the afternoon on Christmas Eve. I sat in the office for the full four hours I had agreed to, then drove back and beeped my horn until my daughter came running. As she trotted down the walk clutching what I could only assume to be some new toy, I saw suddenly in everything she did—the way she flipped back her hair, the way she stepped over the leaning picket fence—traces of her father.

"How did it go?" I asked.

"Fine." She was fiddling with the Extreme Sports Motor-Cross Man that Larry had given her. Basically it was a doll with a helmet and a red jump suit, mounted on a motorized dirt bike. I thought about the Barbies I used to buy Charlie. Immediately abandoned and stacked in an old shoe box, each doll's hair was still smoothly twisted into its original bouffant. "Check out these lights, Ma." She flipped a switch and the bulb flashed on behind the headlight at the same time a recorded revving rose from the little battery-powered engine.

I told her to put on her nightgown when we got home. Then I let her sit up with me and eat icing while I decorated cookies.

Although they never met, it is inevitable that Frannie's story would intertwine somehow with that of Trish, Wade's first wife. I went to high school with Wade, and, although I am a few years younger, it would have been impossible not to know who he was. He was a good boy and a good-looking boy in a clean-cut kind of way, a golden boy, really—honor roll student, all-state football player. I scoffed at his kind back then and sought out boys with long hair and ripped jeans. Younger versions of Larry, boys who carved words into their own skin and smoked dope behind the shop building.

Wade went to the University of Kentucky, and that's where he met Trish, a Tri-Delt from Nashville. She had intricately highlighted blond hair. She took Dexatrim pills like vitamins, and they kept her slender and full of energy. She had a way of staring intently at whichever boy on whom she had chosen to bestow her attentions that made him feel as if he were her entire world. Wade, who had been a local hero here in Conrad's Fork, was ripe to be someone's entire world again.

She was a partier; that much is clear. And I can imagine the details: the sound of shot glasses slamming back to the bar, tiny Mickey Mouse faces dissolving onto their tongues, her hair making a tent around their faces as she leaned over him in the back bedroom of a strange apartment.

Their life changed shortly after he brought her back to the valley, though. Wade was making plans to open the insurance agency, and they were living in an apartment on Lee Avenue. He wanted to carve out a little place for the two of them. He thought he could settle Trish into such an existence if they had each other, and for a while it seemed he might be right. They attended a revival held over by Wildwood Dam. As they ate fried chicken with the other young married couples, sitting on the dock and listening to the crickets start up in the tall grass on the other side of the river, a kind of peace welled up inside Wade's head, and he wanted to hang onto it, let it slide down his throat like a warm nosebleed. He and Trish took out one of the paddleboats, and they paused for a minute in that deep pool above the dam. They stopped paddling and let the strange mumble of believers rocking and whispering in tongues carry across the water from the prayer tent. They decided they were born again. They went to church every Sunday morning and had brunch afterwards at the Valley Vista Grill or Ray's Diner.

I started working for Wade right after they had Nick, and I guess that's when things started to change between them, too. I'm not sure when she first cheated on her husband, but I have a feeling Trish unraveled a little with every encounter. After a while I started to hear about things she did—crazy, unbelievable things—like showing up for her son's entrance interview into Genesis Preschool wearing only a raincoat. I can remember cleaning old files from the cabinets in the sitting area and listening to Wade just across the hall, picking up his phone and dialing the same number again and again.

Wade never would have considered a divorce. No matter how long it continued, he never would have been able to wash his hands of the situation. That's why, if you ask me, it was a kind of blessing that when the new middle school gym teacher lost control of his Bronco and barreled past the guard rail while crossing the mountain into Wise County, Trish was strapped into the passenger seat next to him. Wade mourned her, though, like it was the most natural thing in the world for your wife to die on the way to a rendezvous with another man. He paid for a lovely funeral and delivered an elegy that made throats swell, even in those who knew firsthand what kind of a woman Trish Rogers had really been.

While Frannie's innocence drew Wade to her, it is important to remember that he was used to a woman who knew exactly how to touch him, a woman who could, with one well-manicured hand, work him into an unbelievable heat beneath an airplane blanket. His first night with Frannie was magical in the true sense of the word. She wore a long white gown with intricate beadwork that glittered in the candlelight. He wanted nothing more than to hover all around her in the half dark and know she was his. But as the months passed, and he tried to guide her hands, he couldn't hide his bewilderment and—there's really no other word for it—disappointment.

Wade tried to talk to me about it. One morning he came into my office and shut the door. He pulled a doughnut from a paper bag and set it on a cocktail napkin in front of me. Raspberry filling was leaking out the side. "Breakfast," he said, settling into one of my chairs holding an eclair. For a while he sat and stared out the window at the cars trickling down Main Street, housewives heading out to Wal-Mart. Finally, he spoke.

"You got married pretty young. I'm guessing you weren't terribly," his eclair moved through the air after the right words, "*experienced.*"

"You could say that." I looked up from my report.

"It probably took you awhile to pick up on certain things, huh? You know, to get in synch."

"What do you mean? Sexually?" I thought about the first few months with Larry, how we barely knew each other. We couldn't make it through a meal without fighting. One morning at a motel diner, I actually picked up a three cheese omelette and threw it across the table. Outside, waiting for Larry to finish his breakfast, I had rinsed the grease from my fingers in the patio fountain. Sex was the only part we ever got right. I didn't know anything, but when I was alone with Larry, pieces of me took over. My mouth and hands and hips got away from the rest of me in the dark.

I looked at Wade waiting, so earnest, still clutching his pastry by the window. "Sure," I said. "It takes some time. You just have to be patient."

Wade began to learn and record to memory the details he had rushed over as a hurried suitor. Things like his wife's pistachio allergy, or the way the feet of all her jeans were ragged because she wore them just a few centimeters too long. These eccentricities only made her more fascinating to him. Frannie insisted on continuing her job at Walker Manufacturing Company, despite Wade's protests that they didn't need the money and that the commute across icy roads wasn't a good idea. "You know what," he confided to me, "I'm glad the girl won't quit. I love that stalwart attitude." That's what he called her— *the girl.*

It must be pointed out that Frannie never grew to love her job. She was summoned to the foreman's office after lunch. One Monday morning there was a notice paper-clipped to her blank time card, and following the directions therein, she made her way to the cluster of offices she had seen the morning of her first interview. When she reached number 17A and knocked tentatively, a small voice called her inside. Behind an enormous desk was the foreman of her line, the man who drove by and observed their work at regular intervals, watching a few moments before marking his clipboard. He looked different inside his office, off his little golf cart. It was like seeing Father Daniel without his robes for the first time.

"Francesca," he said. "Am I saying your name right, dear?" Then when she nodded, "Come inside, please. Have a seat." He motioned to the two chairs against the wall, and Frannie seated herself on the edge of one of them. She watched as the man moved aside looping reams of computer printouts. He folded his hands in front of him and smiled at her. "Do you have any idea why I've asked you to come see me?"

"No, sir."

"Well, each line has a quota—a certain number of parts that must be pushed through each shift, as well as a certain percentage of that number that must pass inspection." He looked at her kindly as he explained this. "I'm afraid our line has not been regularly reaching its quota since you joined the team."

"It's just taken me awhile to get the swing of it all," she said.

"I understand, Francesca, I surely do, but I need you to work faster for me and more conscientiously." He looked across the sprawling surface of his desk top, right into her watering eyes. "I need to see more turn-out. Can I count on you?"

"Of course." She said this as if she were accepting a grave mission.

The only problem was Frannie couldn't work any faster. I believe this because I had tried to put her to work doing something as simple as hole-punching in the office. She tried to hurry herself. She imagined music in her head and pretended she had to keep time in some intricate, smoldering metal dance. *Bend. Place. Press. Bend. Place. Press.* But the faster she went the sloppier her work became. She melded pipes into the doughnuts in crazy angles and had no choice but to toss them into the scrap metal bin, the one that doesn't even go to the inspection center.

One morning a few weeks after her summons, when her scrap bin was filling much too quickly, she realized the pieces she had just placed were misaligned and made a frantic grab for them after she'd already pressed her palms to the buttons. The steel jaws of the machine caught her left hand, and she felt a strange pressure as she watched them tighten, hearing the mechanical groan as the machine crunched against her outstretched fingers. She waited for the pain, like when she tripped and caught a slice of broken pop bottle in her knee in the vacant lot behind her grandmother's house. In the milliseconds before the machine released her hand, she imagined herself passed out on the cement floor, and wondered if they would know to call Wade at his office. Then, suddenly, she was free, and her hand was whole. She stepped back and turned it over in front of her face, wiggling her fingers. Then she walked away from the line, leaving the gaping cluster of men staring, some of them calling out to her, "Hey, where are you going? Are you okay?"

Driving home for the first time in the afternoon, she cracked her windows and breathed in the spring smell of wet asphalt and damp pasture. She kept stretching her fingers out then gripping them around the steering wheel. She had heard of amputees who wake from surgery and think they can move their toes, only to discover their leg has been removed below the knee. Only the sight of her long fingers and chewed nails reassured her that she still had a left hand.

She made one stop before reaching the office, at St. Isadore's. She knew Father Daniel would be out making his visits on a Friday afternoon, so she went up the stairs to the alcove above the catechumen classrooms. She had not been to mass since weeks before her wedding, and as she knelt at the altar below the tabernacle, she could feel the wafers and wine, the resurrected body and blood, radiating out from the locked plywood cabinet. Her own blood was racing in her ears so that she could not find the words for the prayers, the ones she had known forever. Inside her brain one word kept playing over and over and it was a kind of prayer. *Miracle.*

By the time she let herself into the office, she had begun to doubt her own experience, and she was talking around the accident in veiled circles. I was able to piece the story together, though. "There's probably some kind of safety release built into the machine," I told her. "I haven't heard of any accidents over there in years."

We agreed it might be best not to tell Wade, who believes God witnesses directly through the souls of those who are born again and is wary of any other kind of miracle.

I noticed a change in Frannie immediately. The next morning she dropped her husband off at the office and helped him carry in the components of our new computer system. It made me sick watching that girl, who had somehow broken one of our keyboards and the coffee maker in an attempt at basic data entry, lug boxes of expensive office equipment down the sidewalk. Then, when the computer rep came down from Garrison, she actually helped him set everything up. I could hear them over in Wade's office as we both worked in mine. "Just plug that in over there," the guy said. "Perfect. Now thread that up to me."

"What's going on?" I said. Wade looked up at me, confused. "With Frannie." I nodded my head toward the door.

"Oh, can you tell something's different?" He looked up at me with a ridiculous grin. "She quit her job yesterday. I think she's going to be a lot happier," he said. "And all of a sudden *things* are better."

"Things?" I didn't know what the hell he was talking about.

"Yeah, things, you know, at home. It's like all of a sudden when she touches me, whoo! Maybe all these months she's just been stressed out from working in that factory, or maybe we just needed some more time."

After that it was their yard over on Laurel Place. She dug flowerbeds all around the property. She took the car down to the boat landing and waded out into Dry River, the cold water riffling around her legs. She scanned the riverbed for rocks, and when she found one that she thought might work, she picked it up and turned it over in her hands, running her fingers all along its surface. She filled the trunk and drove back up Main Street, with the back end of the car only inches off the road. She stacked the stones into retaining walls to hold in place all that dirt she'd turned up. She felt her way along the rocks she'd already placed until she found the right spot for the next one. They were held together tighter than if she'd secured them with mortar.

She started doing all sorts of crafts, the things ladies around here call handiwork. She embroidered butterflies on pillows and cross-stitched a sampler for Wade to hang in the office. She knit me a turtleneck tank for my birthday in April. She made a wreath for her grandmother's grave and took it down to the cemetery on Mother's Day. She tried to talk me into taking a folk art seminar with her over at Mountain Empire Community College—basket-weaving techniques of the Appalachian people.

And all the while things kept getting better and better between her and Wade until he finally couldn't take it anymore. He started to doubt her.

"I'm telling you," he said to me as I stood at the Xerox machine, copying the previous week's accident report forms, "it's too much." He was hovering over my shoulder, obsessing over Frannie's latest accomplishment in the sack. Something he called the swirl.

"No, Wade," I said, "You're too much. You married a woman practically half your age, and now you're insecure."

"Listen, it's like she knows something new every night. Where's she getting all this stuff, and why didn't she ever do any of it before?"

I considered describing for him the way they looked to me—walking home from the office holding hands, their shadows stretching forward together on the sidewalk. Perhaps I should have told him how, by the end of their first date, he knew Frannie better than I ever knew Larry.

"I don't know," I said. "I'm your assistant, not your marriage counselor."

"I won't go through what I did with Trish all over again," he said. "That's too much to ask of any man."

Charlie started getting off the bus with Nick toward the end of the school year. Since Frannie was free, she offered to keep an eye on her until I finished up at the office. They were trying out for majors that year, Nick for shortstop and Charlie for pitcher. They tossed the ball back and forth for hours while Frannie yanked dandelions out of her vinca beds or soaked thin strips of oak in a basin of warm water to loosen them up for her baskets. She spray-painted a strike zone target on the side of the woodpile. My daughter was the only girl left in the league. Over the years the others had all switched to softball. Charlie fired away until Frannie thought the girl's arm would fall off.

"You're hitting that target every time," she said when she brought the kids Popcicles.

"It doesn't matter because I can't throw hard enough," Charlie said. The previous spring Wade and I had taken the kids to King's Dominion, and Charlie insisted on going into the booth that clocks how fast you can throw a baseball. She got three throws, and they all looked perfect to me. Even Wade said she had great form, but none of them clocked higher than 60 miles per hour.

"How hard do you have to throw?" Frannie looked at Nick, who shrugged his shoulders and sucked on his popsicle. He wasn't sure how to treat his new stepmother, and that's understandable since she was only eight years his senior.

"Our coach says in the seventies at least," Charlie said, "or else you have to be able to throw junk."

"What's junk?" Frannie unwrapped her own popsicle.

Nick sighed, exasperated. "Screwgies, knuckle balls, sliders."

"If I could get a knuckle ball, he'd let me pitch," said Charlie. "You don't have to throw those fast at all. You just push it off your fingertips like that." She flicked her hand out in front of her like she was finishing up a magic spell. "So it won't spin. Then the wind makes it do all kinds of stuff."

"They go all squirrelly," said Nick.

Frannie laid her popsicle down on the plastic wrapper and picked one of the balls up off the lawn. "So it's something like this?" She didn't bother pulling the ball in to her chin or drawing up her leg, she just hurled it toward the target, and the kids, even Nick, watched in awe as the ball pushed straight off her fingers, dipping crazily just before hitting base of the woodpile.

"No one could've hit that," Charlie said. "It dropped right off the table. Can you show me how to do it?"

As the summer wore on, Wade started to lose control. If Frannie was a few minutes late with lunch, he was sure she had met someone on the sly that morning. He would accuse her of all sorts of indiscretions right in front of me, right in front of customers a few times. She left the office in tears, and eventually she stopped bringing over our meals. The little league coach heard about Frannie's pitching, and asked her if she wanted to volunteer to work with the kids on Wednesday evenings. Wade was positive she had something going on with the coach.

Things finally came to a head in August, and Frannie, tired of defending herself, decided to leave, at least for a while. She moved back into the little house by the vacant lot, almost a year exactly after her grandmother's death. She's a different person now, Frannie is. I don't know that I've ever seen someone come into her own like that, all in the course of a year.

Throughout the winter I had Wade over to eat dinner once or twice a week, just to keep him from getting too down, but mostly all he did was ask me if I'd talked to Frannie. It amazes me what I once would have done for him. I've stopped by to see her a few times, too. She says she's not ready to file for divorce, but she won't move back in until Wade agrees to see a counselor. We don't talk about her accident, or whatever it was that happened to her on the line at the muffler factory. We sit on the steps and stretch our legs out because the cement holds onto the sun, even after the lights go on in the shop windows downtown and the breeze picks up off the river. We sit there in the dark like high school girls

She's been working for an orchard outside of town. All their autumn help disappears after the fruit harvest. In the past few weeks they've begun pruning trees, and she thinks it's wonderful the way the light shines through the branches when they're done. She tries to tell me what it feels like to run your fingers along last season's growth, finding the right place to cut so that the leaves keep reaching up.

NAKED LADIES

Charlie 1996

If my mom were here, she would tell me to paint my toenails. I prop my feet on the coffee table and tighten the Velcro straps on my sandals. About three inches up my ankles I can see the thick white line from the heavy socks and boots I wear at work. Mom would say Deric and I shouldn't spend his first night back fishing, that we should get dressed up and drive into Garrison, have dinner at the Bluestone Inn where we can stare into each other's eyes and talk over those fancy mushrooms stuffed with crab meat. She wouldn't understand how Deric and I can spend a whole evening together and hardly talk at all. We've been apart so much this summer that we need to just relax and do what we do best.

Last summer we used to always go driving up in the mountains, right at twilight when the shadows were starting to creep up the tree trunks. We'd stop at Cumberland Gap up at the visitors' center. Inside they have filmstrips like *Daniel Boone and the Westward Expansion,* but that's not our kind of thing. We would always walk around to the backside of the building where a grassy slope extends toward the meadows and sit right below the observation deck. We'd hear the footsteps of kids clamoring around above us and the sharp voices of their parents drifting down. It can get chilly up there in the evening, even in midsummer, so we always sat real close. The first time we went, I didn't even know what I was looking for, but Deric shushed me and said to just be patient and keep watching.

The fields were a hazy copper color in the low light, with gold-enrod and ragweed in the meadow, cinnamon ferns all along the tree line. Slowly the animals came into focus. There must have been at least ten, mostly mothers and fawns nosing their way through the brush, deer standing with their heads up and their ears pricked and others just grazing right out in the open.

After you knew how to look for them, they were obvious. Deric's got a really good eye for seeing things other people can't. Otherwise someone like him never would have picked me out of the crowd.

I pull back the blinds a little, scanning the curb for Deric's black truck. Since he graduated, he's been working as a rafting guide on the New River in West Virginia. It's a long drive, and most weekends he has to lead overnight tours, so this will be only the second time I've seen him since June.

I've been spending my summer working at Outdoor Effects, a landscape company. I pulled a help-wanted flyer off the bulletin board at Piggly Wiggly the day after Deric left. Last summer I got so used to hiking and fishing with him that I thought working outside every day would make me feel almost like he was still here. I had to go in for an interview and everything. I can still hardly believe I did it. Of course, it wasn't scary once I got there because I discovered I knew one of the owners, or I used to know her anyway. Fran. She went by Frannie back then, back when she was married to my mom's boss. She looked just the same when I saw her again that first morning—jeans frayed, hair curling around her face as she lifted a garden hose to reach the petunias hanging in iron baskets.

Mom wasn't too thrilled about the job. You should see the pair of us climbing into the car in the morning. She's dressed in a silk blouse and a pencil skirt, her hair pulled back in neat combs, while I'm wearing Deric's old ball cap and a pair of second-hand work boots.

Most days she drops me off at 7:00 AM, and I open the greenhouse before Fran and her boyfriend Bryce arrive. That early the whole building smells clean in a way I never knew dirt could, and the air is warm and wet with transpiration. I have to crank open the big air vents at the front and the back. Every morning I get almost sad when I feel the cool morning air start to rush into where the plants have just been soaking in themselves all night. I work on a crew with a guy named Dave. We mow lawns on a rotating schedule, and sometimes we plant trees or annuals. It's seasonal work, and that's good because I've still got another year of school. But I'll miss it in the fall. Fran says they may be able to keep me on part-time because there will be trees to prune and bulbs to plant once it gets cooler.

I run a hand through my hair. Still damp, it looks darker than usual against my fingers and smells faintly of shampoo. Mom says the one good thing about my job is that the sun has brightened up my hair. Deric and I are just going fishing near Island Ford, so I haven't bothered to use the blow dryer or to put on any make up. Deric likes it better when I don't anyway, although Mom would surely say something if she were here.

"Go put on a little blush, babe. You look pale." That's what she would say, even though after two months working eight- to ten-hour days outside I'm anything but pale. Then, when Deric got here, she might add, "I don't know why you want to leave the house with that ragamuffin. I told her not to wear those cut-offs."

I'm not really sure what I look like. In the mall, I usually see fat little girls with funny hair hanging onto the hands of even fatter mothers with even funnier hair. I'm not sure what happened to me. My mom, Mary Joyce, is slender and blond. She knows how to walk across a room and will men to look at her. She can turn a forty-five minute wait for a table into a five minute one just by shifting her hips and sighing in the right direction. I've seen pictures of Mom at sixteen standing on the steps in front of the church or sitting on a picnic bench in the park, always the same penciled brows and feathered hair, like the paper dolls she tried to get me to play with when I was little.

There's a girl at school named Amanda McClintock who's the same way. She wears her hair in a shiny black bob like a flapper or something. She's always on the homecoming court, and for all the dances she orders dresses to match the decorations. I know I couldn't be that way, even if I tried. Still, every time I pass a storefront with my mom I glance over to see if I can find any of her in my face or in my walk. I'm always disappointed.

Deric and I met in World History class the beginning of my sophomore year in high school. It was time for the annual Social Studies Fair. The year before I had molded salt dough into the shape of Kentucky, pinching up the Appalachian Mountains and gluing blue sparkle for the lakes and rivers. Turns out salt dough was a very common medium, second only to sugar cubed monuments, and my map didn't place. Still, I had gotten a respectable grade, and I didn't care to exert myself any further this year.

I was paired with Deric Fawley who was taking the class a year late and was already starting as quarterback on the football team. He had more elaborate plans. He had been saving the box his mom's new refrigerator came in for months. He wanted to fashion it into an Egyptian sarcophagus and paint it with hieroglyphics.

Later that week, we met after practice in one of the coach's offices. Deric had covered a table with newspaper, and he had a cardboard box full of supplies.

"How much did all this stuff cost?" I asked him.

"My dad had all this crap in his workshop," he said. "Don't worry about it."

We got into a rhythm applying the base coat, and Deric started to talk. At first he talked about the projects that he'd heard other students were working on. Then he talked about the new head coach and how far the team had run that day. He talked for a long time about a 7.5 lb. trout he had caught in Cedar Creek. Finally, he said, "What do you do?"

"What do you mean?" That was the kind of question adults asked each other.

"What do you do?" He dipped his brush carefully, rubbing off the excess paint. "Are you on the track team? You look like a runner."

"No. I'm not on any team."

"Do you have a job?"

"No." I didn't really do anything. I got off the bus and took meat out of the freezer to thaw for dinner. Sometimes I went to my friend Nick's house and we played video games. When I was little, he was like my brother, but we didn't hang out that much anymore. Once in a while I let Mom talk me into a game of Scrabble if nothing was on TV. "I guess I used to play baseball, you know, little league." This was true. "In fact, I pitched on the Conrad's Fork all-star team every year from the time I was seven until I was thirteen."

"That's so cool," Deric said. "Why did you stop?"

"They told me I had to switch to softball the summer before high school. I wasn't as good underhanded." I shrugged. "And I guess I was starting to get tired of it anyway."

He asked me out the afternoon we put the final touches on the project. He had found a *National Geographic* article with a dictionary of symbols. Mostly we painted the pictures for gods and animals. The article showed how to draw things such as grain and lotus and knotgrass, but those symbols weren't very exciting. He wanted the symbol for victory to be on top to ensure that we would place in the fair, but we couldn't find that one, not even in the section on weapons and arms. It came down to either "rule, reign, govern," which looked like a shepherd's staff, or "great," which looked like a sword. He wanted to go with the sword.

"You're awfully competitive," I said.

"More so during football season," he said. "Are you coming to the game this weekend?"

"I doubt it." I hadn't been to a game yet.

"That's too bad," he said. "We're playing Allegheny, so it ought to be a good one. There's a dance afterwards, and I thought, if you were going, you could wait for me after the game and we could go in together."

"Oh, well I might go," I said, "You know, if I can get a ride."

"I tell you what, I'll look for you when we get out of the locker room. If you can get there, I can give you a ride home."

Needless to say, Mom about flipped out. Not because she didn't want me to go on dates or anything. Totally the opposite. Practically since before I had a training bra, she's been trying to set me up. Every time we went to a restaurant and had an even semi-attractive waiter she would say things like, "You're awfully tall. Do you play basketball? Charlie here just loves basketball." Which is not true. She'd nod her head brightly at me until the poor guy turned away, and then she'd whisper, "What's wrong with you? Can't you at least smile once in a while." But I knew what would happen if I did. All evening, every time he walked past our table with a bottle of ketchup or some extra lemons, she'd be ready to burst. "Oh, I think he was looking at you, babe. Seriously."

When I got off the activity bus that afternoon, I could see Mom's car parked on the curb. She works at the insurance agency on Main Street, and she's been there so long that she can come home early anytime she wants, although most nights she works past six. I stood in the doorway for a minute, watching my mom. She had her feet up on the coffee table next to a half-eaten pudding cup, and she had Oprah on the television. I watched her chew on an ink pen and stare into one of her puzzle books. She tapped a Virginia Slims against the lip of the ceramic ashtray I made in fourth grade. Back then she didn't smoke. She picked up the habit after Grams died two years ago. I just made the clay into an ashtray when the sides of the bowl kept caving in. Her stockings looked damp, and there were inky red lines around her heels where the dye had seeped off her satin pumps. She looked up when I shut the door.

"Hey, Charlie, how was your day?"

"Okay." I fanned the smoke away from my eyes. On the bus I had decided to take the most subtle approach possible to bringing up my weekend plans. "Do you think you could give me a ride to a football game this weekend?"

"Since when do you like extracurricular activities?"

I shrugged my shoulders.

"I'm sure we can work it out. What time would I have to come back for you?"

"Oh, I have a ride home already."

"With who? I don't want you getting into just anyone's car, babe. High school girls are about the worst drivers in the world."

When I told her it was a boy, she jumped up, snuffed her cigarette, and crushed my face against her satin blouse. "See, sweetie. I knew it was just a matter of time until they were banging at our door." She smoothed her hands across the back of my head. "You're not going to wind up like your mom."

My father chose my mom on an afternoon in early summer. She and her best friend Ruth had been working all morning, painting the walls of the fellowship hall in the church basement. They peeled their stockings off and hid them beneath the sink in the bathroom. The window, high on the wall with heavy frosted glass, was open because of the paint fumes, and the breeze puffed the white curtains like a sail, calling the girls upstairs and out of the building. I know Grams forbid her to cut her hair, so I can imagine my mom, her ponytail swinging all the way down her back, her calves slender and shiny, as she and Ruth walked along the sidewalk. They went to the Tastee Freeze for vanilla cones, and that's where she first saw Larry Porter.

He was leaning against those glass picture windows in the front, guarding about ten or fifteen slick black motorcycles, and when the girls walked out the door, he grabbed hold of Mom's hand and said, "Baby, those legs would be perfect around my bike. I think I want to marry you." Ruth hurried to tell my grandparents, but by that time my mom was already on the back of Larry's motorcycle heading for North Carolina. The way she figures it, I was conceived about three days later at a Howard Johnson's during a Harley Davidson convention in downtown Charlotte.

I swear my mom must have had more fun in those five months she rode around with my father and his friends than she has had during the seventeen years since. I get the feeling things might have worked out between them had I not come along. When Larry dropped her off at the edge of the driveway around noon on a Sunday morning, just as her parents and her brothers were arriving home from church, she was only beginning to show. Pappy and some of the elders from his church chased Larry down and convinced him to do right by my mom. So he came back, and they got married two weeks later. My mom must have really loved my father because she named me after him, Charlotte *Lawrence* Porter. It didn't last, though. He was gone before my first birthday.

For a while we'd still see him. He drove an eighteen-wheeler back and forth between here and Texas. Sometimes he would be waiting for me on the bus ramp, and I knew that meant his rig was parked sideways back in the teachers' lot. I would get to ride home up in the cab, and the two of us would make "vroom" noises whenever he shifted gears. He moved up to Alaska when I started middle school, and I haven't seen him since then. Once in a while I get a postcard with some amazing picture. My father just scribbles something like, "So, here's the mountain—Dad."

I don't know if she still has it, but long after Larry left for good, I found a black and white picture of him standing beside his bike. It was hidden in the back of Mom's underwear drawer beneath her stockings and slips.

The day before the football game, Mom picked me up from school at lunch time. First we went to Belk's, and she bought me a new pair of jeans and an angora sweater set in light green, to bring out my eyes. I could tell she really wanted to get me a new jacket too, but I knew there was no way we could afford all that, so I told her that Deric wouldn't even see my jacket except for right after the game. Then we would be at the dance.

Next she had made me a doctor's appointment, but in a new office. Just for a check-up she said, but when she switched off the car in the parking lot, she turned to me and said, "We're here for the first of your womanly appointments, and I'm not going to lie to you, babe. This is not going to be pleasant." She took off her sunglasses and put them on the console.

The waiting room smelled like vanilla, and there were a lot of paintings, all of the same woman. She was naked, although you couldn't really see anything, and she was running around with a bunch of horses. The doctor was a younger woman with bangs and thick glasses. She made my mom go back to the waiting room, and then she started asking me all kinds of questions.

"Do you like school?" The same crap Mom asks, only now I had to answer.

"It's all right."

"What's your favorite subject?"

"I don't know."

"Do you play any sports?"

"Not anymore." I stared at the metal box marked hazardous waste next to the regular trashcan in the corner.

"Do you have regular periods?"

"I guess so."

"Do you have any boyfriends?"

"No." I wondered if that question was really on her chart, but, sure enough, she scribbled something down.

"How do you feel about your body?"

"I don't know."

"How do you get along with your parents?"

I looked up when the doctor said that, and I saw she was watching me, her head cocked to the side. She was sort of pretty, but I couldn't help thinking what my mom would say—*Why wouldn't she at least wear some mascara if she's got to put on those big glasses?* "Okay," I said finally. "With my mom, I mean. My dad's not really around."

She left for a minute, and I had to take off my clothes and put on a robe from the corner, where there were several stacked on cardboard shelves, the kind of disposable furniture you buy at Wal-Mart. I put one on that had pale blue flowers—flannel and open in the back. When the doctor returned with a nurse, I had to lie on the table and stick my feet in these stirrups. She spread me apart with a cold metal thing and poked around until I had cramps.

As soon as we were in the car Mom wanted to know what I had told the doctor.

"Nothing."

"Well she came out and told me she wasn't sure if you needed to be on the pill, that she thought maybe you didn't want to be on the pill."

"Jeez, leave me alone. Why would I tell her that? I didn't even know that was what that was about." I put feet up on the dashboard, the way she always asks me not to. "I'm not coming back."

"What's that supposed to mean?"

I stared out the window.

"I'm just looking out for you. Guys want girls who don't have to say no, but they don't want a family till they are good and ready. Look at what happened to me. Baby, I love you," she turned to look at me. "I wouldn't do anything differently, even if I could, but I want something better for you."

We stopped at the pharmacy on the way home. She went in for my prescription, and when she came out, she tossed the paper bag into my lap. Inside was a plastic canister. I flipped open the top and saw the first month's pills arranged in a careful circle of pastels. "They look like Smarties," I said. There was also a box of Trojans. "Rubbers, Mom?" I sighed. "Really?"

It's hard to tell what Deric thinks of my mom. Last November, his family invited both of us to Thanksgiving dinner. His parents are still together. The Fawleys live in a huge house up in Cedar Creek Summit where the ranch house my mom and I share is one of several tiny duplexes that mar the view of Dry River.

I was worried because I know my mom can be a little unpredictable. I could remember too many less-than-perfect parent-teacher conferences where she exploded after a teacher described me as what, to my mom, must have sounded hopelessly average. It wasn't so much that I thought I would be embarrassed by my mom—although, I wasn't sure what Mrs. Fawley would think of Mom's frosted hair and her Payless shoes—I was more worried about how my mom would react when she saw how different our world was from the one she's so ready for me to enter. But we had a beautiful dinner. Mom wore a burgundy blazer and swept up her hair. She spoke of my grandparents and what it had been like growing up with three brothers.

Sometimes, though, I don't think Deric buys all of my mom's smiles. He presses my palm very tightly between his when she starts in with the old routine, and folds me against him as soon as we're out the door.

When I see his truck pulling up to the curb, I grab my reel and my little tackle box from the corner, and I am running down the sidewalk before he can get out. I throw my gear in the back, and he reaches across and flings the door wide open for me. Inside the truck, his shoulders feel hard from pulling oars, and he smells like fabric softener and Rightguard.

"How was your trip?"

"It was okay. I hit a lot more traffic than I expected this late in the season."

I look back and notice the duffel bag behind his seat. "You haven't been home yet?"

"No. You remember that group we were just getting ready to take out when I talked to you yesterday?"

"Sure." The day before, he had been preparing to take thirty Girl Scouts down river.

"Let's just say I've never seen so much screaming and squealing and carrying on. It took forever to get them back in the boats after lunch. We got back so late we had to clean and check all the equipment this morning."

Deric's hand is making slow circles along the inside of my thigh. He takes my hand from my lap and kisses the back of it.

"What did you do the past two days?"

"Well, work was wonderful today. I didn't work with Dave."

"Why not? Did Bryce hire a new guy?"

Deric eyes me with suspicion. In the beginning, he was a little weirded out about me working with all guys. He says locker room talk has showed him that all guys have an agenda.

"No, they can't afford anyone else. It was still too wet to mow, so I worked with Fran at their house. You wouldn't believe their place," I said. "A big farm on the other side of the high school, right at the foot of the mountain. Fran has a million little saplings planted all over. She marks them with pieces of pink yarn so Bryce won't mow over them."

"What for?"

"So they can be trees. In the morning, she had me dig up all the weed trees that were coming up in her flowerbeds—Eastern Redbuds,

Mountain Maples, White Oaks. Dig them up, not pull them. Then, I had to wrap each one in wet newspaper and put them all in a bucket. After lunch, we planted them and marked them. That's where all those saplings come from. She's turning part of their farm back into a forest. Can you imagine? It'll take a hundred years. She won't even see it, not really, but to her it still matters."

"She sounds like a whack job."

"Why would you say that?" I think about Fran, her face tanned and serious, her hair curling damp where it has unraveled from her braid. A strange surge of defensiveness rises in my chest. "Why are you being that way?" I think about the rain barrel next to her back porch. The way the cats smelled like mulch when they rubbed against my legs. I swivel around in the seat so I'm facing Deric. He is concentrating on the road, looking for our turn off.

"We had about an hour left at the end of the day, so we started cleaning up her perennial beds, and there were all these light green stalks. They looked like weeds or maybe leftover stems from spring flowers. I almost pulled them, but she stopped me. She said they're a special kind of lily that sends all its foliage up in the spring, when all the other flowers are blooming." I raise my voice as the truck rattles onto the gravel road. I have to make him see the magic in everything I saw. "Then the leaves die right along with everything else. Later in August, when all the other lilies are spent, this one sends up just the stalk, and within a week it opens into the most beautiful pink flower. They're called Naked Ladies, or Surprise Lilies, and she said they'd probably be blooming next week. It's like all of a sudden I have all these things to look forward to."

"So you're going back there?"

"Yeah, that's the cool thing. Fran requested that I help her, just me. She says I'm the only one careful enough. I told her I only have a few more weeks before school starts, but Bryce said he could probably spare me on Fridays."

Deric eyes me strangely. "Listen to you. I've never heard you talk this much."

The stretch of river we will be fishing is actually private property, but Deric knows the people who own it. They've given him a key to the gate. When I climb out of the truck, I can hear a dog clanging its chain against a clothesline pole up the hill. The trees look darker as the sun begins to slip behind them.

"Check out my new aerator." Deric pulls a Styrofoam cooler out from the truck bed. "See, it's got a little motor that agitates the water. It'll keep the fish alive longer."

There isn't much of a path down to the river. The ground is so soft with silt and deteriorating leaves that our sandals sink down with each step. We step across branches rubbed clean of all their bark by the flood water. They look skeletal in the dwindling light. I choose a spot where I can tell by the riffles that it is shallow enough for me to wade a good ways in. Deric kisses my cheek, then heads upstream about a hundred feet. He needs calmer water to work his fly rod.

The river water looks like black velvet moving around my ankles. I immediately fall into the rhythm of casting and slowly reeling my line back. I can see the spinner skipping across the surface. It's the perfect time of evening, and not many other people are allowed to fish this stretch, so it doesn't take long for one to strike. I can tell it's a bass by how hard it pulls. I have more patience than Deric does for letting a fish tire itself out.

I find a small mouth on the end. She's beautiful, greenish brown and silver, with about a million colors sparkling through underneath, and pretty big. I slide my thumb inside her mouth, where there are rough nubbins of cartilage, and work the hook out carefully. Deric brings the cooler, and I gently slide the fish inside. She sinks to the bottom where her gills flutter rapidly.

Deric heads back into the water, but I wait on the bank and watch him. Usually there is something erotic about the way he moves with his fly rod. His blond hair has been buzz cut because of the heat and for convenience on the river. The line becomes an extension of his body. It whispers, arching behind him, as his shoulders harden and relax. The fly skims the dark surface of the water, and I try to think about later, when the two of us will be beneath the comforter on my bed.

I let Deric take off my shirt for the first time in the tree house in my friend Nick's backyard. It was a typical party beginning to fizzle out. Nick's dad had gone away for the weekend and someone thought they could get a keg, but of course that fell through. Instead there was a six pack of wine coolers and three cases of Natural Light. Nick had strung some Christmas lights along the banister, and every now and then, they illuminated a couple sneaking up the stairs. Twenty or thirty people still crowded into the kitchen and living room. Music videos flashed silver from the TV screen, silent because someone had turned off the sound. Earlier in the evening there had been dancing, but now someone had put Morrissey and Tori Amos and Morphine in the CD changer. A few people were playing truth or dare, but most people were lying around on the sofas, pretending they were wasted, making everything deep.

I led Deric out back, past the woodpile and garden. His hand hovered against my back as we climbed up the ladder. We had to duck through the doorway. Inside everything was black. We sat down on the sanded floorboards. "So," I said, "this is where Nick and I used to play Transformers."

He leaned forward and kissed me behind my ear. "Watch out for the spiders," I said, pinching his ankle.

I felt his breath against my hair. "Charlie," he whispered, "you are so weird."

When we kissed he tasted warm and yeasty from the beer. I let him pull my sweater off, and, when he struggled with the clasp of my bra, I reached behind my back and unhooked it for him. When his mouth moved across my chest, I felt a door opening inside my stomach. He made his way down my belly, and I pulled on his hair and made him stop, made him come back to my mouth.

Back home, we lug the cooler, now heavy with five fish, through the garage into the kitchen. My mom is conveniently absent. She probably headed back to her room as soon as she saw the headlights from the truck. She thinks Deric and I have sex. She's been paying for birth control for two years, and she's so sure he's the perfect guy for me, that I haven't had the heart to tell her anything different.

As soon as we set the cooler on the floor, Deric's arms are around me. We are still damp from the river, and his mouth tastes salty-sour against mine. I kiss him more deeply, waiting for that safe feeling that comes when I feel him all around me. His hands are all over my back, inching my T-shirt up so that I can feel the edge of the sink, cold against my skin. I pull away, "We should really clean those fish. I feel bad about leaving them in that thing while we stand here making out."

"Okay, we have all night." For seventeen years, I haven't been allowed to have one of the girls I know from school spend the night, but Mom doesn't mind if Deric stays over. When he visited back in

July things went pretty far. I guess you could say I freaked out a little, made him stop at the last minute.

He sees me tense up. I place the first fish in the sink and, using the pocketknife Deric gave me the last time he visited, I cut off its head in what I want to be one quick motion. But I have to work the blade back and forth a little before I hear a snap.

"Charlie, I don't mind that you're not ready yet. I'm glad that I have someone like you. You've never been with anyone else. I'll wait as long as you want, because then I know that when you are ready, you'll be all mine."

The blunt end of the knife makes a scraping sound as I run it backwards along the fish's side. The loosened scales float on top of the bloody water that's starting to pool in the bottom of the sink.

He watches appreciatively. "There aren't many girls who would do that. Hell, there aren't many girls who would go tromp around in the river at night."

He watches as I slice open the fish's belly and began scraping out the insides. We both have to turn our heads a little.

His hand is moving up and down along my side. "I'm glad you like to do the same things I do."

"Deric, I don't want to finish cleaning these fish." I throw down the knife.

"Well, I can do it."

"No, I don't want either of us to." I stick my hand into the cooler and watch the remaining fish dart into the farthest corner. "I want to put them back."

"What? That small mouth is the biggest one you've caught all summer."

"Well, I don't want it." My voice is starting to crack. We've been dating two years, and I'm pretty sure Deric has never seen me cry. He hoists the cooler up by himself, and I follow him out to the truck. He flips on the little motor and lowers it into the water where it begins to bubble again.

Inside the truck I sit as still as I can. His fingers are fluttering lightly on my bare knee, like fish gills. We park at the canoe landing behind the dump. It's at least one in the morning. We must look like we are sneaking down to throw a body into the water. The rocks slide around under our feet, and I'm hurrying so much I almost lose my footing.

At the edge of the water, Deric sets down his side of the cooler, then immediately turns around and starts back up the bank.

The fish are barely moving now. I slide my arm into the dark water up to my elbow. They tickle against my arm like wet leaves. I push the Styrofoam down the slick rocks until I can hear the water lapping against it, then I tip the cooler over. The fish shoot into the water like spilled oil, and then disappear. I hold my breath, waiting to see if any of them are going to float up.

There are lights from the bridge sparkling on the surface up stream, and I hear the radio click on in the truck. The sound is muffled by the thick trees and by the gurgle of the water. The windows of a few of the houses in Cedar Creek are still yellow and warm. They look like Jack-o-lanterns up on the ridge.

In our duplex, about a mile downstream, across a vacant lot and a chain link fence, I know my mom is probably in her room working a crossword puzzle. I begin walking quickly toward her along the edge of the river, and pretty soon I can't even hear the radio anymore. I wonder why my mom never dated anyone else after my father, won-der—other than her magazines and puzzle books, other than me—if there is anything in her life that is really important. I know she'll be disappointed tomorrow morning when she discovers I left Deric sit-ting in his truck. I don't know how to tell her that I'm not spent. If she will just wait, I might surprise her.

FLOATING

Casey 1987

Jed says summer starts on Memorial Day, and I believe him because at school we never do anything but watch videos and erase marks from our books after that. So it's really the first day of the summer when I see Shane Spangler lounging next to the lifeguard stand waiting for his shift on the chair to begin. I've been coming to Elk Run Pool with my stepsister three summers in a row. The first summer we could only go in the shallow end and the game room, but now Darla's thirteen, and Jed says that's old enough that she ought to be able to keep us out of trouble. We live on the far side of the trailer park, where there's another hill in back with an old turkey house. Now it's full of moldy hay bales, and one time we found the skin of a black snake.

I saw Shane all those other summers. He used to stand me and Darla up on his shoulders, and his fingers would feel slippery around our ankles, and he'd jump off into the deep end and send us flying. He'd come up first and pull himself out of the pool and stretch out his hand like to help me up. Then he'd fling me back into the water and say, "Come on now, Casey. You got to hang on," until I got mad and had to doggy paddle it over to the ladder, with him doing his damn donkey laugh. Back then he and his friends were all buzz cut and shiver ribs and drippy, cut-off jeans.

So it's Memorial Day weekend. That's when they always open up the pool in Conrad's Fork. We already wasted half the day in town because Mama wanted to watch the parade. Then Jed saw his buddies from Walker, and we all had to go into The Valley Vista Grill and suck on French toast sticks while he had a few beers. Darla and I are in such a hurry we make it up the steps before Jed turns off the car.

"Hey, shut that thing right," Jed yells when we leave the screen door swinging. But I saw him in the car, rubbing his big fingers in the back of Mama's hair the way he does when he's had more than one beer, and I know he's not mad for real.

I got two new suits from the attic shop. That's what Mama calls it when I wear Darla's old clothes. My stepsister's just finishing up the eighth grade, and she's started growing boobs, so nothing fits. One's a red and white two-piece with a big rose in the center of the top, and that's the one I put on. I'm feeling pretty good as I set to untangling our bikes from the mess of junk under the deck until Darla comes out in her new lavender bikini with the ties on the side, looking all slick and slinky and curved. I figure I'll still beat her to the pool, so I hop on my bike and take off pedaling, even on the down hills. There was a thunderstorm last night. Now the sun's breaking through, and the water's sizzling in the potholes. The rain wilted the lilacs in the pool lady's yard, and they smell sticky and heavy like to make you sick.

As soon as I lean my bike against the chain link fence, I realize Darla has our money, so I'll have to walk in with her anyway. I can see her coasting down the hill with her ponytail flying straight and blond behind her, and that makes me madder because I cried till Mama let me cut off my hair last year, and now it's all poofy curly around my head. It's in knots most of the time because it hurts when Mama combs it. Jed calls it my red rat's nest, but Mama says my hair's not red, it's auburn, which everyone knows is not trashy. I sit down and stare at the kiddy pool through the metal fence and start picking through the clover thinking maybe I'll find a four-leafer, and that's when I see him.

He's at the base of the stand wearing those red shorts they make all the lifeguards wear. His hair's grown out, and there are damp curls of it hanging down the back of his neck. He's got sunglasses dangling around his chest on a rubber string next to a whistle chain. I'm not sure it's Shane Spangler until he donkey laughs at something the blond haired girl says up in the chair.

Darla pedals up not even out of breath. She says, "What're you staring at?"

We walk over to the counter, and she pulls a wad of ones out of the front pocket of her cut-offs. She's got them held together with a lavender and pink glitter hair barrette, and I think that looks pretty posh, but I sure don't tell her. Odessa, the pool lady, puts down her

cigarette to count our money. Two times she counts out those four dollar bills. She's real tan and skinny, but her arm is all shaky-sag underneath when she finally waves us inside.

Her husband's a lot older. He worked in one of the coal mines,
but he got hurt in some kind of accident and doesn't ever come outside. They got a load of money—that's what Jed said—because of that
accident. They got the whole pool and the campground next to it and
the trailer park up the hill where we live. Their house isn't any bigger
than our trailer, though. It's a little brick thing, painted white, right as
you start up the hill. They've always got all the blinds closed. Odessa
walks up and down the hill pumping her arms and shaking her butt
every evening. She holds a little dumbbell in one hand and a cigarette
in the other, and every time she gets back to the bottom of the hill she
switches them.

"Hey Hinkles!" yells Odessa behind us as our flip flops slap across
the cement. "You two better stay out of trouble this summer." She's
got stringy brown hair, and she looks like a muppet when she starts
screaming. We don't look back because we know most of the stuff
she's always accusing us of isn't our fault. Last summer we tried to tell
Jed that she was a grump and he needed to come down here and stop
her from picking on us. Mamma laughed and said it's because she's
getting old and she's not getting any from her old man since his accident. They wouldn't tell me any what.

"Well lookie here, it's Darla Hinkle and Miss Casey," Shane says
when we walk under his chair. My sister doesn't look up, but I flip
him the bird as we pass. Shane Spangler shakes his head and laughs.
Last summer that would've been enough to set him after me to throw
me in the deep end, but I figure he's got his duties now.

We put our towels on the smooth cement by the deep end, and
Darla's got to get every wrinkle out of her towel before she'll lie down
on the thing. She's that way, my sister is. Right off she starts oiling
herself up. And by the time she settles down, you'd think she was trying to climb into a too hot bathtub it's such a show. I try to be still for a
while because I know she'll want to sunbathe before swimming.

My sister can lie in the sun for hours and not get burnt, even
though she's got blond hair. Mama and her friend Janelle say that's
unusual to get so tan, with the blond hair and all. My skin turns bright
pink, and Mama rubs me down with Noxzema and pieces of aloe plant
from the pots along the deck. The first summer we came to the pool by
ourselves was the worst because I wouldn't let Darla put lotion on me.
We swam for nine hours that Memorial Day, and that night it felt like

my skin was shrinking around me. Mama smacked at my hands when I tried to reach them around to rake my back. She made me wear a T-shirt to the pool after that. I yanked that thing off once we got here, and when we were lying on our bellies in the grass, Darla pulled the pieces of dead skin off my shoulders for me. They were like little snake skins. We crinkled our noses as she tossed them up into the air and watched them float down like insects.

Pretty soon I can't help but start in. "Come on," I say, "this is boring as shit. Let's go off the slide." There's a huge metal slide at the Elk Run Pool.

"Don't cuss," says Darla without moving or opening her eyes.

This coming from the girl who got a week of in-school suspension up at the middle school for telling the student gym teacher she could put the field hockey stick up her ass. I know why she won't go down the slide. Before the parade, she spent about an hour curling her bangs into a crunchy pouf that's shining like a Brillo pad on the top of her head. I can't help it then. I start making my I-want-my-own-way noises. I make them with my nose, and they're better than crying on Mama and Jed. But Darla just rolls her head toward me and says, "Jesus, Casey, stop whining. I'm not getting in yet. Go down yourself."

I can see the thing looming across the deep end, about as big as a roller coaster. It doesn't just drop you off into the pool. It spits you out about ten feet, with your butt skidding like a big rock on top of the water.

"You're supposed to stay with me."

"I can see you," she says with her eyes still shut.

When I get over there, there's a woman already standing on the wooden platform up at the top, pulling at the back of her bathing suit and hollering at a guy who's sitting on the side of the pool. She finally shuts her mouth and grabs hold of the bar, and for a minute I just hear the splashing of the little jet of water before she goes screaming down the chute. She disappears beneath the surface, and a few seconds later I see her hanging onto the side of the pool. I can tell she got a nose full of water even though she's trying to act like everything's okay.

I figure I'll wait a little while, so I make my way down to the shallow end where you can go in easy. It's so cold I'm all chicken-skinned before the water's up to my waist. I can see the hairs prickling on my legs beneath the water. I'm going to tell Mama I need a razor like Darla. I stand there cross-armed for a minute trying to figure out who I want to play with. There are a lot kids from school around, but I don't see anybody from my class. Two boys are throwing a Wiffle ball back and forth across the water, and when they overthrow it lands near me. I scoop it up as the water starts seeping into the holes to sink it. I'm about to say what's your name to the nearest boy when the other one yells, "Hey, you, girl! Give that back. Hey, lifeguard," he says, "she stole our ball."

Shane turns around to look at us, and right as he goes to blow his whistle I chuck that ball over the fence.

He makes me come over to the stand, and when I get there he calls me Miss Meanness and wants to know why I threw their ball.

So I say, "'Cause my sister won't go down the slide with me."

He looks down the sidewalk to where Darla's lying, all greased up with one knee propped in the air.

"Well go on and get it and give it back to them. Then when I get my break in about ten minutes I'll go down the slide with you."

I do like he says, but when I get around to the back side of the fence I can see they haven't cut the grass yet this year, and I'm not wearing my flip flops. There's a mess of dandelions and Queen Anne's Lace, all of it swarming with bees, so I've got to pick my way through all careful before I can even find the thing. I finally see it, and I grab it and hold it up in the air for Shane to see. When he nods his head, I toss it back over the fence, but I make sure those boys will have to swim for it.

Shane has climbed down from his chair, and that blond-haired girl's climbing back up. He hangs his whistle chain and his sunglasses off the ladder, and he says, "Let's go." Over at the ladder he does this little bow thing and says, "After me lady."

Nobody's at the top this time, and I can hear the little jet of water whistling out. I start to feel like all those bumble bees on the other side of that fence are buzzing around inside my stomach, but I don't want Shane to think I'm chicken shit, so I step up to the ladder. Big shade trees on the other side of the fence keep the metal from getting too hot, and the steps have grippy teeth, and I know Shane's coming up right behind me.

I'm not really scared of the slide so much as cautious. Jed taught me how to go down it last summer after watching five or six times as I had to shimmy back down the ladder to where Shane Spangler and his crowd of boys were booing and laughing. He told me we weren't going home until I went down that slide. He said there's a secret to liking heights, and that's to not ever look down, only up or out. He said that before he met my mama, when he and Darla were living in a trailer on one of Les Monger's farms, she would climb all the way up the silo, and she was way littler than me. Jed says he doesn't want his girls to be scared of anything, and I know that must be true because Darla's not scared of much. Of course, you wouldn't think it now, not the way she acts so prissy.

Once I'm up on the platform I don't look down. I look up at the swirly kind of clouds, the kind that Jed says make for good sunsets, and I look out across the pool for my stepsister. I figure I'll wave at her and make nice, but she's not on her towel. She probably went to the bathroom to check on her bangs. I don't swing myself off the bar or anything. I'm not scared, but I'm not taking any chances. I just scoot my bottom along the metal until I start moving. I don't grip at the sides because even though Darla has told me a zillion times I'm not moving fast enough, it feels like it could cut my hand for sure. I use both hands to hold my nose shut. For a second I hang there with the treetops floating in front of me over in the campground. Then my belly drops out and the clouds rise up, and I close my eyes as tight as I can. By the time I'm bobbing in the water I can see Shane never climbed up the ladder at all. He's leaning against it talking to my sister.

"Shane Spangler," I holler, "you're a goddamn liar."

"I was watching you," he says. "Besides, now you know you can go down all by yourself, and you don't have to be scared no more."

"I wasn't scared!"

Darla's rolling her eyes, and he's telling me I got to exit on the left side so I don't get in the way of the divers. I can't give him the finger because if anything messes up my doggy paddle I get a monster nose full of water, so I paddle right across the row of diving boards to the opposite side of the pool like I never even heard him. He looks at Darla like to ask why I'm so bad, and she just shrugs her shoulders. Then they go off to the game room to play pool.

My stepsister doesn't know how to play pool. Besides, who plays pool when they could be swimming? Last summer me and Darla and Shane and his friends would only go to the game room to play Pole Position II or else the pinball machines, and then only if it was raining. I think I'm not going talk to her again or at least not until tonight, but I mess up when we get out to the parking lot and she wants to know where we left our bikes. When we're walking them up the hill, she asks me why I was so peeved back there. I don't know how to tell her she's fixing to ruin the whole summer.

Mama has Wednesdays off. The dentist office where she's an assistant closes down all day. Jed says it's the cheapest way Dr. Leubner knows to get girls to work for him on Saturdays. So it's Wednesday, and me and Darla and Mama are having our hair done at J & Company on Main Street. "J" stands for Janelle. She's a friend of Mama's who always lets all three of us get our hair done together. She has sparkly eye shadow and shaggy blond hair. She smells spicy when she leans over the sink to lather up your head, and she grows her nails out way long so they give your scalp a good scratching. She's pretty posh with long silver earrings and jingle bracelets and stuff. She sits Mama and Darla down with a magazine and tells them that after she finishes with me there's something she's got to talk to them about.

I always have to go first. Otherwise Janelle says I can't sit still long enough for her to finish giving me a trim. She tried to talk Mama out of cutting my hair off last winter, but Mama told her go ahead and hack it because she was tired of arguing with me. Janelle has to make my hair straight to cut it even. She puts a bunch of goop on it after she's done washing and takes the blow dryer to little chunks of it until it lays all soft and fluffy around my chin. Once she starts snipping I can see the clumps of hair gathering on the linoleum out of the corner of my eye, and they look all straight and pretty. I start to whimper because I know they are way too long, and I won't ever be able to get my hair back in a ponytail now, so finally I yell, "Stop."

"My God that girl's got lungs," Janelle says to Mama. Then she spins the chair around so they can both look at me.

"You need to use the ladies room?" I can tell Mama is hoping that's all this is going to be.

"No!" I smooth my hair down next to my head and hold my hands there so Janelle can't get to it.

"Well, what's the problem then?" Mama is standing up now.

"I changed my mind. I don't want it cut."

"It's a little late. I already finished this entire side." Janelle points to the shortened half of my hair with her little silver scissors. "Do you want to go around with your hair hanging two different lengths?"

"She probably wouldn't mind." That's Darla, sticking her nose into my hair cut.

"Casey, I thought you wanted long hair again." Mama's talking slow, the way she does when she's about to start yelling. "Look, if you don't trim it then it won't grow. It's up to you."

Janelle scoops some of the reddish brown fluff off the floor and waves it in front of my face. "Sweetie, that's all I'm taking off. That'll grow back in a month."

I let go of my head and take the trimmings from her. When no one's looking I slide them under the black cape she has covering me and into the pocket of my shorts.

Later I try looking at magazines, but they never have *Highlights* or *Ranger Rick* like at the doctor's office, only the kind of magazines that Darla's been buying at Rite Aid and taking to the pool all summer. Janelle can't believe how tall Darla's grown when she sits down in the chair or that all the sparkly streaks in her hair just come from the sun.

"You wouldn't believe how many girls come in here wanting me to highlight their hair to look like that," she says. "And I can't do it. You're a lucky one." I know Darla squeezes lemon juice on her hair every morning before we go to the pool. I think about asking Janelle has she tried that.

"In fact," says Janelle, looking at Mama, "I've been thinking she should enter the Harvest Days Pageant."

Conrad's Fork Harvest Days comes every August. There's a big parade. The Lion's Club men and the cheerleaders from up at the high school where Darla's going to be in the Fall and a bunch of the churches decorate hay wagons and pick-up trucks and throw candy. I got a load last year—of course, it's mostly that pick-a-mix stuff from the plastic bins at Piggly Wiggly. There's a big carnival too every year, with funnel cakes and a scrambler ride down in the park. There's even a Ferris wheel that Jed always goes on with me. He takes us on Wednesday because kids can ride all night if they pay five dollars for a little red bracelet.

"Have you ever thought about doing the pageant?" Now Janelle's asking my sister.

"I don't know. Some of the girls from school are doing it."

"Isn't it kind of pricey?" Mama asks. "With a big entry fee and then a dress. I can't really see Jed going for that."

"Well, we could sponsor you," Janelle says. "All those girls have sponsors. We do someone every summer. We do her hair and make-up and pay the entry fee. Then when they call her out they say our name too, and we get a little advertising." She leans down to look over Darla's shoulder into the mirror. "You could be the J & Company girl."

When I hear that, I go rearrange all the bottles in the nail polish display.

For Shane's sixteenth birthday he gets a new truck—a Chevy S10 with a little seat in the back—and on his break he asks us do we want to go for a ride. When he goes to get his keys out of his locker, I tell Darla there's no way I'm going with him because Jed says we're supposed to ride our bikes to the pool and straight back with no lollygagging.

"Well I'm the boss of you when we're here," she says.

The back seat of his truck is so small you have to sit sideways. He says to buckle up, but before I can my head starts bumping against the window because he tears across the potholes, leaving dust and gravel floating above the Elk Run Pool parking lot. I watch Route 38 snake out behind us through the back window, and every now and then I hear Darla laugh about something going on up front. We're heading back towards downtown, which I can't figure out since Bear Gun and Grocery is just half a mile up from the pool, and that's where Jed and Mama always go. Sometimes they just walk up there for no reason in the evening and bring us back candy bars. Shane turns into the 7-Eleven and gets out. He pulls the seat up and hands me a five dollar bill.

"You want to go get us some Cokes?" He stands there with his hand on the back of the seat, and I have to squeeze past him to get out of the truck. I can see the little circle of hair beneath his arm.

"Casey, get me a diet." Darla's started thinking she's got fat thighs.

Inside the store there's a girl standing at the ice cream counter. She's jiggling a baby on her hip and talking to the woman behind the counter about someone they both know and trying to figure out whether she wants strawberry or pistachio. That baby's slurping at his fingers, and every now and then she leans over and shhhhhhs in his ear. I have to make my way through the candy aisle to get to where the sodas are.

Mamma doesn't trust me to go into the store all by myself, especially because of all the townies that like to hang out, so I hesitate at the front for a second, feeling my palm start to sweat around that five dollar bill. I look back through the door for Shane's red truck, but there's really nothing to see since he's got those dark windows. I can hear the women blabbing it up over at the ice cream counter, so I grab a handful of fireballs as I pass by and stuff them real quick inside my back pocket. The doors start fogging up as soon as I open the cooler, and I don't want that lady to come over and get after me for messing up the glass, so I just grab three bottles and head over to the counter. I know I'm not in any trouble for that candy because the woman behind the counter keeps on talking and baby cooing even as she's ringing me up.

"Casey, this ain't diet." My sister does that prissy eye roll as Shane hands her a bottle and I climb back into the little sideways seat.

"Well, Darla, you ain't fat." I can't see what he does, but my sister starts laughing and squirming toward the window.

My sister hears the crinkling of the wrapper as I pull out one of those fireballs. She wants to know where did I get that candy and did I use Shane's money.

He starts to say that's okay, but I thrust what's left between their two seats.

"There!" I say, "Count your stinking change. I used my own money."

"You don't have any money. Jed gave it to me this morning." I can tell by my sister's voice that she knows about the candy. She can't tell on me though because we weren't supposed to be leaving the swimming pool anyway.

When we pull back onto the highway, I see that the candy's not really important anyway, that for some other reason things are different than before I got out of the truck. The two of them are quiet all the sudden, and Shane's got his arm stretched out so that his hand is lying on the head rest of Darla's seat. I use my thumb to pull back my middle finger, and I give him a good thunk right on the knuckle. He swings his head around and smirks at me, but he doesn't move his arm.

"Hey," I say, "ain't you supposed to have both hands on the wheel?"

When I get home I climb up the hill to the old turkey house before it starts getting dark. Inside it smells like year-old hay and sawdust, but there's a faraway smell too of animals and weather. Last summer me and Darla—and sometimes Shane and the boys from the pool—would play in here all the time, hay tunnels and capture-the-flag. Mama wants us to act more like ladies. I tried to get Darla to come up here the first rainy day this summer, but she says it's not fun anymore. Most times when I come up here now, I sit by the air vents and spy down the hill. You can see all the way to Odessa's, where the dark windows in the front reflect the sunlight like mean-looking eyes. Last summer we spent a lot of time hiding out here from the pool lady, although she never was really looking for us. We figured her husband's worse than her, even, lying on the bed with twisted up legs.

I shimmy myself up onto the rounded side of one of the hay bales by pulling at the twine that's holding it together. It's old and moldy, and sometimes it tears apart in your hands. I crawl across the hay until

I find the pile of feathers I use to mark my spot. They're pigeon feathers not turkey—that's all that lives in here now. I showed some of
them to Jed, and he's the one that told me. I reach down between two
bales, carefully, because, like I said, one time we found a snakeskin,
and pull out one of Jed's old hunting socks. I dump the rest of those
fireballs inside with my important stuff. I wiggle my fingers around
inside, making sure everything's still there. I got some of my hair, a
rock from last time we went fishing over at Lake Cumberland, some
change I saved from my tooth pillow and chores, and an arrowhead
that Jed gave me.

That night we cook hamburgers out on the grill, and as we're sitting
at the picnic table eating them, Darla starts talking about some movie.
"It's about this guy who's doing a science project," she says, "and he
discovers how to make himself invisible."

I know what movie she's talking about. In the commercials the
invisible guy gets to follow this girl around, even to the bathroom and
slumber parties. I glare at her across the table.

"Anyway, there's this guy at the pool who wants to go see it, too."
She's just nibbling at a veggie burger because she's thinking maybe she
doesn't want to eat meat anymore. I can tell by the way she's chewing,
that thing must taste awful bad.

"Since when do thirteen-year-old girls go on dates?" asks Jed.

What exactly is she asking, Mama wants to know.

"I want to go into town and see a movie with Shane Spangler." We
don't have a movie theater in Conrad's Fork, so we have to drive half
an hour to Garrison if we want to see a show. Sometimes I get to feeling car sick on the way back, especially if I eat too much candy.

Mama's looking at Jed with her eyebrows raised up all funny.
"Would the Spanglers drive you two love birds, or would we have to?"

"He's going to drive us. He just got his license and a new truck."

"All that means is that he's too old for you," Jed says through a
mouthful of hamburger. "You can't go on that kind of date."

They all three get to talking at once, and Darla's voice starts cracking. So I pick through the pile of grilled burgers, slicing them all open
a little the way Mamma never lets me, until I find one with just the
right amount of pink in the middle.

Later, after they've sent me to bed, I'm standing in the hallway
brushing my teeth, trying to catch a glimpse of the TV, and I can hear

Darla talking real low to someone on the phone in her room, sniffling
a bit every now and then. I stand there until Mama hollers for me to
go on and get in bed. Then I yell back there's no way I can go to sleep
because Darla's still blubbering on the phone. They have a rule about
how she's not allowed to talk after ten-o-clock. When I hear her getting
up, I run for my room and close my eyes like I'm sleeping.

I'm floating in the shallow end with my arms spread wide, head down,
hair fanned out all around my eyes. In the water my hair looks longer
and straighter. It's Wednesday, and Mama took Darla to Garrison to
look for a Miss Harvest Days dress. That means I've got nobody here
watching me, so I'm supposed to stay out of the deep end.

Jed taught me to float like this when he gave me swimming lessons. He would lay his hand flat underneath my belly and balance me
right at the top of the water and say for me to relax. When I finally
did he'd pull his hand away real slow, so I wouldn't even know it was
gone, and sure enough I'd hang right there at the surface like a fishing bobber. He says anybody can float if they try, that the only reason for people drowning in pools and lakes is because they get scared.
I haven't tested the floating thing enough to try it in the deep end,
though. There I always try to hit the water doggy paddling.

I saw them fish a boy out of the water at the boat landing at Lake
Cumberland. Jed's boss took us fishing, and we were coming in for the
day. There was a bunch of commotion so we hung back a ways from
shore with the boat engine making colors swirl on top of the water.
The boy was bigger than me. Later, Jed told Mama he was about Darla's age. He was floating just like Jed showed me, but he never turned
his face up out of the water. Two men pulled him in and stretched him
out over the grass. As soon as Jed and his boss walked the boat up
onto the trailer, Jed pulled me out by my armpits and stood me on the
gravel.

"Casey, go get in the truck right now." He handed me the keys,
and when I turned and stared at the men kneeling over top of the boy,
he shoved my backside. "Girl, I said go get in the truck."

LeAnn Wharton comes over and tries to float with me, but she can't
do it right because she keeps talking. She's splashing around between
me and the lifeguard stand.

Do I want to go under water and have a tea party she wants to
know. I don't say anything because I'm playing like that drowned boy.

"Do you want to dive for pennies?" I can hear her voice even with my ears under the water. It makes me think of at school this past year how she would try to make all of us fifth-grade girls do cheers with her out on the playground. I could hear them chanting even on the days I was in trouble and sitting cross legged facing the brick wall. "How about if I let you use my new diving mask and I use my sister's goggles? Then do you want to?"

LeAnn's got cheerleader twin sisters up at the high school. Darla's been talking to them a lot at the pool this summer because she's thinking maybe she's going to try out for cheerleader in the fall. They both have boyfriends, and they float around the edge of the deep end holding onto them like they can't swim. I've seen them with their mouths locked and I think it must probably taste like chlorine to kiss on a boy in the pool like that. One time I asked my sister had she kissed Shane.

"What do you think?" she smirked.

"I bet you do, and I bet Jed would get mad. It looks so dumb anyway. Why'd anybody want to just sit there with their face hooked onto some boy's?"

"You don't just sit there," she rolled her eyes. "You touch your tongues and stuff."

"Nasty!" I made gagging noises to show her how disgusting that was.

"If you ever grow up you won't think so."

I don't want to try it for real, but sometimes when I'm in my room or else up the hill at the turkey house I try kissing on my hand. Or if nobody can see my face, like when I'm floating in the pool this way, I try turning my tongue over on itself inside my mouth. Just to see how it would feel to touch it against another tongue.

All of a sudden I feel someone yanking at the straps of my swimsuit.

"Hey!" I jerk up with my arms flying. I slick my drippy hair back out of my face. I know it's Shane with his red shorts and whistle chain. He drags me over to the side of the pool by my straps and sits me up on the warm cement. He's fired up and wagging his finger in front of my face. What's wrong with me he wants to know, and haven't I ever heard of the boy who cried wolf? When he tells me I have to sit out of the pool for twenty minutes, I figure I'll just get my bike and ride home.

Back at the trailer I have to squeeze into the bathroom sideways because Darla's standing naked in a puddle of pink satin. Her arms are folded across her chest like she doesn't want me to see her, but it's just smooshing her boobs up making them look even bigger. She twists herself around trying to see her bottom in the mirror. "That one makes me look too wide in the rear."

"Well I think it might be too big, and I don't know about the sequins on this one." Mama's perched on the edge of the toilet, and she fingers the dress that's laying across her lap. "Casey, you want to help us make a decision?"

I roll my bathing suit down to my calves, then kick my feet free. I sit down on the tub to look at my toenails. They're turning kind of yellow. I thought I might have some kind of toe disease, but Mama says it's just from the chlorine and running around without shoes all the time.

Darla pulls another gown from the counter and hoists it over her shoulders.

"Did you see Shane at the pool?" Her voice is muffled by all the material.

"No."

"Really? He's supposed to be working today."

Mama says I've got a lying problem, and that may be so because sometimes I'm not sure why I say things the way I do. I better start fixing it, though, because the Presbyterian church has vacation Bible school this month, and they let you play dodge ball and make sculptures with matches.

I ask Mama how'd she afford so many dresses. We're not poor. One of the Sluss girls was in my class last year. There's a Sluss in almost every grade, and some grades have more than one because a couple of the boys have failed. She didn't have but two changes of clothes. That's poor. We're saving, and that's different than poor. We've been saving money to build a house ever since Mama got married to Jed. They keep all the bills in a green shoebox underneath the counter, and every so often they dump everything inside out onto the kitchen table. I know they won't be going on one of their walks on those evenings.

"I charged them, nosy," says Mama. "But we have to take two of them back. We couldn't decide, so we figured we'd ask you and Janelle." She plucks my rolled up bathing suit off the floor like it's poison and tosses it in the tub. "That means we definitely don't want them to get wet."

Darla's worked the last gown over her head, and she's trying to get it fastened. This one's a shade lighter than the others, and it shimmers when she moves, like insect wings.

I stand up on the edge of the tub where I can see into the mirror on the medicine cabinet. I put my hands on my hips and suck in my stomach until my middle looks lean and stretched out like Darla's. I turn sideways and look at myself until I have to breathe. Then my belly bows out like a bubble.

"So which one do you think?" my sister asks. I say I don't really like any of them, but when I look up at her she's turning in a circle in front of the mirror holding her arms out wide, and I see she looks like Cinderella.

For the next two weeks that dress is hanging in the coat closet. Mama's got it wrapped in layers of plastic. Whenever I walk by, I remember it's in there hanging like the squirmy webs of tent worms in the trees around the turkey house. I think about sneaking in there during the day while Darla's yapping on the phone or sitting on the toilet and maybe plucking off one of the pearl buttons. I could hide it up the hill in my sock and nobody'd ever know, but I can't get past opening the door. That shimmer material is all wound around itself and then covered in plastic like the pink underside of a shell. It makes me feel crowded.

A lot of stuff's been making me feel that way lately. The cloud of Love's Baby Soft perfume my sister's always leaving in the bathroom. The tissues with pink lipstick marks piling up in the wastebasket and stuffed into the ash tray in the car.

Darla keeps her foam hair curlers under the bathroom counter. She's got them stashed in a suitcase her real Mama forgot when she left her and Jed. It's one of those old fashioned round ones with hinges that snap it shut and a brass clasp that's pretty posh. I figure I'll load it up instead of my knapsack because it's way more stylish, plus sturdier, and I'm not sure how long I'll be on the road.

I make my exit when Darla's tanning out on the back deck. She's got the ribbons to her bikini undone because she's got a strapless dress, and Janelle says the judges count off for tan lines. I bring my special sock down from the turkey house. I load it along with an apple and three Twinkies into that little suitcase.

Under the coffee table we've got a mess of maps. I pull one out that says *Daniel Boone National Forest, Pine Mountain Ranger District* across the side. When I unfold it, I can't make any kind of sense of it, and I'm sorry I tried because it's a chore to fold that thing back up, but I throw it into my suitcase with the other stuff. I leave all those pink rollers piled on the linoleum floor. I'm a little disappointed that they didn't clatter more or roll behind the toilet when I dumped them out.

I can't take my bike because I'm only allowed to ride it around the trailer park and up and down our road. I can cross the highway, but only to get to the pool. I'm pooped by the time I make it half way down the hill. Darla and I already rode our bikes down once today and then walked them back up. I sit down on one of the whitewashed rocks marking the end of Odessa's driveway.

I'm feeling brave because I know the pool lady's still down there behind the counter, making change and scooping snow cones. I rattle the spit around in my throat the way Jed's buddies do when they're working on his truck. I hock a loogie onto the pool lady's driveway, and when I see the way my spit looks when it splatters against the black top, I hock another one.

"If you use the hose, that job'll probably go faster." Those words come out of nowhere, and for a second I think about God talking to Abraham and God talking to Moses and God talking to all those other people at the vacation Bible school. I see somebody standing inside the dark rectangle of the front doorway, and I suck in my breath real hard because I know it's got to be the pool lady's husband, and that's worse than God. He asks me do I want to come inside and have a Coke.

Now, I don't get Cokes too often on account of Jed says they make me hyperactive. Plus, there's nothing like a Coke when it's hot outside. So I walk right up the steps, and the pool lady's husband points me inside with his cane. It's not really a cane but more like a walking stick, carved up to look like a snake. It's just the kind of thing I figured he would have except it's got some kind of jewel where the eyes are, which is pretty posh for an invalid man. I sneak a look around as I'm following him through the living room. They don't have a sofa, just two big black leather recliners in front of a TV that's so big I don't even see it at first.

He's got to shift his stick to the other hand when he opens the refrigerator. He pops the top of my Coke after he sets it on the table, and he pulls out a Coors Light for himself. "This is my silver coke," he says. Then he holds out his hand and says his name is Whitey.

I don't know if that means Mr. Whitey or Whitey and then Mr. something else, so I just shake his hand and say, "Casey Hinkle." Then he looks me over and asks me where it is I'm heading today.

"I'm heading over to the lake," I say. Then I tell him probably Lake Cumberland or Laurel River Lake when he wants to know which one.

"What are you going to do there?"

I'm thinking he's awfully nosy for an invalid, but he gave me a Coke, so I don't want to be rude. "I'm going to take a job as a professional fisherman," I say.

"Oh, well, I do a lot of hunting and fishing myself," he says.

I tell him straight out then that I don't believe him because everyone knows he never leaves his house.

He thinks that's pretty funny. "Sometimes I do," he says when he's done laughing. "Only I don't tell anyone where I'm going."

"Not even the pool lady?"

"The pool lady?" he laughs. "Well, sometimes I might tell her." He's got a gray beard that's longer than I'm used to seeing and hair that's combed back with grease so that it's a little bit darker. His eyes are pale blue. "I got to keep some secrets," he says.

He asks me do I want to see another secret, and I say I guess I do. I have to follow him down the hall with his cane making a thump-scrape-thump that's still kind of scary. He opens a door at the end of the hallway, and inside there's a lighted table and work bench. Along one wall, there are shelves with clear sliding trays, and I can see they're full of feathers, wire, glass beads, and tiny bottles of paint.

I ask him is this his craft room.

"You could say that," he says. "This is where I make my lures."

"Lures?"

"Sure, fishing lures," he says. "I make them myself. I'll show you." He limps over to the table and dangles one from his fingers beneath the lamp. It's larger than I would have thought. I'm used to the rubber and plastic lures Jed buys at Wal-Mart. They're all shaped liked crayfish, worms, or little frogs. This one's more like a piece of jewelry. It has a silver shield at the top like Jed's spinners, but it rests on a mess of feathers and beads that glow all kinds of pastels when he shakes it in the light.

"I can't see nobody catching anything with that," I say.

"Oh, I catch some big ones."

"Well then let's see them." Jed's got two big bass mounted on the living room wall back at the trailer and probably ten more sliced up in plastic bags in the freezer.

"I never keep them," he says. "They look so much prettier swim-ming around, and the pool lady"—he looks at me and winks when he says that—"is not much good at cooking fish."

I tell him I better get going, seeing as how I still got a long way to go yet today.

"Why don't you go on home," he says. "I tell you what, you keep that lure because I always have good luck with that kind. But don't go off to be a professional just yet. Come back down here and visit me again, and you can help me make some more. Then you'll be ready for the tournaments."

I shake the lure in front of me in the fading light as I trot back up the hill. I decide it's the kind of treasure I should keep with me instead of in my sock. I watch it shimmer, and I like the way it feels to have a secret.

It's a Sunday night, and Jed's holding our seats in the auditorium. I'm disappointed because I figured that if this pageant is part of Harvest Days there would at least be cotton candy. Mama forced me into a yellow sundress from the attic shop, and I'm not even in this stupid contest. Me and Mama and Janelle are in the middle school choir room helping Darla to get ready. It smells like hair spray enough to make you gag.

My sister had to keep curlers in her hair all day long plus last night. She tied a scarf around them for the ride here. Janelle's pulled them out and piled all the hair up onto Darla's head with a bunch of stray curls hanging out here and there. She takes a long time to do Darla's face. She opens a box with pencils and powders and all kinds of stuff. It folds out in two directions like a tackle box and has tiny drawers like the shelves I saw in Whitey's workshop. Every time my sister turns to see who's coming in the big double doors, Janelle jerks her chin back under the light. She says Darla's got to be still.

My mom asks my sister is she ready, and she nods her head.

"How are you going to walk?" asks Janelle.

"Squeeze my butt cheeks together and pull back my shoulders."

Darla looks scared, and it makes me think of how last summer we used to plan to camp out up in the turkey house. Just talking about spending the night in there with the woods behind us and the old animal smells all around us was enough to spook us. We didn't ever need to actually do it.

"Don't touch that too much." Janelle pulls my sister's fingers away from where the curls are fastened like a crown on top of her head. "You're going to make it fall."

We have to kiss the air next to Darla's face so as not to mess anything up. After we leave, I run back real fast and find her pinning a slip of paper onto her hip. It's got a big "12" written on it in black magic marker.

"I forgot to give you something," I say, thrusting the lure into my sister's hand.

"What's this?" She fingers the feathered tail.

"It's just a lucky thing," I say. Then I run like hell to catch up with Mama.

The contest is long and boring and kind of like the Christmas pageant at the Presbyterian Church. The one where they make all the kids come up to the microphone and say a little poem. It's hard to tell all the girls apart when they're up there on the stage. They're all standing the same, and they've got on so much make-up. When Darla steps forward, though, there's something shimmery dangling from her hair.

My sister doesn't win, and after the show everyone tries to stand around and tell her it's okay, that she was definitely the prettiest one anyway. She just wants to know can she please, please go down to the carnival with Shane.

Jed looks over to the corner of the chorus room. There's Shane Spangler standing against the wall, wearing brown pants with the shirt tucked in all tight instead of his red shorts and whistle chain.

"I'm sorry, Sweetie," says Jed. "I just don't think that's a good idea. You can invite him to go on the rides with us on Wednesday."

She walks over to Shane real slow and whispers something in his ear. He nods his head and hugs her, then goes on without her.

That night Darla and I catch fireflies like we used to along the hillside behind our trailer. The grass is all damp with night, and I feel like my bare feet sliding over it must leave a wake in the moonlight. The woods behind us are full of fireflies because it's almost the end of the season. They hang like far off Christmas lights, and every so often the leaves rustle around over our heads. Then I have to look up because it's like they're sighing, "Summer . . . ."

We sit down with our backs against the deck and try to count how many insects are lighting up our jelly jar. Darla's scrubbed her face clean, and now her nose is shiny beneath the porch light. I get a little hurt in my heart then and a feeling like something's about over. Like when Jed and his boss start unloading the boat for the day up at Lake Cumberland.

I'm not sure how much later that same night I hear the window screen pop out in the room next to mine. I rise up and, holding onto to the white iron bars of my daybed, standing in the middle of a twisted pile of Holly Hobby sheets, I can see myself reflected in the mirror. There are tufts of red hair matted against my face, and my night gown, one of Jed's old T-shirts, has slid down across my shoulder. My breast looks like a little pink moon. The jar of fireflies is sitting on my dresser. Most of the insects have settled to the bottom, but a few float up every so often, flashing quiet and sending light creeping up my bedroom wall.

The rocks are stirring on the ground outside, and my sister's flip flops slap against the gravel. I know pretty soon I'll hear the engine start in a red truck somewhere down the hill.

SEEING RED

Casey 2000

I had my own little bedroom at Darla and Lincoln's place, but usually I fell asleep on the couch where I watched movies after they had gone to bed. The first month I worked at the Video House, I took home three, sometimes four, movies every shift. I must have thought somehow I could forget my own story. More often than not, I'd wake up when the credits were rolling, and then I couldn't fall back to sleep. Lincoln always turned off the air conditioner at night to save electricity, so I would walk outside where there was at least a breeze.

The apartment where my stepsister and her husband lived was above an antique shop on Main Street. The previous year the town had passed an ordinance giving investors tax incentives, and one by one, the facade front buildings were painted in bright colors with names like Colonial Yellow. During the day it was all patio music, chalked lunch specials, red and white awnings. But at night you could tell all the buildings hadn't been fixed up yet, and neither had the people. The streets were never empty, though. Couples embraced deep in the alleyways, and every so often the bravado of male voices would rise off the basketball courts across from the police station.

Some nights I walked uphill past the elementary school to the stretch of road that overlooks the ballpark. There was the smell of cut grass and the silhouettes of ball players leaning against open tailgates. Other times I walked toward the river and stood with my chest pressed against the cement railing on the bridge, watching the reflected street lights continually bend and disappear into the black water.

Surprisingly, no one spoke to me. Once, on a night when the wind was blowing trash across the sidewalk and blue lightning was forking over the mountains, Jeff Sweeney, the deputy sheriff, pulled up alongside of me and said through the open window of his squad car, "Casey, they're calling for a real bad one tonight. Maybe you ought to cut your walk short. Can I give you a ride back to your sister's?" All those nights, he was the only one to ever say anything. As we made our way back up Main Street in the quiet police cruiser, I realized that people were watching and waiting to see if I was going to snap out of it.

Abandonment led me to pass the summer with my sister. Darla found me in my underpants on the laundry room floor, clutching a bag of kitty litter as if I could no longer remember its purpose. I couldn't tell her how long I'd been sitting like that, pressing my spine into the cool metal of the washing machine.

She scooped me up by the armpits the way I've seen soldiers do their comrades in black and white movies. "How long has he been gone?"

"Less than a week."

Her hands stayed on my shoulders. "Casey, why didn't you call us?"

I didn't have an answer.

"Do you know how I found out?" she said. "Do you?"

I didn't look at her.

"I found out in the teacher's lounge. Amy Radabusch told me. 'So,' she says to me, 'That Murkey boy finally ran off on your sister, huh? I knew he was no good.'" Darla took an empty duffel bag off the back of the door. "She had hired him to remodel her kitchen cabinets, and he left them half finished. Just stopped showing up."

She started stuffing underwear and T-shirts into the bag. "What do you need for the next few days?" she asked. "We'll send Lincoln back for the rest of your stuff." Then, when she noticed I was standing there, "What, Casey? What were you planning on doing? Just hanging out here and waiting? You can stay with us, or I'll take you to Dad's."

I followed her through the house. She had the bag slung over her shoulder and the cat squirming under her arm. "Thank Christ he never married you," she said. We were in the living room, the only room in the old farmhouse that Jackson and I had actually finished, but she rolled her eyes in a way that included the empty rooms around us with their half-sanded floor boards and stripped wallpaper, as well as the mess on the coffee table in front of us. Jackson had separated seeds onto a napkin and left a pile of rolling papers. "Now you can make a clean break."

I lay down as soon as we got to her apartment, and the cat circled into a little nest on the back of my legs as Darla pulled the door shut. That's pretty much how we stayed for a week. When I awoke that first night, it was dark outside. I could hear the clink and splash of dishes moving in the sink and the quiet murmur of Darla and Lincoln's voices.

I lay awake a long time, stretched out on top of the covers. I never knew my real father, and my mother left when I was ten, but suddenly I recalled her crouching next to me as I lay on my daybed. I could feel the hot itch of a rash on my neck and the heaviness of fever behind my eyes. She had placed a cool washcloth on my forehead and was trying to massage away my headache. My mother worked her way up my legs and then back out my arms, making tiny circles with her fingertips, whispering, "Your toes are warm and relaxed, your feet are warm and relaxed, your ankles are warm and relaxed . . . ." My mind moved up and down my body so many times that night, turning her voice into a kind of mourning chant for Jackson.

I thought, "He will never touch you here again, he will never touch you here again . . . ."

That week Darla dragged me up and to a shower once or twice, and Lincoln came home every day during his planning period. He tried to make me eat deli sandwiches or canned soup. He told me, "Casey, if you need to talk to someone, we'll pay for it."

I stared at the soft lumps of carrot floating in the vegetable beef. That's how everything felt, soft and shapeless. I couldn't find the edges anymore.

It must have mystified Lincoln, that I could feel so much—feel to the point of physical exhaustion—when I was raised in the same house with Darla, who is always steady, always in control. He never met my mother. When the hour was up, Lincoln rose from the table and rinsed the dishes. Once, as he was leaving, he stood behind my chair and set his hand on top of my head and sighed. His hand felt large and foreign and charged, like a kind of baptism. I thought about Jackson's hands, his fingers almost as slender as mine, always splintered, the edges of his nails rough from work.

Finally, one night, I rose and slid open my window. The warm air sighed through the screen. I responded by leaving my bedroom and walking outside, still in pajama bottoms. I didn't go far, just down Main Street to the car wash and then back up the alley, where I stood and stared at the rectangle of light that was my room. The cat was walking back and forth across the windowsill, pressing her fur against the screen. The next morning, I got up and had a bowl of cereal with Darla and Lincoln.

I wanted to give them something toward rent, and that meant finding a job. I'd never had a real job. Since I met Jackson I'd spent my days helping him. When he lined up a project, his friend Dane Shifflett would drive his big van down from Sandy Bottom, and they'd work sometimes from seven in the morning until eight at night. It was my job to drive out to Dean's Hardware after tubs of nails and extra extension cords, or else to the 7-Eleven for Dr. Peppers, which is all they would drink when they were working. It was not uncommon for Dane to bring a girl along. During the summer he always had different people in and out of his cabin. I would sit with the other girl, or we would run sheets of extra fine sandpaper back and forth across base boarding or carved pieces that were to become the edging for new cabinets.

Usually Jackson didn't have a project, though. He was fixing up the farmhouse his mother had left him, and sometimes we would work inside, but he spent most of his time out back. When we went for walks or took his boat to the river, we were always looking for the right wood, smooth slabs that had been bobbing in the water or lodged in the fields and half covered with leaves. He brought them into his studio where he carved them and, using all sorts of materials—river rocks, broken pop bottles, clothes hangers, old car parts—turned them into people or animals. Some of the pieces he sold in town—he had a few pieces at a studio in Garrison, and he always set up a booth at Harvest Days and at the Sugar Maple Festival. But most of them he attached to the army of wooden creatures he was creating in the backyard. He had begun the project long before I met him, and over the years he carved an intricate arbor with a table and benches and two free standing towers that rise above the house. The structure became a kind of cocoon, encasing half the house and creaking with the weather. Once I saw the same couple in a car with Ohio plates drive by three times in one afternoon, slowing down and craning their necks, leaning out windows with their chunky cameras. The Appalachian Arts Guild did an article on Jackson, and they said the house is the most amazing example of contemporary folk art in the eastern United States.

Really, the only job experience I had was running after hardware and sodas. Darla suggested I ask about waiting tables. She made a killing doing that when she was in college. There are only two real restaurants on Main Street, though: one sells Jackson's sculptures, and he and Dane built the booths in the other. I wore one of the long, flowered skirts my sister teaches in, and took off up and down Main Street anyway. The owner of the antique store below the apartment told me he already had a high school girl helping him in the evenings. At the United Way Thrift Store, two old women were digging through a box of clothing and kitchen utensils someone had just dropped off. They told me all their workers were volunteers. At the top of the hill, I saw a help wanted sign in the window of The Video House, and I asked the owner, Mrs. Howdyshell, about it.

"I don't know anything about a sign," she said.

I pointed to the piece of notebook paper scotch-taped to the glass. Magic marker had bled through the back. "That's Mr. Howdyshell," she said. "He thinks if he gets someone else in here, he can talk me into a trip to Dollywood."

I stood there and smoothed my damp hands against the sides of Darla's skirt.

Mrs. Howdyshell pointed to the TV mounted in the corner. Robert Redford was in a biplane, wearing aviator's goggles, looking back one last time to Meryl Streep. "You can't just hang out and watch movies here," she said. "You might think that's what we do, but this is a very complicated process."

I nodded my head.

"You have to keep careful track of what movies are checked out to which accounts." She flipped open a stained three-ring binder, and spun the pages of names around for me to read. "You know we don't have those fancy cards like they do in Garrison."

"I wouldn't know how to work those anyway." Although Garrison is less than twenty miles away, and many people have started running over there for groceries, it was rarer than once a month that Jackson and I made the drive.

"Your fella left last week, didn't he?" Mrs. Howdyshell probably had a better idea where Jackson was than I did. "You living with your sister?" She snapped the notebook of names shut. "Well," she said, "I guess if my husband is determined to hire somebody, you'll do as good as anyone."

We drove out to see Jed that Sunday, just like always. Lincoln took the long way out, east on 38, then looping around the back way by Old Nag Mountain. It's a prettier drive, with grazing horses and farm ponds that reflect pieces of sky. But I know he just didn't want to drive past the house. I turned toward it anyway when I stepped out of the car, knowing it was there past the cluster of trailers, the half mile of woods and corn fields. You can't see the towers from Jed's place, but I leaned into the breeze, imagining that I could hear the whining of the wood spiraling above the house. Some of the carvings, the ones emblazoned with glass shards and pieces of shell would be blinking in the afternoon sun.

Jed hugged me harder than usual. I could feel the pack of Winstons crinkle in the pocket of his uniform. Like a lot of men in town, Jed has worked at Walker, the muffler factory, for nearly twenty-five years. He wears his uniform even on the weekends. He spends most of his time off working on a Chevy Corvair he keeps covered in the driveway. After lunch, there would be no sitting on the porch and watching Jackson's back bending with his into the raised hood.

Jed still eats off the same table he and my mother bought when they first married. Its enameled surface has been scratched over the years, and the seats of the matching red vinyl chairs have sunken and hardened. If my mom had not left us, he surely would have another table, polished walnut with extensions that fold out for family Thanksgiving dinners. We took our seats while Darla slid a casserole dish covered with aluminum foil into the refrigerator. She always leaves Jed an extra dish to supplement the Sunday leftovers. Darla began to move her chair around the table like usual, then caught herself. There were only four of us now. I could see the aluminum lawn chair we usually set up for Jackson. It was still folded against the wall beneath the telephone.

After our meal I went outside with Jed while Darla and Lincoln loaded up the dishes. He sat down and lit a cigarette. He has one of those metal couches that move along a runner, a green and white old lady couch. He dropped his match into the empty flower pot he keeps next to it for butts and ashes. He won't use a lighter. I picked up a stick and began poking it around the leaves in one of the window wells the way I used to hunt salamanders.

"Are you okay over at your sister's?" he asked.

"Yeah."

"You can always come back here if you want." He flicked ash off his cigarette.

When I met Jackson, I was still in high school. I never came home from our first date. Jackson dropped me off at school each morning in his same varnish-splattered pair of jeans. He asked me if there wasn't someone I should call, and I said probably. But I just waited. By the time I had worked up the nerve to come back and explain to Jed, more than a week had passed and he had figured it all out through the rumor mill anyway. He turned off some part of himself to me then.

Jed formally adopted me when he married my mother. He used to take me fishing, and he taught me how to shoot. He would set aluminum cans along the fence posts. Darla's aversion to these activities made me like them more. They were my secret alliance with Jed, the thing that made him my father, too.

He stared across the field, and the couch whined as he slid it slowly back and forth. "I'm probably better off at Darla's right now," I said. "I found a job."

"Oh yeah?"

"At the video store." My voice was touched with pride, and when I heard it, it sounded silly. "Just a few evenings a week."

"That Erma Howdyshell's the biggest gossip in Renfro County."

I met Jackson Murkey half way through my senior year in high school. Jed had taken his truck up to West Virginia for a long weekend of hunting, so I had to suffer riding the bus for two days. The older boys sat in the back. They slapped their hands against the seats in front of them and stabbed butterfly knives in and out of the spaces between their spread fingers, trying to see who could move the fastest. The bus lurched over the back roads like a wounded animal. Two boys sat behind me snickering. They were young enough that they had not stopped wearing their blue corduroy Future Farmers jackets. I thought I felt one of them pull my hair, but when I spun around they were looking at a weather map in an Earth Science textbook.

My hair is thick and wavy. It's never been any use trying to comb it out straight. When we were little my mother used to take me and Darla to the salon on Main Street, and her friend Janelle would trim all of us in one afternoon. Jed always dropped us off at a beauty parlor in Garrison and watched television in the bar across the street. There were mottled gray floor tiles, and the whole place stank of chemicals. The woman who trimmed my hair had warm, fat hands. "Look at this hair," she would call to the women flipping through magazines on the brown sofa. "Have you ever seen hair like this girl's got?" My hair used to be bright red, but it darkened as I got older, and by high school it hung down to the waist of my jeans.

Once I got to school that day, I found two fishing bobbers knotted in the back of my hair. They were twisted up so tight I couldn't get them out. I went to the guidance counselor, and she told me I could leave in her car and go see a hair dresser if I wanted. She said she hoped they wouldn't have to cut it. I went to the fancy salon, but Janelle wasn't there. The stylist took one look at the mess on the back of my head and said she'd have to do some heavy layering, at least to chin length. I told her to just take it all off then.

"Well, how do you want it styled?" She sighed and shook her head as she lifted little sections.

"I don't know," I said. "You decide."

"Okay, let's do a pixie."

I didn't freak out when I saw my hair hugging my face like a dark cap, but I could tell the stylist thought I was going to.

"Here's some free hair pins," she said when she was ringing me up. "You can pull the bangs over if you want."

My new shadow looked strange as I walked through the faculty parking lot. I liked the way the sun felt on my neck. I felt lighter.

If it wasn't for those fishing bobbers, I might never have met Jackson. Months later he confessed it was my hair that first got his attention. He said I looked so different than the hundreds of other girls he had seen wander in and out of the building that afternoon. He was constructing a new trophy case next to the office, consulting figures he had recorded on a beaten-up notepad. He smiled at me the first time I walked by, and after I had signed in with the secretary, he called me over to where he was standing. His body was small and hard beneath a plain white T-shirt. His tool belt hung low around his waist.

"What's your name?" he wanted to know.

"Casey."

"You go to school here?"

I nodded.

"How old are you?"

"Eighteen."

He kept looking back over his shoulder to see if the office secretary was watching us. He asked if he could take me out that night, and I wrote down directions to our place on his notepad. I had been on my share of dates. I got excited every time there was a school dance, told the right people so that whoever I wanted to ask me would find out, talked Jed into gowns that cost more than the money he had allotted. I knew this date would be different, though.

We went to the Country Kitchen. I ordered a 12 oz. rib eye, the kind with onion rings on top. I had missed lunch getting the haircut. Jackson acted surprised, but I could tell he liked the fact that I ordered real food. There were antique kerosene lanterns on each table, and the owner came by and lit ours. I could tell Jackson knew her by the way they laughed, but he didn't introduce me.

"How old are you?" I had been scared to ask him before. He had real sideburns and the corners of his eyes crinkled a little when he laughed, but I didn't think he was any older than my brother-in-law.

"Twenty-six." He looked at me and took a long sip of his beer. That was good, twenty-six. That was younger than I thought.

I said, "Did you go to college?"

"Nope." He slid his fingers up my hand, paused and smiled when he got to my class ring. It had a lavender stone and was engraved with a Trailblazer on one side and a volleyball on the other. "I was lucky," he said. "I didn't have to."

"Why not?" I liked the way my exposed neck felt. I was somebody else.

"Well, my mother died of ovarian cancer several years ago, horrible stuff, but I've been able to get my own business going with what she left me."

"Making trophy cases?"

"Among other things." He laughed and brushed his hair out of his face. It was brown and longer than mine. Suddenly I wondered if he might not be nervous. "I do carpentry projects, but I really consider myself an artist. I did all those." He pointed to the sculptures hanging along the opposite wall and behind the bar. There was one in particular. It was a fish, over five feet long. Shards of colored glass scales sparkled in the lamplight. It was a fairytale fish. Wasn't there a story with a fish who granted wishes?

"You didn't make those." I really didn't believe him, and I wasn't sure about his age either.

"I'll show you," he said.

Then he took me to the house. At first I thought he was taking me home, back to the trailer park, but he pulled off the road too soon. We drove down a long gravel lane, and I started to be a little afraid. The teachers were forever warning us about date rape in Health and P.E. I let him lead me up the porch and through the dark house. Inside it smelled like sawdust and varnish. "This isn't even your house," I whispered. "You're just doing work here."

He took something out of a closet. "You'll see."

We went straight through the back of the house, and when we were in the middle of the patio, he flipped a switch and decorative lights twinkled on above and all around. There was a maze of intricate carvings overhead—foxes and hawks and squirrels and others all suddenly watching us.

"It's amazing." I sank down on the flagstone. "I think I've seen this from the road, but I never knew what it was."

He sat down beside me and covered us with a blanket. I let him kiss me for a long time. Insects hovered around the lights. He worked off some of my clothing, and I had to tell him *no*. But then hours later, because he had stopped before, I let him start again. I didn't tell him it was my first time, but he must have known, the way I had to keep stopping and shifting and beginning again. We finally got to moving together beneath the blanket, and I felt like the two of us were an animal hatching out.

I had already decided to move in with Jackson by the time Jed returned from West Virginia, and I quit going to school a few weeks later. Jed wasn't happy about the arrangement, but he didn't pitch a fit or try to force me back. He had learned with my mother years ago that it backfires when you try to pressure people into making good decisions.

Darla and Lincoln said things every day.

It's really all for the best. You can go back to school now.

That relationship became an addiction. You cut yourself off from everything you used to love.

That man was trash. He was a pothead. He had no idea what partnership means or commitment.

He could have ruined your life.

At work Mrs. Howdyshell let me reorganize the shelves. I made a special display of old movies, and these were the ones I liked to take home the best. Black and white films where the actresses had penciled eyebrows and could cry, really cry, without messing up their faces. When I watched the end of *Casablanca* or *Roman Holiday*, I told myself that this is how it should be, that the final good-bye wasn't always tragic, that sometimes even it wasn't enough to cancel out what had been.

We took note of who checked out which movies, and, for Mrs. Howdyshell, it was like reading horoscopes. She knew who was having sex and who wasn't, who was having a babysitter, who was having trouble at work, all by which movies they selected. Not many people took the old ones. They would come in and glance at the new arrivals, always picked over on a Saturday night. "Everything's already gone," they'd say. "I guess we'll have to drive to Garrison."

One customer did rent old movies and nothing else. Mrs. Howdyshell showed me his list, and it was impressive. At that time he had out *Double Indemnity* and *A Streetcar Named Desire*. His name was Stirling Norvell, not a local name, and he had opened an account only that summer. Curious, I checked the folder of membership agreements to get a look at his signature. It was sprawling and old-fashioned. Jackson always printed, and he only used capital letters. "Are you sure he's a man?" I showed the paper to Mrs. Howdyshell.

"Yes, and he's not bad looking either," she said. "He usually comes in early, so you've never seen him."

When he finally came in, one afternoon in July, Mrs. Howdyshell hustled over to the counter to announce his arrival. I watched him move down my display. He picked up *African Queen*, then put it back. There were two videos tucked beneath his arm. He had light brown hair, a little sun-bleached, and the back of his neck and ears were burnt red. I guessed from driving a tractor.

When he arrived at the checkout, he placed *West Side Story* and *Summer of '42* on the counter. "I want to return these two," he said, "And I want to rent this one." He looked back over his shoulder as if he might change his mind, then he set *Double Indemnity* next to the cash register.

"You checked this one out a few weeks ago," I said as I recorded it again in the big notebook. "Fred MacMurray."

"You've seen it?"

"One of my favorites." I handed him his change, and he looked at me kind of funny before turning to go.

He returned in about half an hour to invite me to a Fourth of July cookout that weekend. "Just as friends," he said when I hesitated. "I've got a girlfriend back at school."

Darla told me to wear my khaki pants because I don't look so skinny in them. She tried to smooth down my hair, but it wouldn't hold. "It looks a little fluffy," she said after she had coated it with hairspray. "Now maybe you can grow it out again." When I showed Jackson a picture of me with long hair, he said that I should keep it short. Hair that long looked white trash. Darla and Lincoln had taken to speaking about Jackson's absence without mentioning him at all. *Now you can concentrate on you. Now you have nothing to hold you back.*

Stirling stepped inside to say hello to my sister and Lincoln. I wondered if the two of them would take advantage of being alone again in their apartment. Once a week or so, Darla made a big show of how tired she was at dinner. She took a long bath, and then came out in her terrycloth robe to tell Lincoln it was time for bed. Those nights I knew she would reemerge from their room within the hour and slink into the bathroom, that I would hear the toilet flush and the faucet turn on. I always pretended to be asleep.

I had sliced a plate of fresh tomatoes from Jed's garden. Stirling held the car door open for me to climb inside. I had expected a truck. All the men I knew drove trucks. Jackson had left in one with a boat trailer rattling behind it. Lincoln drove a Suburban. I had assumed Stirling was a farm hand, and I was right. Technically, he was doing an internship for his Agricultural Engineering major at the University of Kentucky, but I was wrong about his wheels. He drove a blue sedan.

The year before, Jackson and I had gone to a picnic at Dane's cabin up in Sandy Bottom. We'd been dating about eight months. It was the only time he ever took me up there. The road was strewn with huge rocks like an empty creek bed, and I had to brace my palms against the dashboard. We started to see smaller cars parked over in the trees, guests who had given up and gotten out to walk. It was getting dark. Eventually the road leveled out and emptied us into a damp field, where we parked with others who had made it all the way up the

mountain. Goats met us as we climbed down from the cab. They nib-
bled at the hem of my skirt, sniffed my sandals.

Dane's cabin was more like a shack. It looked as if it began as an
old aluminum RV, but it had been added onto again and again. Honeysuckle vines crawled up onto the roof. Some people milled around
the front of the building and others clustered around three bonfires
in an adjacent field. When we reached the fires, they were passing
around a bong, and a girl in a gauzy halter top offered it to Jackson.
She had loosened the straps so they hung way down off her shoulders.
One of her nipples showed a little as she leaned forward.

"How about you, baby?" she asked me. Her eyes looked sleepy.

Jackson said, "No, thanks. We brought some stuff." He took one of
the cigarettes he had rolled earlier from his pocket and looked around
for a lighter. That was the first time I realized he smoked pot. Until
then I just thought he made his own cigarettes.

Dane had killed a goat and roasted it in a pit in the ground, but I
couldn't eat it, not with the other ones bleating and nosing our palms.
Some of the guys said it was time for the fireworks, and they told us
to turn and look down the hill. After the first explosion, we had to lie
on the ground for the rest. They had fixed five-gallon propane tanks
into homemade bombs. I lost Jackson in all the commotion, so I talked
to the girl by the fire for a while. Her name was Promise, and she was
learning to be a massage therapist.

I finally found Jackson inside the building. He was sitting on a
lumpy futon with two girls. Promise had told me about this room. It
was where Dane had used fluorescent paint on the ceiling to create
the night sky during the summer solstice. One girl's hand was draped
across Jackson's knee, moving along the inside of his thigh. "I want to
go home," I said. "Now."

"Okay." He moved the hand and set it on the cushion. "I've got a
surprise for you first." He rose and propelled me from the room with
his hand on the small of my back. "Goodnight, ladies," he called over
his shoulder. On the backside of the house there was a screened porch
where a litter of kittens squirmed inside a cardboard box. "Pick one
out," he said. "I think you need a pet." I chose a gray and white one
and inhaled the warm milk smell from his fur.

On the way to his cookout, Stirling tried to make nervous talk
about movies, then work. *Breakfast at Tiffany's* was his all-time favorite,
and he was living in a guesthouse on a farm near Rockhouse Creek. I
felt sorry for him. Who knows what he had heard about me and Jackson? Finally we arrived at the Methodist Church, where there were

two tables set up on the lawn. One was just for desserts. We placed my tomatoes on the other one, in the salad section, and then Stirling introduced me to the farmer he was working with for the summer.

After dinner, Stirling got a softball game going with some of the kids, but I didn't want to play. I sat on the grass and watched him run. He had taken off his loafers, and I liked the way his bare feet looked in the grass. He came and sat down with me when the families began dispersing to go watch the different fireworks displays. He asked if I wanted to go see the show on the hill in the park.

We got back in the car, and I was surprised but mostly happy when he drove me home. "Do you want to walk down toward the river?" he asked when we were parked at the curb. He had shut off the car. "I bet we can see some over the water."

He took my hand as we walked, but I didn't curve my fingers around his. I folded my arms across my chest when we got to the railing. The sky was full of popping and whizzing, and every now and then one cracked in just the right place so that we could see its color in the air and on the surface of the water. Every time he exhaled I could feel his breath against my neck, a quiet offer. I leaned over the water, thinking about his girlfriend back in Lexington. I had given Stirling my number when he asked me out, but I knew he wouldn't call me again that summer, and I was glad. I was glad Jackson had left me because he loved me, not because he didn't.

I asked Stirling why *Breakfast at Tiffany's* was his favorite.

"It's such a love story," he said. "It makes me have faith that when people are really in love it will always work out."

I didn't tell him how that was complete horseshit.

I only went back to the house once, on a Sunday after we had eaten lunch with Jed and I had put away the clean dishes. I watched Darla and Lincoln through the kitchen window as they made their way across the garden. Lincoln held a plastic grocery bag filled with beans, and Darla was pointing out cucumbers that would make good pickles. When she knelt to pick the ones that were overripe or too large, her blond hair swung across her shoulders. Something about the ease with which she moved down the row suddenly repulsed me. She tossed the bad ones into the tall grass on the other side of the barbed wire fence. I turned and walked out of the trailer, past Jed and the greasy tools he had arranged on the ground.

A "for sale" sign was posted by the road, and I took a brochure from the plastic box. *Own a home with a 140 year history. A handyman's dream with a fantasy patio already completed.* Grass had started to spread across the gravel lane, and the front fields were brambly and full of Brown-Eyed-Susans. The turrets of the backyard structure rose like ramparts over the edge of the roof. I knew the door would be locked, but I tried it anyway. I sat down on the porch and stared down the road. Pretty soon I could see Lincoln's Suburban coming up the hill out of the woods.

We didn't know my mother was going to leave us. She went shopping on her day off and never came back, but she left a note for Jed and a note for each of us. I can remember things from when I was really little. I can remember when my mom and I lived alone and shared a bedroom with flowered wallpaper, but I can't remember what my note said. Why wouldn't I have held on to something like that? I've asked Darla what it said, and she says she can't remember but probably the same stuff hers said.

I knew Jackson would leave eventually. In fact, I think he was preparing me for it all the time. We never used anything when we made love. He just pulled out and left a mess all over my belly, but a few months before he left he starting doing it inside me. He even positioned a pillow under my hips. We never talked about it, but I think he wanted me to get pregnant, so he could leave me with a part of himself. At the time I convinced myself it meant he wanted to marry me, but a part of me knew even then. I was disappointed every month to find the familiar stain there in my panties.

Toward the end of the summer, I started going to the Country Kitchen for pancakes in the morning. The fish was still there. Its price tag said nine hundred dollars. One by one, the other sculptures came down from the wall, but the fish stayed. The owner must have known where to send the money. I guessed somewhere out West. Jackson always told me we'd go to New Mexico when he was talking like he'd take me along. I never thought about asking the owner for an address or even news about where he was, but I thought about shaking her and insisting she give me that fish.

One night at the end of August, Darla had to spend the evening at the elementary school for orientation and open house. Lincoln ordered a pizza, and we ate it at the table. I cleaned everything up, while he paid bills. Afterwards, I put in *Picnic* and lay down on the sofa, pulling the afghan over my legs. I had watched it the night before, and I knew how the girl would set out in the end after the guy who didn't really deserve her. I liked it, because what would happen if she found him? *Nothing,* I thought as the cat walked back and forth beneath my outstretched hand. That's what made it so good—even though it was over, it had been the real thing.

In a little while Lincoln came in and sat down on the other end of the couch. He pulled the blanket over his feet, and we watched the screen in silence. His feet were heavy and alive next to my legs. "Are you doing better, Casey?" he asked. "It seems like you are."

I didn't answer.

"What was it about him?" he wanted to know. "What made you lose your head so much?"

Our calves were touching then, the top of his foot curling around the back of my thigh. All I had to do was move in his direction, crawl down the length of the couch, slide my hands into his sweatpants. I could see myself straddling him, his chest large and soft and pale beneath my fingers. In that moment, I knew I could make it happen. I could show everyone how hypocritical they all were, disintegrate their word *loyalty.* "I'm tired," I said, scooping the cat up on my way to the bedroom, shutting the door behind me.

That weekend Darla and I finished the last of the canning. I sat at the table snapping pole beans from Jed's garden, watching her lower a ring of tomato jars into the pressure cooker. She had turned down the thermostat, but the air was still hot and full of steam.

"Lincoln and I've been talking," she said. "We were thinking maybe it's time you looked into getting your own place." She twisted the top into place and turned to face me. "We haven't deposited any of your rent checks. We want you to take the money and use it for a down payment on a studio. You could live in Garrison, or over in Big Stone Gap if you're really planning on going back to school."

I had signed up at Mountain Empire Community College to take the test for my GED at the end of September. "All I'm saying," she said, pulling out a chair and sitting down beside me, "is that maybe you should start looking."

The next week I dropped Jed off at Walker and took his truck. I had an interview at Blockbuster Video later that morning, but I stopped at the Valley Mall just as it opened and walked around a while. They had already put out the fall sweaters. I picked one that was red and cashmere. I wouldn't even be able to wash it in the sink with shampoo, but I carried it back to the dressing room anyway, even though Jackson always said only whores wear red. I unbuttoned my blouse, and draped it on a hook so it wouldn't wrinkle. My shoulders were pale and only vaguely freckled. I realized I'd spent the whole summer inside. Suddenly I wanted to be fishing with Jed, wanted it so bad my throat hurt. I wanted the steady hum of the trawling motor propelling us slowly forward, wanted to watch the dragonflies land and, for a moment, balance on the edge of the boat.

I pulled the sweater over my head. It settled soft on my shoulders, the way my long hair used to, and when I turned around there were three of me—an army facing off in the mirrors.

EXPECTING

2008

Cora

As soon as your brother-in-law gives you word, you begin making the room ready. One of the upstairs bedrooms. The one with the east facing window. The room that was never filled.

You paint the walls a pale lilac. Elden and one of the farmhands drag an old iron bed in from the storage room in the barn. You sand off the rust and paint it white. You hang sheer curtains and spread a bright quilt—one of dozens your grandmother made over the years—across the bed. As a final touch, you add an antique vanity—a splurge purchase—with flowering vines stenciled across the front of each drawer and a matching velvet-covered stool. You position it in such a way that the mirror will catch the light from the only window, making the room seem larger, sunnier.

In the days before her arrival, you sit for hours at a time on the edge of the bed. You expected a kind of upwelling, working up here behind this door that you and Elden have been careful to keep shut for so long. But what you feel is quieter. You can't even tell your husband.

When he finds you like that, you stand up as if you've been caught doing something sly. You turn and run your fingers over the quilt. *Prairie Star*, Mamaw called this pattern. You know the answer, but you ask him anyway, "Is it too much of a little girl's room?"

And he wraps his arms around you. "Stop worrying," he tells you. "She'll make it her own."

The morning of her arrival, a humid August morning, the White Oaks form a dense, green canopy overhead. They've poured new black-top since the last time you crossed the mountain, and the air is thick with the scent of tar. Elden's hands tap a nervous cadence against the steering wheel, and you stare out the open window, hearing the insects rattle the brush. You don't know what to expect. It was easier with your older nieces and nephews, easier to remember birthdays and gradu-ations, and easier, too, to engage them in talk, in play. You know this must be your fault. Once that desire rooted in you, so different from the sexual desire you spent decades nursing—even more consuming—you started to forget how to be a proper aunt. Perhaps you had to.

And now this one. Your sister's sixth, and five full years the young-est. How is it that you can hardly remember her infancy, hardly remem-ber her in diapers or toddling around the parsonage, while you can remember the wet, needy mouths of the others, especially the oldest boy, the way his fingers would curl around yours when you touched his palm. Jane always dismissed it. *Reflex.* But you knew it was more. Like stirring buttermilk into fat and flour, the sudden thickening you felt in your womb. And now that boy, Peter, is soon to be an architect, finishing an internship in Seattle. When did you grow so old?

You think this as you and Elden approach the airport entrance. You can see yourself there, reflected in the dark glass. Your hair, which you finally stopped dyeing when you started the fertility treatments, now contains almost as much gray as brown. And the weight you lost—the doctor said it would add years to your life, but somehow it added years to your face instead—carving crow's feet and pulling down the corners of your mouth in a few short months. More than this, though, it is the way you walk that marks you. Hesitant. Your arm linked with Elden's. The way he pauses for you to step up onto the curb. The last two years have taken their toll.

You don't know what to expect. It has been ten months since the funeral. You try to conjure up a picture of your niece from that day, but it is difficult. Your own grief put a caul over everything. You can only remember later that evening, after the visitors finally left, when you and Elden went around to hug all the kids (funny to call them that, since the rest of them are all in college or working, living on their own). "Goodbye," you told them. "Call if you need anything." Most of them were still clustered around the kitchen, wrapping food, rinsing plates. You found her sitting in the carport, even though it was forty degrees and getting dark.

Now, watching people stream off the escalator in the Tri-Cities International Airport, you try again to remember, try to reduce that last conversation to a series of stills. She was wearing those too-tight jeans—cigarette jeans the magazines call them—and a concert T-shirt. She didn't look particularly criminal. Maybe a little too much eyeliner. She was sitting in a plastic lawn chair, texting away on a phone, and she looked up, for just a second when you called to her, thick bangs cutting a black slash diagonally across her face. "Okay," she said. "Bye."

Grace

On Monday morning, she knocks on your door. Soft. Overly polite. "Pancakes are on," she says. This is new.

The last three days she has allowed you to sleep in, said nothing more than—"Hey there! Would you like a sandwich?"—when you finally wandered downstairs as late as one o'clock. But you have been awake. That is what she doesn't realize. You have been awake in this ridiculous purple room, awake as soon as you heard their muffled alarm clock sound from somewhere down below, heard the two of them start to shuffle around, heard the dog yapping at the back door. *And barely a thread of silver light through your window!* Each morning, stretched—*like death*—beneath the heavy quilt as his coffee starts to percolate, as her tea pot shrieks, as the silverware rattle in the drawer, everything eventually fading into voices and stomping boots—the arrival of the morning help. And even after the men left to start the feeding, you could still hear her padding around down there, rinsing the dishes.

Your mother, each time your father was reassigned, would make her way slowly through whatever house the new church had provided, tapping door frames, opening and shutting cabinets, running water from each tap. "They don't make houses like they used to," she would say. Or, once your family had settled in, when the noise level rose as it was sure to in a house so crowded, when your brothers were strumming their electric guitars or your sisters were bickering over some piece of clothing, she would shake her head and mutter, "These walls are like paper."

Yet here you are, in the house where she grew up, and you can hear everything. The last three mornings, you waited as long as you could. *Not like it's easy to keep busy.* You can't even text your friends since your dad took back your phone. So you slowly unpacked your suitcases. You thumbed, again and again, through the same three magazines, the ones your father bought for you at the airport. *Star, People,* and *Glamour.* Thankfully, without commenting on the scandalous covers. *His usual custom.* You're not sure what keeps you anchored in this room, the room you hate—*would've hated even when you were six years old.* Each day you waited as long as you could to go downstairs, waited until the smell of her midday baking rising warm and yeasty finally pulled on your empty stomach.

But today is the first day of school. The first day of eighth grade. *Well, really it is like what—the 260th?—day of eighth grade since you'll be repeating it this year.* You saw the middle school on the way back from the airport. You'd just made it out of the mountains and you were a still little slurgy from that curving road, your forehead pressed up against the glass. *They didn't even turn the air conditioner on until you asked!* You drove right past it—a limestone building with an arched entryway, a cinder track, a few basketball hoops minus the nets. *Totally 1950s.*

She is yelling up the stairway now: "Thirty minutes till departure!" *Like this is a train station or something.* You pull on some jeans.

The men are already at the barn. She has cleared away their dishes and set a place just for you—three pancakes, bacon, a glass of juice, and a glass of milk. You shudder when you see the milk. Your uncle has explained that they only raise beef cows, but you can't get the thought out of your head: *Probably right out of a cow.*

And Peppy, her miniature poodle, is already there—hardly what you'd call a farm dog, white and fluffy, *half blind from inbreeding.* You can actually feel him panting beneath the table, waiting to gobble up any morsel you drop.

"Coffee?" She's holding the stainless carafe, waving it vaguely in your direction.

You shake your head.

"You young people don't need caffeine to get going," she says. "Me, I can't roll out of bed unless I know Elden's put my teapot on."

You think about telling her that back home you have sometimes three Mocha Frapuccinos a day. Or you did anyway until other stuff started eating your allowance. You think about telling her that your mom considered herself lucky to get all of you out the door with a Pop Tart and a multivitamin.

The clock on the microwave blinks 7:16. *Jesus.* You'll hurl if you take a bite this early, especially without having had a cigarette. She is smiling at you, waiting. You take a little sip of the juice.

It works. She turns away, opens up the fridge. "What do you want in your lunch," she asks. "We have turkey and honey ham." She looks back at you, all expectant. "I could make you up a PBJ."

"Oh," you say, "I always buy my lunch."

Then she opens a drawer and pulls out a little plastic card. "Well," she says, "I got you $50.00 in Blue Knight bucks. That should be enough for a few weeks' worth of lunches and any school supplies that weren't on the list they sent me."

She sets it next to your plate. It is like a credit card, only blue and gold with the words *Conrad's Fork Middle School* across the front.

"Cool, huh? I can put more on it online each month. They didn't even have those things when I was in college."

And then you know. Your father has told her, told her to give you absolutely no money.

Cora

You and Elden take the cuttings in October, which isn't optimal, you know. You wait as long as you can. The land hasn't been yours for months. Your grandmother always grafted in early spring because the incisions didn't have to be as deep, because less jointing material was required. And less time. You would know within weeks whether the new limbs were going to blossom.

Fifty acres. Nearly a third of the farm, steep—not the best land for grazing, but, still, your favorite spot because of the view from atop the ridge. You can see the river from up there, especially in winter. You can see the shacks that still dot the shore down in Sandy Bottom. And the trees. Those apple trees, decades old, really at their peak in terms of production—the trees your father planted!—will be thinned and cleared, and over the next two years twenty tudor-style houses (with Mansard roofs and three-car garages) will be constructed. You wait until they've staked each property with little orange flags, until bulldozers are parked just below the tree line.

When you ask her if she wants to come along she shakes her head, doesn't even look up from her sketch book. Those pads cost $30 at Hobby Lobby, and she goes through one every two weeks. But she says art is the only class she really likes. Early on you asked her if you could look at what she was drawing. "Oh." She slammed the pad shut, looked absolutely horrified. "It's not finished yet." She's been sitting out back all morning curled in one of the deck chairs.

You try again: "Are you sure? It was your grandfather who planted those trees."

This morning she's pulled her hair back with a bandana, and you're amazed at how pretty she looks while she's sketching—her brown eyes, downcast and glittering, her face open.

But she looks up then. "Was he *really*?"

"Sure," you say. But then you see the way one of her carefully tweezed eyebrows is arching. And you understand she's not alluding to the orchard. She knows the truth, somehow she knows. Your sister must have told her. Jane didn't even know until a few months before her death. She didn't even tell you right away. At first, she just said you were not a donor match. You know she would have left it at that had the circumstances been in any way different. The fact that she told you shows just how desperate she was to live.

She flew down to spend a few days with you, despite your worry that she was too weak. The two of you stopped for lunch at the Valley Vista Grill, and that is where she told you, didn't even wait for the food to arrive. Just came right out and said it: "The reason you are not a match is because you're only my half sister."

You looked up, holding a lemon slice, suddenly unable to squeeze it into your sweet tea.

"My oncologist told me so," she said. "He encouraged me to talk to my family and see if there is any possibility of another sibling out there. A full sibling."

She reached for your hand, across the table. "I was shocked too, Cora. I told Dr. Adler that. I told him there is only you. That everyone else is gone. And he told me to start with you, that you are where I start looking."

But you were not completely shocked. That's the thing. There were signs. Jane's hair, so black and thick and shiny before her treatment. Her olive skin. Her calm, no-nonsense attitude. Even her ability to leave the farm, to leave the valley altogether. She wasn't drawn back to that tether the way you were. And in that moment you knew something else: If your father had lived (and, even now, you still think of him as yours and hers) the secret would have been exposed.

You can't be sure how much the girl knows, so you just say it again. "Your grandfather planted all those trees," you say. "The sweetest Staymens in the state. And your mother and I crated and sold them each fall."

The girl looks down, and her charcoal pencil begins to scratch the paper again.

The ground, always soft and mossy beneath the apple trees, feels spongy from several days of rain. The branches are slick and cool. You and Elden work quickly. Years have passed since you have done this—Mamaw directed you the last time—but your hands remember. It is not unlike feeling a human limb, something you did back when you were a nurse. Your fingers move over the ridges in the bark, feeling for tenderness, testing the joints. Elden works the clippers, cutting only where you direct him.

You wrap each branch in a wet towel from the pile soaking in the wheelbarrow. And once you have finished, the hillside is dotted with the bundles—you try not to think it: like casualties marking a battle-field. Elden dumps the remaining water and starts to gather the cuttings into the wheelbarrow, but you stop him.

"Wait," you tell him. "This is our only shot."

If they are heaped like that you fear the branches will jostle and crack. Instead, the two of you carry them in your arms, across the front of your bodies.

Grace

They have been together, it seems, since kindergarten, these kids at Conrad's Fork Middle School. And the girls, even more than the boys, have long since established certain cliques. They move around each other in careful arcs, like the electrons and protons Mr. Martin blabbers on about in Chemistry. You don't belong. You throw off the balance.

The worst group wears sundresses or designer polos with chunky, plastic jewelry. They tie their long, streaky hair back in matching blue ribbons for school spirit days. The teachers like these girls, always ask them to run notes to the office. And you can understand. In the classroom, they are all, "Yes, Ma'am. No, Ma'am." Their hands shoot up with the appropriate answers. But in the hallway, they are all whisper and head toss. They slip each other intricately folded notes. In the cafeteria at the big trash cans, they reach across you to dump their trays, splash chocolate milk or spaghetti along the arm of your favorite sweatshirt. "Sorry," they say, but, always, with a carefully contained smirk. *Two-faced bitches.* Only a few teachers can see through the act: Ms. Hinkle in Art, maybe Mr. Espinoza in Civics.

The school doesn't have air conditioning, and the classrooms are unbearable in the afternoon. You look forward to winter. Then, when the temperature suddenly dips in November, and you have to wait for your uncle to scrape the truck's windshield each morning, the old broiler kicks in and the rooms are even hotter, even stuffier. Your eyes grow heavy after lunch.

In English, you ask for a hall pass. In the empty bathroom, you smoke so you can make it through the rest of the day. You climb onto the far toilet. Then, standing on the seat, you blow smoke through the cracked window. The relief, in your chest and your head—*in your fucking fingertips!*—is instantaneous.

You are nearly out of cigarettes. Back home, you got them from Scottie, the guy who worked at the 7-Eleven near your house. You fooled around with him sometimes, and he always slipped you a pack whenever you went in. The last time you saw him, in the basement of his parents' house, he gave you three cartons. "Here you go kid," he said, "a little going away present." When you were packing you emptied them all, stacked the cigs in supersize tampon boxes—just in case your dad decided to search your luggage.

You only bring two cigarettes with you each day because you'd be tempted to stay in here if you had more. You're trying. You really are. You hurry back to class. After English, it's on to Health and P.E., which you can tolerate. Outside, clad in the standard issue blue and gold sweat suits, you and twenty-three other girls spread across the field. You try to stand ready with your hockey stick, stomp your feet against the chill, but your eyes wander along the line of the mountains. They are always there, and you can't get used to them. They make you feel even more caged. Last month, the slopes which had at first hovered blue or green, depending on the light, burst into autumn color. Now the leaves are almost gone, and you can see outcroppings of gray rock through the bare trees.

Back in the locker room, you delight in the squeemish way the other girls undress, even the blue ribbon click. They slide their athletic bras off through the sleeves of their gym shirts, and then slide their regular bras on the same way, hunkering by their lockers. *Flat-chested prudes.* You've worn a C-cup since sixth grade. Scottie would always suck in his breath when you removed your shirt, *practically swoon.* You make a point of walking bare-chested through the rows of wooden benches. You look straight ahead, but you can feel their eyes flit toward you for just a second as you make your way to the bathroom stalls.

Seventh period. The tables that have been covered again and again in shellac, the smell of oil paints and linseed oil from the storage cabinets in the back of the room, the faint breeze through the windows—always cracked—for ventilation. Today Ms. Hinkle moves through the tables in a Boho skirt and ankle boots placing a roll of butcher paper in front of each student. You hear the jingle of her bracelets when she leans over your table. Her curly hair carries just a whiff of her shampoo. *Something citrusy.*

Back at the front of the room she unrolls her own piece of paper. She says, "Today you're going to begin a kind of self-portrait." And you see immediately that she is also there, on the paper. Well, really it is just an outline, but it is clear that it is Ms. Hinkle, not so much in the outline—just a shadow shape, really—but in the swirling colors and words. Her hair, springy even in silhouette, has been filled in with tiny magazine cut-outs—hundreds of shades of red that capture just the way her hair looks to you, *almost glowing.*

"The first step," she says, "is to partner up. Get someone else to trace the outline of your body onto your piece of paper." The class quickly divides itself down amid a sudden rush of mumbling and screeching chairs. You look around. Paired students are already staking out locations, spreading their rolls of butcher paper. And for just a moment you consider this possibility: perhaps the class is not numbered evenly. Perhaps Ms. Hinkle will have to be your partner. But then you see him. The quiet kid by the window is looking around too—Eliot, you think his name is. He shrugs his shoulders and points his finger at you.

Cora

They have broken ground in the orchard, reduced the ridge to three leveled tiers, left just a few of the trees, enough, you suppose, to earn the name. They haven't begun pouring the foundations yet, but already workers have constructed an elaborate entrance, a limestone and brick wall featuring the words *Orchard Heights,* a key pad to control the heavy wrought iron gates.

"Don't look at it," Elden says. "We'll plant a giant hedge row."

But for now that is your view from the kitchen window. And you torture yourself, hand-drying the dishes, making slow circles with the towel.

You make excuses to duck behind the old barn, trudging out to the compost pile three or four times a day. It's not like you owe anyone an explanation, and besides, Elden spends the bulk of the day at the cattle barn. Finished last year, this new barn is as long as a city block, with birthing stalls and a state of the art ventilation system.

It was your idea, really. You laid it out for Elden, the specific allocation of the money: you would undergo one more round of in vitro, and then use the rest to outfit the farm for beef cattle. And you know you could have stopped it. Elden said so himself. "We'll keep trying," he said. "I'll go back to work for Les. Hell, I'll get a factory job. You just say the word." But you were tired. You had already given up.

So here you are, emptying the slop bucket again, then pausing to inspect the crab apple trees behind the old barn. The jointing material is resinous, still clean and amber-colored in the afternoon light, making the grafts look like grotesque Christmas balls. It is different in texture from the stuff your grandmother used. She fashioned her jointing material herself, out of hardware store compounds. One of many things you failed to pay enough attention to.

You had, you suppose, thought it would fall to your mother, that she would be the one to impart all that knowledge. But then she went first, just lost control of the pick-up on her way home from the farmers' market. She might have fallen asleep, that's what they told you later when you were trying to make sense of how her truck wound up at the bottom of Elk Run Gorge. And then your grandmother was gone not three years later—an embolism following what was supposed to be a routine hip replacement.

So, not wanting to take any chances, you called the local landscape company to help with this project. The young woman they sent out— you were secretly glad it was a woman who climbed out of the big white truck—said this is the best stuff there is. She had a man's name, Charlie, but her movements were soft and feminine. She wrapped the branches while you held them in place. You held them so steady and so long your arms started to ache, and all the while you watched her movements—precise, yet almost tender.

You said, "Charlie, you would have made a good nurse."

And she laughed, said, "Well, I guess what I do isn't that far off. Maybe that's why they call it a nursery."

You run your fingers carefully along the fused cuttings, knowing all the while it is pointless. There is no way to tell if they will take, not until March, February at the earliest. But it is not unlike praying.

"The laying on of hands," Jane called it when she asked you to touch her head and pray that day in the attic. You had spent an entire morning going through boxes of photographs and old letters, searching for anything that might provide a clue.

"I'm not sure I'm the right person to pray like that," you said.

But she unwrapped her scarf. "It doesn't matter if you believe," she said. "I do."

So you closed your eyes and placed your hands against her warm scalp.

You don't force the girl to go to church, but you do call Steve on Sunday evenings. It is a good reminder that this is temporary, that he is still, after all, the girl's father. You dial his number and hand the phone to her once it begins to ring. It is important, you think, that he hear her voice first. After the initial, "Hi, Dad," her conversation tapers into a series of one word responses. It is painful to listen. Finally, she pushes the receiver back to you and trots upstairs.

You try to give him all the details you can, but it seems like you end up ticking off the same things: her grades have improved, she's finally eating, she's doing some chores. He doesn't ask if she is making friends. He doesn't ask about her drawing. He really only wants confirmation of one thing: "Is she clean?"

It's wrong to judge him, you know. You can't imagine how much embarrassment he must have felt when she was expelled last spring. But you were still shocked when he said he wished she had been arrested instead, that it might have been easier to keep that quiet.

You sigh, try to tell him the truth. "Her jacket still smells like cigarette smoke, but I don't think she's doing anything else."

There hasn't been alcohol in the house in months. You don't even have a glass of wine anymore when your friend Amanda stops by to gossip after work. You hear news reports about all the meth being manufactured over near Somerset, but the girl never goes out. She hasn't asked to go to a party, or even to be dropped off at the mall. In your mind that's a bigger problem.

Girls never call the house, and you think that is strange. When you and Jane were in middle school, you kept the one phone, a red rotary style contraption that hung on the kitchen wall, tied up all evening. A boy has called a few times. You wouldn't have even known he was a boy, except you asked, "Who may I say is calling?"

And he said, "Eliot." Although, you suppose, that doesn't really mean anything either, not the way people name their kids these days.

But then last week, you made salon appointments for the two of you, hers at 6:00, yours right after. Against your better judgment, you said nothing, just kept flipping through a magazine when she told the hairdresser she wanted to shave her head. It was Amanda, getting up from her station at the cosmetics counter, who intervened. "Or how about some purple streaks?" she said, catching your eye, for just a second, in the mirror.

And then, when the foils were in place, the evening started to unfold more like you had imagined it, the girl almost giddy with her head under the dryer. "What do you think it's going to look like, Aunt Cora?" And later, when her hair was blown soft and straight, the streaks shimmering out like fairy wings, she actually sat in the make-up chair and let Amanda remove the thick make-up and redo her eyes. She was so lovely, suddenly, without all that eyeliner. You felt your own eyes start to tear up, and she misunderstood. "Hey," she laughed, fingering the streaks in her hair. "It will grow out. Besides, it matches my room."

You laughed, nodded your head when she asked if she could take a walk and look in some of the shops. And a few minutes later, when Amanda motioned you over to the front window, there she was, standing next to a boy. He was thin with a sandy crop of hair, and he was holding a skateboard. They leaned toward each other, and you felt your breath catch in your throat. You thought, are they going to kiss? But he only reached his hand up to touch her hair.

Grace

The weather turns bad two weeks into December, and you hole up for a string of snow days. In the morning, a lacy film of frost coats your bedroom window. You scratch the word FUCK with your fingernail, and then realize you should have done the letters backwards. You used to write in the hymnals back home. You don't know where it comes from, this need to mar things, to mess things up. You have begun marking the little white dresser—*vanity, she calls it!*—with a Sharpie, a twisting connected pattern, like the tattoo you plan to get as soon as you're eighteen.

You stay in your pajama pants all day, play Tetris on the computer, lounge on the sofa in the living room where the pellet stove exudes a warm smolder. When you settle in, that dog moves in right beside you,

curls up in a little ball. You've got a theory about why she's so attached
to the thing. He can't weigh more than ten pounds: always the size of
a newborn. When you shift to stretch your legs, Peppy's suddenly all
snarl, and you hear her voice from the kitchen. "Don't get him riled
up!"

Later, you shake your head when she asks if you want to make
Christmas cookies, but you eat a couple when she brings them to you,
warm and sparkling with red sugar.

It is your uncle who finally gets you out of the house. "You want to
earn some cash?" he asks the third day when you show up downstairs
in time for breakfast. "We're mucking out the barn today."

It is her reaction, turning and glaring at him—you remember seeing that look (*Cut it out now!*) on your mom's face—that makes you say,
"Maybe."

By the time you get out there, you are having second thoughts.
You've watched the cows from your window or the back deck, but
here in the barn you're surrounded by them. You're amazed at the heat
that so many bodies can create. Already your winter coat feels suffo-
cating. You loosen your scarf and get a sharp whiff of ammonia. *And
shit.* Because that's what it is really. That's what you're standing in. The
straw slurps and sucks at your boots—*gum shoes the men call them*—with
each step.

Up close, the cows seem a lot bigger. They nose their way into the
troughs the men have filled, until all you can hear is the sound of their
chewing. *Seriously. Like something out of a horror movie.* Elden makes his
way from animal to animal, running his hand along their backs. *Like
they're freaking pets!* They finish quickly and start swinging their heads
around, butting each other. Then your uncle hollers, "Alright, let's move
them out."

You climb up on a railing and watch as Elden and the men fan out
to shoo the cows from the barn. Once they get the animals going, the
herd moves together like one giant creature, flowing through the big
doors and spreading across the snow-covered pasture.

Then it's on to the cleaning. *Nasty!* One of the men drives the tractor, scraping muck from the middle of the corridor, and the rest of you
work the edges and the corners one scoop of the pitchfork at a time.
The tractor lumbers out to the manure tank and back.

After a little while, Elden comes over. "How you doing?"

You point to the tractor, which is orange with the word *Kuboda* on
the side, "I want to drive that thing," you say.

And he just laughs. "Not a chance."

An hour or so later, when the cement floor of the barn is exposed, you gather just outside the door, where the air is fresh and cold. The sun is up over the ridge now, and you have to squint your eyes it is so bright against the snow. The cows have gravitated to the back of the field, and you think how you would like to draw it—the cows against the fence in the foreground and the construction up on the hillside in the background. *Talk about surreal.*

One of the men takes a pack of Lucky Strikes out of his coveralls. "Anybody want a smoke?" he asks as he shakes one into his palm.

Elden is looking away, granting you permission. But you realize, for the first time since you ran out, that you don't want a cigarette. You just shake your head.

Cora

Usually Elden cuts down a Cedar or a White Pine that is twisting its way up one of the fence rows, the uglier the better. That's part of the ritual. The two of you decorate it buzzed on eggnog. Before she was married, Amanda would come by too, sometimes one or two of the farm hands.

This year you go to the lot outside the Farm Bureau, just you and the girl. In the cab of the truck, is a box of frosted cookies—little baggies tied up with festive ribbon. They're for an errand you're planning afterwards, if you can talk her into it.

The lot itself is a little overwhelming—Blue Spruces and Douglas Firs trimmed into perfect towers of greenery, prices ranging from forty to well over one hundred dollars.

She takes off. "Wait!" you shout in her wake. "They all look the same. You're going to have to choose."

And she comes back dragging the scrawniest looking tree of the bunch. It can't even be five feet tall, gaping holes, needles turning brown at the ends of the branches.

"Seriously?"

"What? You don't like this one?" Her skull cap is pulled low, making dark wisps of hair fan her face.

You wonder if this is a test, an attempt at sabotage.

"I love it," you tell her. "Talk about family tradition."

Back in the truck, the tree wrapped in twine and tossed in the bed, you ask her if she's up for lunch at the Valley Vista Grill.

"Sure," she says, but then, when you two are seated in a booth and looking over the menus, you can tell she's worried about the tree. She keeps looking toward the door.

"What if somebody steals it?" she asks.

You laugh. Because this is Conrad's Fork. You and Elden don't lock your doors, not even when you head over to the Land Between the Lakes for a week in August. And besides, who would want that tree?

But you ask the waiter if you can move to one of the window seats. There the two of you eat French fries and greasy burgers, watching snow flurry through the picture window.

You decide to split a piece of apple pie, and after a bite or two, forks jabbing across the little dessert plate, she looks up and says, "It's not as good as yours, huh?"

You want to pull off her hat, reach across the table and ruffle her hair. But instead, you use that as your in: "Listen," you tell her, "I have to ask you a favor."

She slumps back in her seat, arms crossed, eyes narrowed. "What?"

"I need to stop by Black Mountain Manor on the way home."

"Whatever." She's barely listening, or else she doesn't even know what Black Mountain Manor is.

"It's the nursing home," you say, "the one where I used to work. I've got a box of cookies, and I was hoping you'd come in with me and deliver them to the residents."

She's really glaring now.

"You have no idea what it would mean to them," you tell her. "They love to see young people."

"So," she says, "this wasn't really our afternoon at all. You were just trying to get me to do something."

Parked under the nursing home's green awning, exhaust fogging the air, you try one more time. "Are you sure?" You turn to look at her. "It would mean a lot to me."

"No way." She pulls her hat down lower and starts to scan radio stations.

Grace

It takes some work to convince her. In the end, his mom has to call. *Mortifying! Like you're six years old and they're arranging a play date.* But it works, and two days before you fly back to St. Louis you are walking around the mall with Eliot. Eliot, who is *not* your boyfriend, but who is sweet and cute. *Well, kind of.* He's only thirteen, *a kid,* after all. But he exists in the same sphere you do—that netherland outside the cliques. And that is enough to draw the two of you into a friendship of sorts.

His mom is tall and serious with big sunglasses, her hair pulled back in a low bun. *Chignon.* That's what Amanda calls that style. She always wants to do your hair when she comes over—*French braids, French twists. Are there no American hairstyles?* Sometimes you let her, but the last time you weren't in the mood. "Sorry," you told her, "I'm not your personal Barbie doll."

And your aunt about cracked up, said something like. "Goth Barbie, that's hilarious."

Eliot's mom is young and pretty. But she doesn't wear any make up, *so it's in a Little House on the Prairie kind of way.* She says, "You two meet me back here in four hours," and you part ways at the fountain.

The Valley Mall is awash with faux flocked greenery and Christmas muzak. You've only been in two stores, and you're sure you're hearing "Jingle Bell Rock" for the second time. You are within ear shot of at least three crying babies.

Eliot has a list he's working off of, a crumpled piece of paper where he's penciled in the presents he wants to get each member of his family. *Typical.* He still writes his homework assignments down in a little spiral notebook. *Keeps it in his back pocket!*

Your dad has always insisted on a noncommercial holiday. When your mom was alive she made sure he did the Santa thing, but you and your siblings were supposed to exchange homemade presents. This rule always led to an array of poorly knit scarves, glitter-pasted ornaments, and papìer mâché under the tree. *Total crap.*

You try, briefly, to explain this, hear how crazy it sounds. "My dad's just weird," you say. "I mean he gets pissy when people abbreviate Christmas—you know with an X."

Eliot's list includes things you've never heard of. His grandparents are doing a house exchange *(whatever that is),* spending New Year's in Colonial Mexico, and he wants to get them a French press from a store called Williams Sonoma.

"For their afternoon espresso," he says, "Last year Nana about died without it." And then he asks, "So, what are you getting your . . . family?"

You notice he doesn't say either "your dad" or "your aunt and uncle." Like your family is some kind of mysterious nebulous thing. *Which it kind of is.*

"I'm not sure." You've thought about giving your dad the self portrait you made in art class, and you've also thought about giving him nothing at all. *It would serve him right—after all, he sent you away.*

You two are weaving through the racks in the men's section of one of the big department stores.

"Handkerchiefs are nice," Eliot says picking up a package. "I've gotten them for my dad before. There's a place here that can monogram them in less than an hour."

You start laughing then because it's the most ridiculous thing you've ever heard. *Monogramming hankies, something you put snot in.* You think about telling him your dad doesn't even use handkerchiefs. He uses Kleenex, or if none is handy, toilet paper. You know because you found them everywhere during your mom's final days, when his eyes just seemed to constantly leak and yours, strangely, had gone dry—shredded tissues in every trash can in the house.

But what you say is, "Can we get out of here?"

And later, sitting on the loading dock behind the furniture store, you reach into his coat pocket and pull out that piece of paper. "Hey," you say, "How come I'm not on this list?" You're joking, finally feeling like yourself again now that you're out of that crowd. You like the cold feel of the concrete against your jeans.

"Because I already got you your present," he says. And you must look surprised because he adds, "Seriously. You want it now?"

He reaches into his other pocket and removes a little paper bag, hands it to you. "It's not wrapped yet."

You draw out a cross on a black leather cord. At first glance it looks like it could have been purchased at one of the jewelry stands in the mall, but when you look closer and turn it over in your hands, you see the cross is like nothing you've ever seen, carved with flowers and dancing skeletons.

"That's a Day of the Dead cross," he says, "the skeletons and stuff. It was actually a key chain. My nana brought it back from Mexico last year. I told my mom what I wanted to do, and she found a jeweler who could make it into a necklace."

Irony—that's what your English teacher would call it. Eliot making you a Christmas present. You don't know what to say.

"Do you want me to help you put it on?"

You hand the necklace back to him and lift up your hair. "I feel bad," you say. "I didn't get you anything."

He leans in to clasp it, and you can feel his breath, warm on the back of your neck. "Just come back," he says, "even if your Dad tries to get you to stay. And don't do anything with that Scottie guy."

Cora

On the farm it begins like any other morning. The alarm clock sounds, and Peppy begins to stir first, pushing his way out of the warm quilts. You get up and get breakfast on the table while Elden goes out to break the ice on the water troughs. With all the help gone, it falls on you to assist him with the feeding. Most of his girls are moving slower now, their bellies swollen around the spring's calves. It's Christmas for them too, a warm bran mash instead of the usual silage, the troughs steaming in the cold air.

"Merry Christmas, babe," Eldens says once the cows are jockeying for their food. The first mention of the holiday. You're both a little too bundled to really embrace—you've got your down stadium jacket over your flannel gown, wool socks inside your boots—but you lean in and accept his kiss.

Back inside the farmhouse, there is no rush to the gifts which have circled the tree for the last week or so. Elden gets a shower, and you dress the turkey, set the rolls to rise on the stove top. You take note of the time as you slide the heavy roasting pan in the oven. 8:34.

You spent only one Christmas with your sister's family. You were twenty-five, working in Minneapolis, and Jane convinced you to drive down. She only had Peter and Jesse back then, but those boys had everyone in the house up by 5:30, and by this hour everything was finished—the living room a mess of torn paper and emptied boxes, the kids sticky with candy cane and chocolate. You know it's best the girl flew back home, but you can't help but wonder. How would the day uncoil if she were here?

You and Elden don't get around to unwrapping presents until almost noon. As always, it is a slow, contained kind of ritual. In between gifts—for you there is a new nightgown, perfume, a few hardback novels, as well as an antique hand mirror (silver, inlaid with mother-of-pearl)—you see to the final preparations for the midday meal, mashing the steaming potatoes, whisking broth into gravy.

When the food is ready, you set the table in Mamaw's china, plates painted with delicate cherry blossoms. This set was mailed in narrow boxes of tissue paper all the way from Manilla back when her second oldest son, your great uncle, was in the navy.

The sound of the television rises from the living room. The same Christmas movie has been playing over and over all morning, the one with the kid with the glasses. You set the silver next to each plate, pour a little wine into the glasses. How criminal it felt yesterday, after taking such pains to keep the house absolutely dry over the last four months, to walk out of the liquor store clutching the paper sack.

You call your husband in then, just as you call him and the men in from the barn or the fields every other afternoon: "Dinner's on!"

And he appears in the doorway, looking back over his shoulder, laughing at the TV. He is clearly shocked, once he sits down across from you, to see the tears streaming down your face.

He comes to you then, hunkers next to your chair. "What is it, babe?"

By that point, you're bawling. You can't tell him what's wrong. You don't know what's wrong. And what's worse is it's not even that uncommon, this crying. For months now, the slightest thing can set your throat tightening, your nose running in an effort to hold back the tears. You think you must be nearing your change, even though it seems a little early. It wouldn't be that uncommon, your doctor has told you, to be perio-menopausal with all the fertility problems you've had. If you were a Hereford, the men would have loaded you in the truck and driven you to market a decade ago.

"Hey," Elden whispers, "she got you something. I was just saving it as a surprise." He gets up then and rummages around in the mudroom.

Your sobbing is quieting now, even though you haven't been crying over any present.

When he sits back down he is holding two more packages. "She gave them to me when I drove her to the airport. I was waiting until after dinner to pull them out."

They are wrapped in plain white paper, sketch paper. You peel it back slowly and break the tape sealing the box you find beneath. You don't care that the food is getting cold on the table.

"Well, what is it?"

You lift it out of the box to show him. "A pie plate." It is heavy ceramic, glazed blue on the outside, cream within. Twice as deep as the aluminum pans you baked in last night.

"What about you, hon?" you ask, sniffling. "What did she get you?"

"I'm not sure. It's sort of half glove half windshield scraper." He holds it up for you to inspect—large and fleece-lined, stitched by a hand unaccustomed to a needle, it looks like those muffs women used to carry, only with a plastic blade protruding from one end.

You laugh, but immediately you feel guilt creeping against your ribs. You gave her some art supplies, an envelope of gift cards to use at the after-Christmas sales.

Later that night you enter her room for the first time. You've made a point, all fall, to offer her privacy wherever you could. You've left her clean laundry stacked on the table in the upstairs hallway. You've always handed her the dust rag and broom, said, "Why don't you go tidy up your room?" You're not planning on cleaning today. Your plan is to peek in her drawers and see if she left behind any of her ratty T-shirts, the ones with the names of her favorite bands. You will write down the names of the bands and then find some posters in the music store downtown, or if you have to, you will order them online. Whatever it takes.

It's not such an ill-conceived plan. The morning she left, she came down the stairs with just her backpack.

And you asked her, your heart thumping because you were scared, even though it wasn't part of the plan, scared that she might be staging a campaign to stay in Missouri and finish out the year at her old school. "Where is your big suitcase?" you asked her. "You want me to send Elden up for it?"

But she shook her head. "I don't want to have to check anything," she said, and then, with that smirk you've come to know so well, she added, "Besides, Dad asked me to bring something other than black clothes. That limited my choices a little."

The shirts are there, just as you had known they would be, carefully folded in the chest of drawers, worn thin from repeated washing. So these are the bands she listens to when she's hunched silent on the deck chair or in the front seat next to you, those buds in her ears. At first you think there is some kind of mistake because the names all sound so much alike: *The Cure. The Cult. The Smiths. The Strokes.* You write them down in your day-planner, thinking maybe you will do better than buy posters. Maybe you will buy concert tickets. She deserves that. Yes, she's been a bit surly at times—what fourteen year old girl isn't?—but she hasn't really given you such a hard time.

And that is when you see the vanity. You suck in your breath, pace across the room, and run your hand across its surface. How could you have missed it a moment ago? The top is covered in black magic marker—a viney, twisting design, breaking at times into fish and trees and skeletal faces, what might be letters. You turn and leave, slamming the door as you go.

"Did you find them?" Elden asks when you slide beneath the quilt a few minutes later.

"No," you say, "they weren't there."

Grace

He's on your case right away. *Before you're even out of the airport!*

"What are you wearing?" he wants to know.

And you look down. You're wearing a red leotard under a gray wool jumper. The skirt isn't that short. The only thing black is your tights and, if shoes count, your Doc Martins.

"Around your neck, sweetie? What is that?"

"A cross," you say. *You know, like Jesus died on.*

In the parking deck he looks at it more closely. He can't stop looking at it. "What's all over that thing? Skeletons? Where did you get it?"

You tell him, "It's a Mexican cross. My friend gave it to me."

"It seems really inappropriate," he says. "Almost blasphemous." He waits to start the car, keys in the ignition. "I want us to get off on a good foot, really I do, but I'm going to have to ask you not to wear that thing around me. I think you should think long and hard about wearing it at all."

Your room is the same. Your Hello Kitty collection still lines the shelves. The same gray branches fork outside your window. You know, if you press your face to the glass and look down, you will see the edge of the patio, the top of the barbecue grill. But the lock has been removed from your bedroom door. The new, smooth knob calls out a subtle warning: *Go ahead and just try any of that crap again.*

At first the house feels strangely quiet. Peter has flown in, but he is busy on some design, tinkering away on his laptop. Your sister Ruth and her husband drive up on Christmas Eve, and Jesse is there, too, with his wife and their little girl, but the other boys are staying away this year, celebrating with college friends. And you can't blame them.

It's the second Christmas without mom, but it feels even more wrong than the first. Last year you moved through the holiday under the fog of Demerol or Oxycotin or something, you weren't even sure.

You kept them in a zippered pencil case in your backpack, the pills you had siphoned from your mother's bedside over a period of months. Sometimes you shared them with select friends, traded them for other things at parties.

After the Christmas Eve service, various members of the congregation trickle in and out of the house. "You look good," they tell you, or "We're so glad you're here." *The Prodigal freaking Son.* No one says, "You know you caused us a lot of worry." No one even asks, "Are you keeping out of trouble?"

Most just deliver fruitcake or plates of cookies and then go on their way. But one woman, blond in a boiled-wool blazer, sits all evening in one of the dining room chairs that have been arranged around the perimeter of the den. Occasionally, she looks up at you and smiles, the lights from the tree casting her face in color. Someone introduced her—your dad, or maybe your sister—when she arrived, but you can't remember her name, don't even think there is cause to try. Not until you see your dad bring her a mug of coffee, see his hand rest a moment too long on her shoulder.

An hour or so later, the house all but emptied, he says, "I'll be back soon, Sweetie. I'm just going to drive Sandra home." And then you know.

You corner Ruth in the kitchen. "Who the hell is that woman?"

And it comes back that fast, the careful touch, the condescension you remember everyone treating you with before. She moves so slowly and methodically—turns off the water, puts down the cookie platter she has been rinsing. "Now, Gracie," she says, "take a deep breath. It's not really my place to tell you."

"So what—she's his girlfriend? He's got a girlfriend?"

"First of all, it's been more than a year." She raises one hand, palm up—*like a traffic cop: stop, stop, stop*—pulsing the air between you. "He has a right," she says, "to at least try to be happy."

If she had just stopped there, you might have been alright, but she said. "They want to give you the news themselves. They're planning on taking you out to dinner, just you and them, right after Christmas."

And then you know he's planning on marrying her.

You leave that night. You shove everything back in your pack, and you walk right out, right past Jesse and his wife sleeping on the fold-out couch, the baby snuggled in the pocket of space between them. At first you just walk. The weeds along the shoulder of the road shine silvery in the moonlight. When you look up, you feel the night sky. *The stars like little pin pricks in your chest.*

Somehow, you've left your gloves behind. Even inside your coat pockets, your fingers have gone completely numb. You think about your mother in the final days, waking only for a few moments at a time and saying the strangest things, looking right at you and not seeing you. "Are these my hands?" she asked. "Why can't I feel my fingers?"

You are walking with no destination, just certain you have to get away from there. But when someone slows down and throws open a car door, you tell him, "East toward Kentucky."

Cora

You ask her for the exit number off the interstate, but you don't ask any other questions.

You think about calling the police, asking a state trooper to wait with her until you arrive. Wasn't somebody found murdered at a rest area on that stretch of I-64 just last year? But she could be on something—you don't want to scare her. Instead, you tell her to wait in the bathroom. "I'll be there in three hours," you say, "three and a half, tops."

Elden has to stay on the farm for the evening feeding, and alone in the car, you can hardly contain the rage you feel toward your brother-in-law. You think about calling Steve and really giving him a piece of your mind, asking him why your niece is calling you collect from a payphone the day after Christmas, asking why he didn't call you as soon as she left, demanding to know just what has happened in the last four days. After all, she was fine when Elden dropped her off at the airport. But right now you need to drive. That conversation will have to happen, but maybe, you think, it's not a bad idea to get the girl's story first.

You leave the car running and take off up the hillside, sliding a little in the thin crust of snow. You call her name, your voice hollow against the tiled walls. She doesn't answer, but you hear a shuffling from one of the stalls, knock—harder than you meant to—on the metal door.

"Hey," you say, "it's me. Open up." You brace yourself for anything. Who knows what she may have gotten into, you tell yourself. She could be completely out of it. She could be injured, bleeding.

She opens the door slowly.

"Thank, God," you say, "you're okay." And you move forward, wrap your arms around her, amazed at how small she feels. "You are, aren't you?"

She nods her head.

You pull back, take another look. Her eyes are puffy, her hair flat and unwashed, but other than that, she seems fine.

"Well, come on," you tell her. "Let's get going."

You've decided that you won't grill her in the car, that you won't ask the really hard questions until you get her home safe. So you just hand her a turkey sandwich zipped in a little baggie. She goes at it like she hasn't eaten in days, and you realize she may not have. At first, she's chatting away, talking with her mouth full, even, but she's not saying anything. Not really. She's asking about Elden and the dog, describing her brother's baby, going on about how they will get to use the new kiln in art class next semester. And as soon as she finishes eating, she falls silent, leans her head against the window. You keep glancing across the seat. You can't help it. Because now she's crying, crying without a sound, smoothing that plastic baggie, folding and refolding it in her lap. And it goes on for miles, this crying, goes on until you realize you have to say something.

So you exit, stop the car in a McDonald's parking lot. "I'm going to get some coffee and use the restroom," you tell her. "Do you want anything?"

She shakes her head. It has grown dark in the last half an hour, and when you turn off the car her face looks almost gray in the dimly lit parking lot, like wet stone.

"Hey," you say, "I didn't get a chance to tell you yet. I love that pie plate. That was really thoughtful."

She doesn't say anything, so you start to get out of the car, and that is when she grabs your arm. You can feel her fingers, like a vice, even through your down coat.

"It was sickening," she says, "everybody being so nice and so careful. But they don't even know. They don't know half of what I've done."

"What are you talking about?" The car door is open beside you, and you can feel the night air creeping into that warm space. "Honey, you're not as bad as you think, not as bad as your Dad's made you think you are, anyway. Besides, there's nothing that can't be forgiven, not if you're willing to start over. Lord knows I've started over enough for three or four lifetimes."

"Sometimes I ignored her," she whispers. "We gave her a little bell like on TV, and sometimes she would ring it just because she wanted to talk, and I would stay up in my room. I'd pretend I couldn't hear it."

You want to tell her that it's her dad, not her, who should be feeling guilty, that he put ridiculous pressure on Jane right from day one of their marriage. There was a certain look expected of a preacher's wife. Her suits had to fit just so. Her hair had to lay just right. And even at the end, when she accepted hospice, he made her feel like she was giving up, like she wasn't praying hard enough, like she was refusing to believe in the possibility of a miracle.

It's like she knows just what you're thinking because she looks up at you then, eyes glittering, voice sharp. "He's marrying somebody else."

You can't help it, you're stunned.

"Look," she tells you, reaching down to unfasten a roll of paper from the outside of her backpack. "I was going to give him this."

You unroll it, knowing she'll be watching you, judging your reaction. It is a body tracing, like the outlines chalked around murder victims on old television shows. The inside is filled in with layers of torn tissue paper. The effect is not unlike stained glass. Then etched across the surface is a design in black ink. You squint, trying to recognize words or shapes. It reminds you of the destroyed vanity.

"It's lovely," you say, although you know you don't get it, not like she wants you to.

She sinks back into her seat and folds her arms across her chest, and you understand that some cord has been snapped by what you said or failed to say.

Back home, you let her be for a while. You let her eat dinner in silence. You let her sit, catatonic, in front of the computer. A few days later, when that boy calls, you let her slink into her bedroom and close the door. More than a month passes. You know you're losing ground.

In February, the first calves arrive, weeks before Elden expects them, during a stretch of ten-degree days, cold enough to freeze a calf to the ground if its mother doesn't get right to the cleaning. Men are in and out of the mudroom all day. You keep the coffee pot going.

In the middle of the night, it is you who accompanies Elden out to the birthing corral, you who helps pull the calves from this year's heifers. You wear gum boots and long rubber gloves, but by the time you are washing up at the basin in the mudroom, you're still covered in blood. It is good blood, you tell yourself, watching as the water clouds and swirls down the drain.

But you can't help it. Your mind slides as it does every spring along the spectrum of your own disappointments. The way, that afternoon twenty years ago, you kept lifting the pad from your panties after you left the clinic in Kingsport. The way you had to keep looking before wrapping it and tossing it in the wastebasket. The way you couldn't stop thinking—it's not the same, it looks the same, but it's not the same. And the way, four years ago, as if in secret confirmation of that other afternoon, when the blood ran warm down your legs as you stepped out of the shower, it wasn't just blood you saw, but clumps of something gray and shriveled there on the linoleum.

Grace

She brings the calves right into house, sets them up in the mudroom, where she has spread cardboard and straw.

"Their mother is gone," she tells you, when you are shocked to hear their lowing that first morning. "I didn't think we'd get them out alive, honestly." She has secured a baby gate across the open doorway. "We have two or three orphans every year, and this is what we have to do to keep them warm and fed."

You peer around the corner and find them curled in the straw like little deer. "They're brother and sister," she says, "and still shaky on their feet. We haven't even been able to get any colostrum into them yet."

One of them looks up, emits a little cry. You are surprised at the sound, a bleating more like the cry of a human baby than the moo of a full-grown cow. They are black and white like the cows you see through the fence each day, but their fur looks softer, curlier. You see the pile of towels, stained and still damp from where she must have finished cleaning them.

"You'll have to get your own breakfast today, okay?" She is removing the plastic baggies which have been in the freezer for days now, since last week's still birth. The milk inside is creamy-colored, frozen in a solid cube. "If I can get some of this in them, their chances are much better." She dunks the bags in warm water. "But this is all we've got."

You watch as the ice melts and swirls into liquid, almost golden. She siphons it out with a baster—you're too fascinated to even wonder if it is the same one she uses in the kitchen—then kneels in front of the larger of the calves and works the liquid into its mouth. He is standing up now, and his long tongue keeps working even after she's moved on to the other calf. "Look at that," she says. "He's going to have no problems with the bottle."

You hope she is right. You start to barter. *The closest you come to prayer.* As you watch her in front of the other calf, the smaller of the two, you think how you will be good. You will find a way to be better.

"I don't know about this one," your aunt says. "She's definitely the weaker of the two."

You tick off the things you will do if they survive. *Stop cutting English class. Toss the Sharpies you use to mark up certain lockers. Find a way to make up with your dad.*

She steps back, looking pleased and then turns to you. "What do you say? You want to try to give them a bottle?"

They have to nurse every few hours, and this chore falls to you. *Yet another chore.* But it's preferable to some of the other stuff they expect you to do—spreading gravel over potholes in the driveway, for instance, or turning the compost pile with a pitchfork. You scoop formula from the plastic bin under the sink and funnel the powder into two empty Coke bottles. At first the thick smell rises up, catches in the back of your throat. But soon there is a familiarity in that scent, a constancy in the motions, repeated several times throughout the day. You add warm water and snap the black nipples in place.

You have to ride the school bus home until the calving is finished. You hurry up the half mile lane, and when you step into the kitchen they are leaning into the baby gate, vying for position. Peppy trots back and forth, egging them on. His claws need trimming, and they click against the linoleum. The lunch and breakfast dishes are still stacked, crusty, on the counter. Everything, it seems, has been put on hold these past few weeks. After three days, the calves butt the mesh plastic, strain their heads past the gate. Already they have grown that tall.

"I'm coming," you tell them. *Hinkle and Morrissey.* That's what you call them, although you don't say their names aloud. The girl for your favorite teacher, and the boy for your favorite singer. They nearly tore the bottles from your hands at first, but you have learned how to hold on, and now you can feed them both at once. When they finish, they bellow and suck on your fingers, searching for more.

After a few more days, they transition to milk buckets, and your uncle moves them to the tiny paddock off the old barn. You still want to be the one to feed them, though.

Your aunt is skeptical. "Are you sure? Things are slowing down out there. I can have one of the men take over."

But you insist. You tell her, "They're expecting me. I feel like they're my responsibility now."

You want to show the calves to Eliot, so he rides the bus home with you one afternoon. Your aunt is making meatloaf, kneading ground beef and bread crumbs and spices together in the big steel bowl. She looks up, all smiles, when the two of you come through the door. "Well, hello there," she says.

"This is my friend Eliot," you say. "I'm just going to show him the calves."

"That's fine," she says. "Is he going to stay for dinner?"

He looks at you then, waiting to see how you will answer. You just shrug.

"Well," she tells him, "there's plenty. If you want to stay I can have Elden run you home after we eat."

"Come on," you tell him. "This way."

He watches as you mix the milk buckets at the big basin. The mud-room has been sprayed down and disinfected, but last week the temperature shot up, and three straight days of rain have left the space almost as dirty as it was when it served as a calf stall. The linoleum looks scarred with long streaks of muck and sour straw. Along the far wall, a line of gum boots are caked with damp mud. "Take off your tennis shoes and pull on a pair of those," you tell him. "It doesn't matter if they're a little big."

Each of you carries a bucket. The milk sloshes a little as you cross the barnyard, wetting your jeans. Hinkle and Morrissey are waiting, bellowing. You show Eliot how to lean over the fence, using it as a brace while the calves slurp down the formula. He laughs, nervous, you can tell, as his bucket jostles against the boards.

The two of you climb up on the fence and sit awhile after the milk is gone. "Come on," you tell him, hopping down, "I'll show you something else." The mud sucks at your boots as you cross the paddock.

You open the double doors a crack, just enough for both of you to pass through. Inside the old barn everything is dry, and you remove your boots and socks. The wooden rungs of the ladder are worn smooth. You wonder, for a moment, how many times your mother climbed this same ladder. If she, too, did it barefoot. If she ever snuck in here with a boy.

Up in the loft, a skim of rich dust coats the floor, along with little seeds and pieces of hay. You've been coming here almost every day. A window opens out the back of the loft. Sometimes you sit there and let your legs swing over the side, look up the ridge where the bones of all those new houses look pale and naked on top of the ridge. But more often than not, you just lie back in the dust, and that is what you do today. You don't mind that it clings to your hair and coats your skin like powder.

Chestnut. That's what your aunt says this barn was built from. "You can't even get that kind of wood, anymore," she says. "Those trees are all gone now, but that barn will last forever."

Your eyes are closed. You can smell the heady scent of the compost pile rising up from behind the barn, and you can feel Eliot's breath, the tickle of his hair, as he leans over you. You think he is going to kiss you, and you think that is okay, that you wouldn't mind that so much. You think that soon he will cup your breasts, that you will feel the weight of his body along your own. You wonder though, at the inevitably of it, wonder why things must always move forward in that way.

You don't let yourself think of others. Not here. Not Scottie's heavy tongue. Not that man's fingers back in December, tangled in the back of your hair as he pulled you toward his lap, said, "Hey, why don't you come over here and wake me up a little bit so I can keep driving."

But instead of Eliot's mouth, there is only breath. His fingers are moving around you, around your face, along the perimeter of your limbs, yet you can feel them, electric. *He is tracing you into dust.*

Cora

You watch them through the kitchen window as they lean over the pad-dock fence, and it dawns on you how the two of them together look kind of like you and Jane—his hair light and wavy, just as yours once was, hers black and thick like her mother's. You realized weeks ago, as soon as the girl took on the bottle feedings, that these calves will have to be dealt with differently. Elden can't just march them up the ramp into the trailer, not even the male. He's got the facilities now to keep a bull.

You pepper the top of the meatloaf and measure out flour and fat for biscuits. It feels good to be moving through the kitchen this way again, slowly, building a meal from scratch. For weeks now, in the excitement of calving, dinner has been whatever you can get on the table—micro-wave pizza, chicken nuggets and vegetables out of a bag in the freezer. In a few more weeks it will be time to start the seed trays for the garden. And you think how it will be good if you can get her to help with that. Then the tilling and the transplanting.

You allow yourself, for a moment, as you roll and cut the biscuits, to have a little faith in the sheer certainty of the seasons. You need to get a couple of jars of beans out of the pantry, and you look for them again, out there on the fence, as you move across the open window.

But they are gone. The calves have gravitated over to the old barn. The presence of the animals there—persistent, waiting—draws your focus to the cracked doors.

So you hurry out, not bothering with boots or a jacket. As you slide through the wet barnyard, you're not sure what you're going to say to her, to them. She's only fourteen, but then again, it's different now than when you and Jane were girls. You were still building hay forts at fourteen, still playing hide and seek in the cornfield.

The calves meet you at the gate, and you have to battle your way past them. "Hey," you tell them softly, "You've already had your milk." And you wonder then, why you're talking so softly, almost whispering.

You hesitate at the barn door, your fingers hovering just over the rough wood. Should you knock, you wonder. They could be doing anything in there. They could be smoking. One spark could send the whole place up in flames. Or they could just be talking, sitting up in loft, shoulder to shoulder, as you once saw them on the steps outside the middle school, linked by one set of headphones. Your hand floats in the cool air.

All week, rain has pelted against the aluminum roof, poured out of the gutters. You are standing in a foot of mud. You realize you have been so busy these past few weeks that you have forgotten to check the apple trees. It has been weeks since you ran your fingers along the slick bark of the grafted branches, straining to feel sap running beneath.

First you had to find Grace. Then there were the problem calves, and not just the two in the kitchen. Three nights ago, when the vet didn't arrive in time, you and Elden did damage control for a heifer with a prolapsed uterus. He braced her in the corner of the birthing corral while you stitched her up, drawing the thread in a calm, careful arc as if you were mending the toe of a sock. These past weeks you have chosen, without realizing it, to focus your energy where it matters, to tend to the crises over which you have a shred of control. Triage, they called it back when you worked at the hospital.

Yet the trees have been there all along—tissue growing, or not, beneath the resin. They are there now, behind the barn. You move your hand away from the door, draw it up into the warm flannel of your shirt sleeve. You're okay not knowing.

That's what your sister said the last time you saw her alive, the day after you laid your hands on her head and she prayed up in the attic. The two of you were in the kitchen clearing the breakfast dishes, and you asked her if she wanted to try and talk to some of your mom's old friends. "Dotty's still living over by Mount Solon," you said, "and there's another lady she used to run around with who's in assisted living at Black Mountain Manor. They might be able to give us some information."

But she shook her head. "I'm glad we didn't find anything up there. I'm okay not knowing. That's not really why I came anyway. I just wanted to be here again, you know?"

Slowly, you step away from the barn. You will go back inside the house and watch the biscuits rise in the oven. You will set four plates at the table, and serve the meatloaf, hot and fragrant. And then you will scrape the dishes and dump the slop bucket out behind the barn. Tonight you will choose not to feel the branches in the dark.

THE NON/FICTION COLLECTION PRIZE
(formerly The Ohio State University Prize in Short Fiction)

Landfall: A Ring of Stories
JULIE HENSLEY

Hibernate
ELIZABETH ESLAMI

The Deer in the Mirror
CARY HOLLADAY

How
GEOFF WYSS

Little America
DIANE SIMMONS

The Book of Right and Wrong
MATT DEBENHAM

The Departure Lounge: Stories and a Novella
PAUL EGGERS

True Kin
RIC JAHNA

Owner's Manual
MORGAN MCDERMOTT

Mexico Is Missing: And Other Stories
J. DAVID STEVENS

Ordination
SCOTT A. KAUKONEN

Little Men: Novellas and Stories
GERALD SHAPIRO

The Bones of Garbo
TRUDY LEWIS

The White Tattoo: A Collection of Short Stories
WILLIAM J. COBB

Come Back Irish
WENDY RAWLINGS

Throwing Knives
MOLLY BEST TINSLEY

Dating Miss Universe: Nine Stories
STEVEN POLANSKY

Radiance: Ten Stories
JOHN J. CLAYTON

CPSIA information can be obtained
at www.ICGtesting.com
Printed in the USA
LVHW092017160719
624313LV00001B/1/P